Penguin Books
The Little Nugget

P. G. Wodehouse was born in Guildford in 1881 and
educated at Dulwich College. After working for the
Hong Kong and Shanghai Bank for two years, he
left to earn his living as a journalist and storywriter,
writing the 'By the Way' column in the old *Globe*.
He also contributed a series of school stories to a
magazine for boys, the *Captain*, in one of which
Psmith made his first appearance. Going to America
before the First World War, he sold a serial to the
Saturday Evening Post and for the next twenty-five
years almost all his books appeared first in this
magazine. He was part author and writer of the
lyrics of eighteen musical comedies including
Kissing Time; he married in 1914 and in 1955 took
American citizenship. He wrote over ninety books
and his work has won world-wide acclaim, being
translated into many languages. *The Times* hailed
him as 'a comic genius recognized in his lifetime as a
classic and an old master of farce'.

P. G. Wodehouse said, 'I believe there are two ways
of writing novels. One is mine, making a sort of
musical comedy without music and ignoring real
life altogether; the other is going right deep down into
life and not caring a damn ...' He was created a
Knight of the British Empire in the New Year's
Honours List in 1975. In a BBC interview he said
that he had no ambitions left, now that he had been
knighted and there was a waxwork of him in Madame
Tussaud's. He died on St Valentine's Day in 1975 at
the age of ninety-three.

P. G. Wodehouse

The Little Nugget

Penguin Books

Penguin Books Ltd, Harmondsworth, Middlesex, England
Penguin Books, 625 Madison Avenue, New York, New York 10022, U.S.A.
Penguin Books Australia Ltd, Ringwood, Victoria, Australia
Penguin Books Canada Ltd, 2801 John Street, Markham, Ontario, Canada L3R 1B4
Penguin Books (N.Z.) Ltd, 182-190 Wairau Road, Auckland 10, New Zealand

First published by Methuen 1913
Published in Penguin Books 1959
Reprinted 1974, 1978, 1981

Set, printed and bound in Great Britain by
Cox & Wyman Ltd, Reading
Set in Intertype Times

Part One

In which the Little Nugget is introduced to the reader, and plans are made for his future by several interested parties. In which, also, the future Mr Peter Burns is touched upon. The whole concluding with a momentous telephone-call

The Little Nugget

If the management of the Hotel Guelph, that London land-
mark, could have been present at three o'clock one afternoon in
early January in the sitting-room of the suite which they had
assigned to Mrs Elmer Ford, late of New York, they might well
have felt a little aggrieved. Philosophers among them would
possibly have meditated on the limitations of human effort; for
they had done their best for Mrs Ford. They had housed her
well. They had fed her well. They had caused inspired servants
to anticipate her every need. Yet here she was, in the midst of
all these aids to a contented mind, exhibiting a restlessness and
impatience of her surroundings that would have been no-
ticeable in a caged tigress or a prisoner of the Bastille. She
paced the room. She sat down, picked up a novel, dropped it,
and, rising, resumed her patrol. The clock striking, she compared it with her watch, which she had consulted two minutes
before. She opened the locket that hung by a gold chain from
her neck, looked at its contents, and sighed. Finally, going
quickly into the bedroom, she took from a suit-case a framed
oil-painting, and returning with it to the sitting-room, placed it
on a chair, and stepped back, gazing at it hungrily. Her large
brown eyes, normally hard and imperious, were strangely
softened. Her mouth quivered.

'Ogden!' she whispered.

The picture which had inspired this exhibition of feeling
would probably not have affected the casual spectator to quite
the same degree. He would have seen merely a very faulty and
amateurish portrait of a singularly repellent little boy of about
eleven, who stared out from the canvas with an expression half
stolid, half querulous; a bulgy, overfed little boy; a little boy
who looked exactly what he was, the spoiled child of parents

7

who had far more money than was good for them.

As Mrs Ford gazed at the picture, and the picture stared back at her, the telephone bell rang. She ran to it eagerly. It was the office of the hotel, announcing a caller.

'Yes? Yes? Who?' Her voice fell, as if the name was not the one she had expected. 'Oh, yes,' she said. 'Yes, ask Lord Mountry to come to me here, please.'

She returned to the portrait. The look of impatience, which had left her face as the bell sounded, was back now. She suppressed it with an effort as her visitor entered.

Lord Mountry was a blond, pink-faced, fair-moustached young man of about twenty-eight – a thick-set, solemn young man. He winced as he caught sight of the picture, which fixed him with a stony eye immediately on his entry, and quickly looked away.

'I say, it's all right, Mrs Ford.' He was of the type which wastes no time on preliminary greetings. 'I've got him.'

'Got him!'

Mrs Ford's voice was startled.

'Stanborough, you know.'

'Oh! I – I was thinking of something else. Won't you sit down?'

Lord Mountry sat down.

'The artist, you know. You remember you said at lunch the other day you wanted your little boy's portrait painted, as you only had one of him, aged eleven – '

'This is Ogden, Lord Mountry. I painted this myself.'

His lordship, who had selected a chair that enabled him to present a shoulder to the painting, and was wearing a slightly dogged look suggestive of one who 'turns no more his head, because he knows a frightful fiend doth close behind him tread', forced himself round, and met his gaze with as much nonchalance as he could summon up.

'Er, yes,' he said.

He paused.

'Fine manly little fellow – what?' he continued.

'Yes, isn't he?'

His lordship stealthily resumed his former position.

'I recommended this fellow, Stanborough, if you remember. He's a great pal of mine, and I'd like to give him a leg up if I could. They tell me he's a topping artist. Don't know much about it myself. You told me to bring him round here this afternoon, you remember, to talk things over. He's waiting downstairs.'

'Oh yes, yes. Of course, I've not forgotten. Thank you so much, Lord Mountry.'

'Rather a good scheme occurred to me, that is, if you haven't thought over the idea of that trip on my yacht and decided it would bore you to death. You still feel like making one of the party – what?'

Mrs Ford shot a swift glance at the clock.

'I'm looking forward to it,' she said.

'Well, then, why shouldn't we kill two birds with one stone? Combine the voyage and the portrait, don't you know. You could bring your little boy along – he'd love the trip – and I'd bring Stanborough – what?'

This offer was not the outcome of a sudden spasm of warm-heartedness on his lordship's part. He had pondered the matter deeply, and had come to the conclusion that, though it had flaws, it was the best plan. He was alive to the fact that a small boy was not an absolute essential to the success of a yachting trip, and, since seeing Ogden's portrait, he had realized still more clearly that the scheme had draw-backs. But he badly wanted Stanborough to make one of the party. Whatever Ogden might be, there was no doubt that Billy Stanborough, that fellow of infinite jest, was the ideal companion for a voyage. It would make just all the difference having him. The trouble was that Stanborough flatly refused to take an indefinite holiday, on the plea that he could not afford the time. Upon which his lordship, seldom blessed with great ideas, had surprised himself by producing the scheme he had just sketched out to Mrs Ford.

He looked at her expectantly, as he finished speaking, and was surprised to see a swift cloud of distress pass over her face. He rapidly reviewed his last speech. No, nothing to upset anyone in that. He was puzzled.

She looked past him at the portrait. There was pain in her eyes.

'I'm afraid you don't quite understand the position of affairs,' she said. Her voice was harsh and strained.

'Eh?'

'You see – I have not – ' She stopped. 'My little boy is not – Ogden is not living with me just now.'

'At school, eh?'

'No, not at school. Let me tell you the whole position. Mr Ford and I did not get on very well together, and a year ago we were divorced in Washington, on the ground of incompatibility, and – and – '

She choked. His lordship, a young man with a shrinking horror of the deeper emotions, whether exhibited in woman or man, writhed silently. That was the worst of these Americans! Always getting divorced and causing unpleasantness. How was a fellow to know? Why hadn't whoever it was who first introduced them – he couldn't remember who the dickens it was – told him about this? He had supposed she was just the ordinary American woman doing Europe with an affectionate dollar-dispensing husband in the background somewhere.

'Er – ' he said. It was all he could find to say.

'And – and the court,' said Mrs Ford, between her teeth, 'gave him the custody of Ogden.'

Lord Mountry, pink with embarrassment, gurgled sympathetically.

'Since then I have not seen Ogden. That was why I was interested when you mentioned your friend Mr Stanborough. It struck me that Mr Ford could hardly object to my having a portrait of my son painted at my own expense. Nor do I suppose that he will, when – if the matter is put to him. But, well, you see it would be premature to make any arrangements at present for having the picture painted on our yacht trip.'

'I'm afraid it knocks that scheme on the head,' said Lord Mountry mournfully.

'Not necessarily.'

'Eh?'

'I don't want to make plans yet, but – it is possible that Ogden may be with us after all. Something may be – arranged.'

'You think you may be able to bring him along on the yacht after all?'

'I am hoping so.'

Lord Mountry, however willing to emit sympathetic gurgles, was too plain and straightforward a young man to approve of wilful blindness to obvious facts.

'I don't see how you are going to override the decision of the court. It holds good in England, I suppose?'

'I am hoping something may be – arranged.'

'Oh, same here, same here. Certainly.' Having done his duty by not allowing plain facts to be ignored, his lordship was ready to become sympathetic again. 'By the way, where is Ogden?'

'He is down at Mr Ford's house in the country. But – '

She was interrupted by the ringing of the telephone bell. She was out of her seat and across the room at the receiver with what appeared to Lord Mountry's startled gaze one bound. As she put the instrument to her ear a wave of joy swept over her face. She gave a little cry of delight and excitement.

'Send them right up at once,' she said, and turned to Lord Mountry transformed.

'Lord Mountry,' she said quickly, 'please don't think me impossibly rude if I turn you out. Some – some people are coming to see me. I must – '

His lordship rose hurriedly.

'Of course. Of course. Certainly. Where did I put my – ah, here.' He seized his hat, and by way of economizing effort, knocked his stick on to the floor with the same movement. Mrs Ford watched his bendings and gropings with growing impatience, till finally he rose, a little flushed but with a full hand – stick, gloves, and hat, all present and correct.

'Good-bye, then, Mrs Ford, for the present. You'll let me know if your little boy will be able to make one of our party on the yacht?'

'Yes, yes. Thank you ever so much. Good-bye.'

'Good-bye.'

He reached the door and opened it.

'By Jove,' he said, springing round – 'Stanborough! What

about Stanborough? Shall I tell him to wait? He's down below, you know!'

'Yes, yes. Tell Mr Stanborough I'm dreadfully sorry to have to keep him waiting, and ask him if he won't stay for a few minutes in the Palm Room.'

Inspiration came to Lord Mountry.

'I'll give him a drink,' he said.

'Yes, yes, anything. Lord Mountry, you really must go. I know I'm rude. I don't know what I'm saying. But – my boy is returning to me.'

The accumulated chivalry of generations of chivalrous ancestors acted like a spur on his lordship. He understood but dimly, yet enough to enable him to realize that a scene was about to take place in which he was most emphatically not 'on'. A mother's meeting with her long-lost child, this is a sacred thing. This was quite clear to him, so, turning like a flash, he bounded through the doorway, and, as somebody happened to be coming in at the same time, there was a collision, which left him breathing apologies in his familiar attitude of stooping to pick up his hat.

The new-comers were a tall, strikingly handsome girl, with a rather hard and cynical cast of countenance. She was leading by the hand a small, fat boy of about fourteen years of age, whose likeness to the portrait on the chair proclaimed his identity. He had escaped the collision, but seemed offended by it; for, eyeing the bending peer with cold distaste, he summed up his opinion of him in the one word 'Chump!'

Lord Mountry rose.

'I beg your pardon,' he said for perhaps the seventh time. He was thoroughly unstrung. Always excessively shy, he was embarrassed now by quite a variety of causes. The world was full of eyes – Mrs Ford's saying 'Go!' Ogden's saying 'Fool!' the portrait saying 'Idiot!' and, finally, the eyes of this wonderfully handsome girl, large, grey, cool, amused, and contemptuous saying – so it seemed to him in that feverish moment – 'Who is this curious pink person who cumbers the ground before me?'

'I – I beg your pardon,' he repeated.

'Ought to look where you're going,' said Ogden severely.

'Not at all,' said the girl. 'Won't you introduce me, Nesta?'

'Lord Mountry – Miss Drassilis,' said Mrs Ford.

'I'm afraid we're driving Lord Mountry away,' said the girl. Her eyes seemed to his lordship larger, greyer, cooler, more amused, and more contemptuous than ever. He floundered in them like an unskilful swimmer in deep waters.

'No, no,' he stammered. 'Give you my word. Just going. Good-bye. You won't forget to let me know about the yacht, Mrs Ford – what? It'll be an awfully jolly party. Good-bye, good-bye, Miss Drassilis.'

He looked at Ogden for an instant, as if undecided whether to take the liberty of addressing him too, and then, his heart apparently failing him, turned and bolted. From down the corridor came the clatter of a dropped stick.

Cynthia Drassilis closed the door and smiled.

'A nervous young person!' she said. 'What was he saying about a yacht, Nesta?'

Mrs Ford roused herself from her fascinated contemplation of Ogden.

'Oh, nothing. Some of us are going to the south of France in his yacht next week.'

'What a delightful idea!'

There was a certain pensive note in Cynthia's voice.

'A splendid idea!' she murmured.

Mrs Ford swooped. She descended on Ogden in a swirl and rustle of expensive millinery, and clasped him to her.

'My boy!'

It is not given to everybody to glide neatly into a scene of tense emotion. Ogden failed to do so. He wriggled roughly from the embrace.

'Got a cigarette?' he said.

He was an extraordinarily unpleasant little boy. Physically the portrait standing on the chair did him more than justice. Painted by a mother's loving hand, it flattered him. It was bulgy. He was more bulgy. It was sullen. He scowled. And, art having its limitations, particularly amateur art, the portrait gave no hint of his very repellent manner. He was an intensely

13

sophisticated child. He had the air of one who has seen all life has to offer, and is now permanently bored. His speech and bearing were those of a young man, and a distinctly unlovable young man.

Even Mrs Ford was momentarily chilled. She laughed shakily.

'How very matter-of-fact you are, darling!' she said.

Cynthia was regarding the heir to the Ford millions with her usual steady, half-contemptuous gaze.

'He has been that all day,' she said. 'You have no notion what a help it was to me.'

Mrs Ford turned to her effusively.

'Oh, Cynthia, dear, I haven't thanked you.'

'No,' interpolated the girl dryly.

'You're a wonder, darling. You really are. I've been repeating that ever since I got your telegram from Eastnor.' She broke off. 'Ogden, come near me, my little son.'

He lurched towards her sullenly.

'Don't muss a fellow now,' he stipulated, before allowing himself to be enfolded in the outstretched arms.

'Tell me, Cynthia,' resumed Mrs Ford, 'how did you do it? I was telling Lord Mountry that I *hoped* I might see my Ogden again soon, but I never really hoped. It seemed too impossible that you should succeed.'

'This Lord Mountry of yours,' said Cynthia. 'How did you get to know him? Why have I not seen him before?'

'I met him in Paris in the fall. He has been out of London for a long time, looking after his father, who was ill.'

'I see.'

'He has been most kind, making arrangements about getting Ogden's portrait painted. But, bother Lord Mountry. How did we get sidetracked on to him? Tell me how you got Ogden away.'

Cynthia yawned.

'It was extraordinarily easy, as it turned out, you see.'

'Ogden, darling,' observed Mrs Ford, 'don't go away. I want you *near* me.'

'Oh, all right.'

'Then stay by me, angel-face.'

'Oh, slush!' muttered angel-face beneath his breath. 'Say, I'm darned hungry,' he added.

It was if an electric shock had been applied to Mrs Ford. She sprang to her feet.

'My poor child! Of course you must have some lunch. Ring the bell, Cynthia. I'll have them send up some here.'

'I'll have *mine* here,' said Cynthia.

'Oh, you've had no lunch either! I was forgetting that.'

'I thought you were.'

'You must both lunch here.'

'Really,' said Cynthia, 'I think it would be better if Ogden had his downstairs in the restaurant.'

'Want to talk scandal, eh?'

'Ogden, *dearest*!' said Mrs Ford. 'Very well, Cynthia. Go, Ogden. You will order yourself something substantial, marvel-child?'

'Bet your life,' said the son and heir tersely.

There was a brief silence as the door closed. Cynthia gazed at her friend with a peculiar expression.

'Well, I did it, dear,' she said.

'Yes. It's splendid. You're a wonder, darling.'

'Yes,' said Cynthia.

There was another silence.

'By the way,' said Mrs Ford, 'didn't you say there was a little thing, a small bill, that was worrying you?'

'Did I mention it? Yes, there is. It's rather pressing. In fact, it's taking up most of the horizon at present. Here it is.'

'Is it a large sum?' Mrs Ford took the slip of paper and gave a slight gasp. Then, coming to the bureau, she took out her cheque-book.

'It's very kind of you, Nesta,' said Cynthia. 'They were beginning to show quite a vindictive spirit about it.'

She folded the cheque calmly and put it in her purse.

'And now tell me how you did it,' said Mrs Ford.

She dropped into a chair and leaned back, her hands behind her head. For the first time, she seemed to enjoy perfect peace of mind. Her eyes half closed, as if she had been making ready to listen to some favourite music.

'Tell me from the very beginning,' she said softly.

Cynthia checked a yawn.

'Very well, dear,' she said. 'I caught the 10.20 to Eastnor, which isn't a bad train, if you ever want to go down there. I arrived at a quarter past twelve, and went straight up to the house – you've never seen the house, of course? It's quite charming – and told the butler that I wanted to see Mr Ford on business. I had taken the precaution to find out that he was not there. He is at Droitwich.'

'Rheumatism,' murmured Mrs Ford. 'He has it sometimes.'

'The man told me he was away, and then he seemed to think that I ought to go. I stuck like a limpet. I sent him to fetch Ogden's tutor. His name is Broster – Reggie Broster. He is a very nice young man. Big, broad shoulders, and such a kind face.'

'Yes, dear, yes?'

'I told him I was doing a series of drawings for a magazine of the interiors of well-known country houses.'

'He believed you?'

'He believed everything. He's that kind of man. He believed me when I told him that my editor particularly wanted me to sketch the staircase. They had told me about the staircase at the inn. I forget what it is exactly, but it's something rather special in staircases.'

'So you got in?'

'So I got in.'

'And saw Ogden?'

'Only for a moment – then Reggie – '

'Who?'

'Mr Broster. I always think of him as Reggie. He's one of Nature's Reggies. *Such* a kind, honest face. Well, as I was saying, Reggie discovered that it was time for lessons, and sent Ogden upstairs.'

'By himself?'

'By himself! Reggie and I chatted for a while.'

Mrs Ford's eyes opened, brown and bright and hard.

'Mr Broster is not a proper tutor for my boy,' she said coldly.

'I suppose it was wrong of Reggie,' said Cynthia. 'But – I was wearing this hat.'

'Go on.'

'Well, after a time, I said I must be starting my work. He wanted me to start with the room we were in. I said no, I was going out into the grounds to sketch the house from the EAST. I chose the EAST because it happens to be nearest the railway station. I added that I supposed he sometimes took Ogden for a little walk in the grounds. He said yes, he did, and it was just about due. He said possibly he might come round my way. He said Ogden would be interested in my sketch. He seemed to think a lot of Ogden's fondness for art.'

'Mr Broster is *not* a proper tutor for my boy.'

'Well, he isn't your boy's tutor now, is he, dear?'

'What happened then?'

'I strolled off with my sketching things. After a while Reggie and Ogden came up. I said I hadn't been able to work because I had been frightened by a bull.'

'Did he believe *that*?'

'*Certainly* he believed it. He was most kind and sympathetic. We had a nice chat. He told me all about himself. He used to be very good at football. He doesn't play now, but he often thinks of the past.'

'But he must have seen that you couldn't sketch. Then what became of your magazine commission story?'

'Well, somehow the sketch seemed to get shelved. I didn't even have to start it. We were having our chat, you see. Reggie was telling me how good he had been at football when he was at Oxford, and he wanted me to see a newspaper clipping of a Varsity match he had played in. I said I'd love to see it. He said it was in his suit-case in the house. So I promised to look after Ogden while he fetched it. I sent him off to get it just in time for us to catch the train. Off he went, and here we are. And now, won't you order that lunch you mentioned? I'm starving.'

Mrs Ford rose. Half-way to the telephone she stopped suddenly.

'My dear child! It has only just struck me! We must leave here at once. He will have followed you. He will guess that Ogden has been kidnapped.'

Cynthia smiled.

'Believe me, it takes Reggie quite a long time to guess anything. Besides, there are no trains for hours. We are quite safe.'

'Are you sure?'

'Absolutely. I made certain of that before I left.'

Mrs Ford kissed her impulsively.

'Oh, Cynthia, you really are wonderful!'

She started back with a cry as the bell rang sharply.

'For goodness' sake, Nesta,' said Cynthia, with irritation, 'do keep control of yourself. There's nothing to be frightened about. I tell you Mr Broster can't possibly have got here in the time, even if he knew where to go to, which I don't see how he could. It's probably Ogden.'

The colour came back into Mrs Ford's cheeks.

'Why, of course.'

Cynthia opened the door.

'Come in, darling,' said Mrs Ford fondly. And a wiry little man with grey hair and spectacles entered.

'Good afternoon, Mrs Ford,' he said. 'I have come to take Ogden back.'

II

There are some situations in life so unexpected, so trying, that, as far as concerns our opinion of those subjected to them, we agree, as it were, not to count them; we refuse to allow the victim's behaviour in circumstances so exacting to weigh with us in our estimate of his or her character. We permit the great general, confronted suddenly with a mad bull, to turn and run, without forfeiting his reputation for courage. The bishop who, stepping on a concealed slide in winter, entertains passers-by with momentary rag-time steps, loses none of his dignity once the performance is concluded.

In the same way we must condone the behaviour of Cynthia

18

Drassilis on opening the door of Mrs Ford's sitting-room and admitting, not Ogden, but this total stranger, who accompanied his entry with the remarkable speech recorded at the close of the last section.

She was a girl who prided herself on her carefully blasé and supercilious attitude towards life; but this changeling was too much for her. She released the handle, tottered back, and, having uttered a discordant squeak of amazement, stood staring, eyes and mouth wide open.

On Mrs Ford the apparition had a different effect. The rather foolish smile of welcome vanished from her face as if wiped away with a sponge. Her eyes, fixed and frightened like those of a trapped animal, glared at the intruder. She took a step forward, choking.

'What – what do you mean by daring to enter my room?' she cried.

The man held his ground, unmoved. His bearing was a curious blend of diffidence and aggressiveness. He was determined, but apologetic. A hired assassin of the Middle Ages, resolved to do his job loyally, yet conscious of causing inconvenience to his victim, might have looked the same.

'I am sorry,' he said, 'but I must ask you to let me have the boy, Mrs Ford.'

Cynthia was herself again now. She raked the intruder with the cool stare which had so disconcerted Lord Mountry.

'Who is this gentleman?' she asked languidly.

The intruder was made of tougher stuff than his lordship. He met her eye with quiet firmness.

'My name is Mennick,' he said. 'I am Mr Elmer Ford's private secretary.'

'What do you want?' said Mrs Ford.

'I have already explained what I want, Mrs Ford. I want Ogden.'

Cynthia raised her eyebrows.

'What *does* he mean, Nesta? Ogden is not here.'

Mr Mennick produced from his breast-pocket a telegraph form, and in his quiet, business-like way proceeded to straighten it out.

'I have here,' he said, 'a telegram from Mr Broster, Ogden's tutor. It was one of the conditions of his engagement that if ever he was not certain of Ogden's whereabouts he should let me know at once. He tells me that early this afternoon he left Ogden in the company of a strange young lady' – Mr Mennick's spectacles flashed for a moment at Cynthia – 'and that, when he returned, both of them had disappeared. He made inquiries and discovered that this young lady caught the 1.15 express to London, Ogden with her. On receipt of this information I at once wired to Mr Ford for instructions. I have his reply' – he fished for and produced a second telegram – 'here.'

'I still fail to see what brings you here,' said Mrs Ford. 'Owing to the gross carelessness of his father's employees, my son appears to have been kidnapped. That is no reason – '

'I will read Mr Ford's telegram,' proceeded Mr Mennick unmoved. 'It is rather long. I think Mr Ford is somewhat annoyed. "The boy has obviously been stolen by some hireling of his mother's." I am reading Mr Ford's actual words,' he said, addressing Cynthia with that touch of diffidence which had marked his manner since his entrance.

'Don't apologize,' said Cynthia, with a short laugh. 'You're not responsible for Mr Ford's rudeness.'

Mr Mennick bowed.

'He continued: "Remove him from her illegal restraint. If necessary call in police and employ force." '

'Charming!' said Mrs Ford.

'Practical,' said Mr Mennick. 'There is more. "Before doing anything else sack that fool of a tutor, then go to Agency and have them recommend good private school for boy. On no account engage another tutor. They make me tired. Fix all this to-day. Send Ogden back to Eastnor with Mrs Sheridan. She will stay there with him till further notice." That is Mr Ford's message.'

Mr Mennick folded both documents carefully and replaced them in his pocket.

Mrs Ford looked at the clock.

'And now, would you mind going, Mr Mennick?'

'I am sorry to appear discourteous, Mrs Ford, but I cannot go without Ogden.'

'I shall telephone to the office to send up a porter to remove you.'

'I shall take advantage of his presence to ask him to fetch a policeman.'

In the excitement of combat the veneer of apologetic diffidence was beginning to wear off Mr Mennick. He spoke irritably. Cynthia appealed to his reason with the air of a bored princess descending to argument with a groom.

'Can't you see for yourself that he's not here?' she said. 'Do you think we are hiding him?'

'Perhaps you would like to search my bedroom?' said Mrs Ford, flinging the door open.

Mr Mennick remained uncrushed.

'Quite unnecessary, Mrs Ford. I take it, from the fact that he does not appear to be in this suite, that he is downstairs making a late luncheon in the restaurant.'

'I shall telephone – '

'And tell them to send him up. Believe me, Mrs Ford, it is the only thing to do. You have my deepest sympathy, but I am employed by Mr Ford and must act solely in his interests. The law is on my side. I am here to fetch Ogden away, and I am going to have him.'

'You shan't!'

'I may add that, when I came up here, I left Mrs Sheridan – she is a fellow-secretary of mine. You may remember Mr Ford mentioning her in his telegram – I left her to search the restaurant and grill-room, with instructions to bring Ogden, if found, to me in this room.'

The door-bell rang. He went to the door and opened it.

'Come in, Mrs Sheridan. Ah!'

A girl in a plain, neat blue dress entered the room. She was a small, graceful girl of about twenty-five, pretty and brisk, with the air of one accustomed to look after herself in a difficult world. Her eyes were clear and steady, her mouth sensitive but firm, her chin the chin of one who has met trouble and faced it bravely. A little soldier.

She was shepherding Ogden before her, a gorged but still sullen Ogden. He sighted Mr Mennick and stopped.

'Hello!' he said. 'What have you blown in for?'

'He was just in the middle of his lunch,' said the girl. 'I thought you wouldn't mind if I let him finish.'

'Say, what's it all about, anyway?' demanded Ogden crossly. 'Can't a fellow have a bit of grub in peace? You give me a pain.'

Mr Mennick explained.

'Your father wishes you to return to Eastnor, Ogden.'

'Oh, all right. I guess I'd better go, then. Good-bye, ma.'

Mrs Ford choked.

'Kiss me, Ogden.'

Ogden submitted to the embrace in sulky silence. The others comported themselves each after his or her own fashion. Mr Mennick fingered his chin uncomfortably. Cynthia turned to the table and picked up an illustrated paper. Mrs Sheridan's eyes filled with tears. She took a half-step towards Mrs Ford, as if about to speak, then drew back.

'Come, Ogden,' said Mr Mennick gruffly. Necessary, this Hired Assassin work, but painful – devilish painful. He breathed a sigh of relief as he passed into the corridor with his prize.

At the door Mrs Sheridan hesitated, stopped, and turned.

'I'm sorry,' she said impulsively.

Mrs Ford turned away without speaking, and went into the bedroom.

Cynthia laid down her paper.

'One moment, Mrs Sheridan.'

The girl had turned to go. She stopped.

'Can you give me a minute? Come in and shut the door. Won't you sit down? Very well. You seemed sorry for Mrs Ford just now.'

'I am very sorry for Mrs Ford. Very sorry. I hate to see her suffering. I wish Mr Mennick had not brought me into this.'

'Nesta's mad about that boy,' said Cynthia. 'Heaven knows why. *I* never saw such a repulsive child in my life. However, there it is. I am sorry for *you*. I gathered from what Mr Mennick said that you were to have a good deal of Ogden's society for some time to come. How do you feel about it?'

Mrs Sheridan moved towards the door.

'I must be going,' she said. 'Mr Mennick will be waiting for me.'

'One moment. Tell me, don't you think, after what you saw just now, that Mrs Ford is the proper person to have charge of Ogden? You see how devoted she is to him?'

'May I be quite frank with you?'

'Please.'

'Well, then, I think that Mrs Ford's influence is the worst possible for Ogden. I am sorry for her, but that does not alter my opinion. It is entirely owing to Mrs Ford that Ogden is what he is. She spoiled him, indulged him in every way, never checked him – till he has become – well, what you yourself called him, repulsive.'

Cynthia laughed.

'Oh well,' she said, 'I only talked that mother's love stuff because you looked the sort of girl who would like it. We can drop all that now, and come down to business.'

'I don't understand you.'

'You will. I don't know if you think that I kidnapped Ogden from sheer affection for Mrs Ford. I like Nesta, but not as much as that. No. I'm one of the Get-Rich-Quick-Wallingfords, and I'm looking out for myself all the time. There's no one else to do it for me. I've a beastly home. My father's dead. My mother's a cat. So – '

'Please stop,' said Mrs Sheridan. 'I don't know why you are telling me all this.'

'Yes, you do. I don't know what salary Mr Ford pays you, but I don't suppose it's anything princely. Why don't you come over to us? Mrs Ford would give you the earth if you smuggled Ogden back to her.'

'You seem to be trying to bribe me,' said Mrs Sheridan.

'In this case,' said Cynthia, 'appearances aren't deceptive. I am.'

'Good afternoon.'

'Don't be a little fool.'

The door slammed.

'Come back!' cried Cynthia. She took a step as if to follow, but gave up the idea with a laugh. She sat down and began to read her illustrated paper again. Presently the bedroom door opened. Mrs Ford came in. She touched her eyes with a handkerchief as she entered. Cynthia looked up.

'I'm very sorry, Nesta,' she said.

Mrs Ford went to the window and looked out.

'I'm not going to break down, if that's what you mean,' she said. 'I don't care. And, anyhow, it shows that it *can* be done.'

Cynthia turned a page of her paper.

'I've just been trying my hand at bribery and corruption.'

'What do you mean?'

'Oh, I promised and vowed many things in your name to that secretary person, the female one – not Mennick – if she would help us. Nothing doing. I told her to let us have Ogden as soon as possible, C.O.D., and she withered me with a glance and went.'

Mrs Ford shrugged her shoulders impatiently.

'Oh, let her go. I'm sick of amateurs.'

'Thank you, dear,' said Cynthia.

'Oh, I know you did your best. For an amateur you did wonderfully well. But amateurs never really succeed. There were a dozen little easy precautions which we neglected to take. What we want is a professional; a man whose business is kidnapping; the sort of man who kidnaps as a matter of course; someone like Smooth Sam Fisher.'

'My dear Nesta! Who? I don't think I know the gentleman.'

'He tried to kidnap Ogden in 1906, when we were in New York. At least, the police put it down to him, though they could prove nothing. Then there was a horrible man, the police said he was called Buck MacGinnis. *He* tried in 1907. That was in Chicago.'

'Good gracious! Kidnapping Ogden seems to be as popular as football. And I thought I was a pioneer!'

Something approaching pride came into Mrs Ford's voice.

'I don't suppose there's a child in America,' she said, 'who has had to be so carefully guarded. Why, the kidnappers had a special name for him – they called him "The Little Nugget". For years we never allowed him out of our sight without a detective to watch him.'

24

'Well, Mr Ford seems to have changed all that now. I saw no detectives. I suppose he thinks they aren't necessary in England. Or perhaps he relied on Mr Broster. Poor Reggie!'

'It was criminally careless of him. This will be a lesson to him. He will be more careful in future how he leaves Ogden at the mercy of anybody who cares to come along and snap him up.'

'Which, incidentally, does not make your chance of getting him away any lighter.'

'Oh, I've given up hope now,' said Mrs Ford resignedly.

'*I* haven't,' said Cynthia.

There was something in her voice which made her companion turn sharply and look at her. Mrs Ford might affect to be resigned, but she was a woman of determination, and if the recent reverse had left her bruised, it had by no means crushed her.

'Cynthia! What do you mean? What are you hinting?'

'You despise amateurs, Nesta, but, for all that, it seems that your professionals who kidnap as a matter of course and all the rest of it have not been a bit more successful. It was not my want of experience that made me fail. It was my sex. This is man's work. If I had been a man, I should at least have had brute force to fall back upon when Mr Mennick arrived.'

Mrs Ford nodded.

'Yes, but – '

'And,' continued Cynthia, 'as all these Smooth Sam Fishers of yours have failed too, it is obvious that the only way to kidnap Ogden is from within. We must have some man working for us in the enemy's camp.'

'Which is impossible,' said Mrs Ford dejectedly.

'Not at all.'

'You know a man?'

'I know *the* man.'

'Cynthia! What do you mean? Who is he?'

'His name is Peter Burns.'

Mrs Ford shook her head.

'I don't know him.'

'I'll introduce you. You'll like him.'

'But, Cynthia, how do you know he would be willing to help us?'

'He would do it for me,' Cynthia paused. 'You see,' she went on, 'we are engaged to be married.'

'My dear Cynthia! Why did you not tell me? When did it happen?'

'Last night at the Fletchers' dance.'

Mrs Ford's eyes opened.

'Last night! Were you at a dance last night? And two railway journeys today! You must be tired to death.'

'Oh, I'm all right, thanks. I suppose I shall be a wreck and not fit to be seen tomorrow, but just at present I feel as if nothing could tire me. It's the effect of being engaged, perhaps.'

'Tell me about him.'

'Well, he's rich, and good-looking, and amiable' – Cynthia ticked off these qualities on her fingers – 'and I think he's brave, and he's certainly not so stupid as Mr Broster.'

'And you're very much in love with him?'

'I like him. There's no harm in Peter.'

'You certainly aren't wildly enthusiastic!'

'Oh, we shall hit it off quite well together. I needn't pose to *you*, Nesta, thank goodness! That's one reason why I'm fond of you. You know how I am situated. I've got to marry some one rich, and Peter's quite the nicest rich man I've ever met. He's really wonderfully unselfish. I can't understand it. With his money, you would expect him to be a perfect horror.'

A thought seemed to strike Mrs Ford.

'But, if he's so rich – ' she began. 'I forget what I was going to say,' she broke off.

'Dear Nesta, I know what you were going to say. If he's so rich, why should he be marrying me, when he could take his pick of half London? Well, I'll tell you. He's marrying me for one reason, because he's sorry for me: for another, because I had the sense to make him. He didn't think he was going to marry anyone. A few years ago he had a disappointment. A girl jilted him. She must have been a fool. He thought he was going to live the rest of his life alone with his broken heart. I didn't mean to allow that. It's taken a long time – over two years, from start to finish – but I've done it. He's a sentimentalist. I worked on his sympathy, and last night I

26

made him propose to me at the Fletchers' dance.'

Mrs Ford had not listened to these confidences unmoved. Several times she had tried to interrupt, but had been brushed aside. Now she spoke sharply.

'You know I was not going to say anything of the kind. And I don't think you should speak in this horrible, cynical way of – of – '

She stopped, flushing. There were moments when she hated Cynthia. These occurred for the most part when the latter, as now, stirred her to an exhibition of honest feeling which she looked on as rather unbecoming. Mrs Ford had spent twenty years trying to forget that her husband had married her from behind the counter of a general store in an Illinois village, and these lapses into the uncultivated genuineness of her girlhood made her uncomfortable.

'I wasn't going to say anything of the kind,' she repeated.

Cynthia was all smiling good-humour.

'I know. I was only teasing you. "Stringing", they call it in your country, don't they?'

Mrs Ford was mollified.

'I'm sorry, Cynthia. I didn't mean to snap at you. All the same . . .' She hesitated. What she wanted to ask smacked so dreadfully of Mechanicsville, Illinois. Yet she put the question bravely, for she was somehow feeling quite troubled about this unknown Mr Burns. 'Aren't you really fond of him at all, Cynthia?'

Cynthia beamed.

'Of *course* I am! He's a dear. Nothing would make me give him up. I'm devoted to old Peter. I only told you all that about him because it shows you how kind-hearted he is. He'll do anything for me. Well, shall I sound him about Ogden?'

The magic word took Mrs Ford's mind off the matrimonial future of Mr Burns, and brought him into prominence in his capacity of knight-errant. She laughed happily. The contemplation of Mr Burns as knight-errant healed the sting of defeat. The affair of Mr Mennick began to appear in the light of a mere skirmish.

'You take my breath away!' she said. 'How do you propose that Mr Burns shall help us?'

'It's perfectly simple. You heard Mr Mennick read that telegram. Ogden is to be sent to a private school. Peter shall go there too.'

'But how? I don't understand. We don't know which school Mr Mennick will choose.'

'We can very soon find out.'

'But how can Mr Burns go there?'

'Nothing easier. He will be a young man who has been left a little money and wants to start a school of his own. He goes to Ogden's man and suggests that he pay a small premium to come to him for a term as an extra-assistant-master, to learn the business. Mr Man will jump at him. He will be getting the bargain of his life. Peter didn't get much of a degree at Oxford, but I believe he was wonderful at games. From a private-school point of view he's a treasure.'

'But – would he do it?'

'I think I can persuade him.'

Mrs Ford kissed her with an enthusiasm which hitherto she had reserved for Ogden.

'My darling girl,' she cried, 'if you knew how happy you have made me!'

'I do,' said Cynthia definitely. 'And now you can do the same for me.'

'Anything, anything! You must have some more hats.'

'I don't want any more hats. I want to go with you on Lord Mountry's yacht to the Riviera.'

'Of course,' said Mrs Ford after a slight pause, 'it isn't my party, you know, dear.'

'No. But you can work me in, darling.'

'It's quite a small party. Very quiet.'

'Crowds bore me. I enjoy quiet.'

Mrs Ford capitulated.

'I fancy you are doing me a very good turn,' she said. 'You must certainly come on the yacht.'

'I'll tell Peter to come straight round here now,' said Cynthia simply. She went to the telephone.

Part Two

In which other interested parties, notably one
Buck MacGinnis and a trade rival, Smooth
Sam Fisher, make other plans for the Nugget's
future. Of stirring times at a private school for
young gentlemen. Of stratagems, spoils, and
alarms by night. Of journeys ending in lovers'
meetings. The whole related by Mr Peter Burns,
gentleman of leisure, who forfeits that leisure
in a good cause

Peter Burns's Narrative

Chapter 1

I

I am strongly of the opinion that, after the age of twenty-one, a man ought not to be out of bed and awake at four in the morning. The hour breeds thought. At twenty-one, life being all future, it may be examined with impunity. But, at thirty, having become an uncomfortable mixture of future and past, it is a thing to be looked at only when the sun is high and the world full of warmth and optimism.

This thought came to me as I returned to my rooms after the Fletchers' ball. The dawn was breaking as I let myself in. The air was heavy with the peculiar desolation of a London winter morning. The houses looked dead and untenanted. A cart rumbled past, and across the grey street a dingy black cat, moving furtively along the pavement, gave an additional touch of forlornness to the scene.

I shivered. I was tired and hungry, and the reaction after the emotions of the night had left me dispirited.

I was engaged to be married. An hour back I had proposed to Cynthia Drassilis. And I can honestly say that it had come as a great surprise to me.

Why had I done it? Did I love her? It was so difficult to analyse love: and perhaps the mere fact that I was attempting the task was an answer to the question. Certainly I had never tried to do so five years ago when I had loved Audrey Blake. I had let myself be carried on from day to day in a sort of trance, content to be utterly happy, without dissecting my happiness. But I was five years younger then, and Audrey was – Audrey.

I must explain Audrey, for she in her turn explains Cynthia.

I have no illusions regarding my character when I first met

Audrey Blake. Nature had given me the soul of a pig, and circumstances had conspired to carry on Nature's work. I loved comfort, and I could afford to have it. From the moment I came of age and relieved my trustees of the care of my money, I wrapped myself in comfort as in a garment. I wallowed in egoism. In fact, if, between my twenty-first and my twenty-fifth birthdays, I had one unselfish thought, or did one genuinely unselfish action, my memory is a blank on the point.

It was at the height of this period that I became engaged to Audrey. Now that I can understand her better and see myself, impartially, as I was in those days, I can realize how indescribably offensive I must have been. My love was real, but that did not prevent its patronizing complacency being an insult. I was King Cophetua. If I did not actually say in so many words, 'This beggar-maid shall be my queen', I said it plainly and often in my manner. She was the daughter of a dissolute, evil-tempered artist whom I had met at a Bohemian club. He made a living by painting an occasional picture, illustrating an occasional magazine-story, but mainly by doing advertisement work. A proprietor of a patent Infants' Food, not satisfied with the bare statement that Baby Cried For It, would feel it necessary to push the fact home to the public through the medium of Art, and Mr Blake would be commissioned to draw the picture. A good many specimens of his work in this vein were to be found in the back pages of the magazines.

A man may make a living by these means, but it is one that inclines him to jump at a wealthy son-in-law. Mr Blake jumped at me. It was one of his last acts on this earth. A week after he had – as I now suspect – bullied Audrey into accepting me, he died of pneumonia.

His death had several results. It postponed the wedding: it stirred me to a very crescendo of patronage, for with the removal of the bread-winner the only flaw in my Cophetua pose had vanished: and it gave Audrey a great deal more scope than she had hitherto been granted for the exercise of free will in the choice of a husband.

This last aspect of the matter was speedily brought to my notice, which till then it had escaped, by a letter from her, handed to me one night at the club, where I was sipping coffee and musing on the excellence of life in this best of all possible worlds.

It was brief and to the point. She had been married that morning.

To say that that moment was a turning point in my life would be to use a ridiculously inadequate phrase. It dynamited my life. In a sense it killed me. The man I had been died that night, regretted, I imagine, by few. Whatever I am today, I am certainly not the complacent spectator of life that I had been before that night.

I crushed the letter in my hand, and sat staring at it, my pigsty in ruins about my ears, face to face with the fact that, even in a best of all possible worlds, money will not buy everything.

I remember, as I sat there, a man, a club acquaintance, a bore from whom I had fled many a time, came and settled down beside me and began to talk. He was a small man, but he possessed a voice to which one had to listen. He talked and talked and talked. How I loathed him, as I sat trying to think through his stream of words. I see now that he saved me. He forced me out of myself. But at the time he oppressed me. I was raw and bleeding. I was struggling to grasp the incredible. I had taken Audrey's unalterable affection for granted. She was the natural complement to my scheme of comfort. I wanted her; I had chosen and was satisfied with her, therefore all was well. And now I had to adjust my mind to the impossible fact that I had lost her.

Her letter was a mirror in which I saw myself. She said little, but I understood, and my self-satisfaction was in ribbons – and something deeper than self-satisfaction. I saw now that I loved her as I had not dreamed myself capable of loving.

And all the while this man talked and talked.

I have a theory that speech, persevered in, is more efficacious in times of trouble than silent sympathy. Up to a certain point it maddens almost beyond endurance; but, that point past, it soothes. At least, it was so in my case. Gradually I found myself

33

hating him less. Soon I began to listen, then to answer. Before I left the club that night, the first mad frenzy, in which I could have been capable of anything, had gone from me, and I walked home, feeling curiously weak and helpless, but calm, to begin the new life.

Three years passed before I met Cynthia. I spent those years wandering in many countries. At last, as one is apt to do, I drifted back to London, and settled down again to a life which, superficially, was much the same as the one I had led in the days before I knew Audrey. My old circle in London had been wide, and I found it easy to pick up dropped threads. I made new friends, among them Cynthia Drassilis.

I liked Cynthia, and I was sorry for her. I think that, about that time I met her, I was sorry for most people. The shock of Audrey's departure had had that effect upon me. It is always the bad nigger who gets religion most strongly at the camp-meeting, and in my case 'getting religion' had taken the form of suppression of self. I never have been able to do things by halves, or even with a decent moderation. As an egoist I had been thorough in my egoism; and now, fate having bludgeoned that vice out of me, I found myself possessed of an almost morbid sympathy with the troubles of other people.

I was extremely sorry for Cynthia Drassilis. Meeting her mother frequently, I could hardly fail to be. Mrs Drassilis was a representative of a type I disliked. She was a widow, who had been left with what she considered insufficient means, and her outlook on life was a compound of greed and querulousness. Sloane Square and South Kensington are full of women in her situation. Their position resembles that of the Ancient Mariner. 'Water, water everywhere, nor any drop to drink.' For 'water' in their case substitute 'money'. Mrs Drassilis was connected with money on all sides, but could only obtain it in rare and minute quantities. Any one of a dozen relations-in-law could, if they had wished, have trebled her annual income without feeling it. But they did not so wish. They disapproved of Mrs Drassilis. In their opinion the Hon. Hugo Drassilis had married beneath him – not so far beneath him as to make the thing a horror to be avoided in conversation and thought, but far enough to render them coldly polite to his wife during his life-time and almost icy to his widow after his death. Hugo's eldest brother, the Earl of Westbourne, had never liked the obviously beautiful, but equally obviously second-rate, daughter of a provincial solicitor whom Hugo had suddenly presented to the family one memorable summer as his bride. He considered that, by doubling the income derived from Hugo's life-insurance and inviting Cynthia to the family seat once a year during her child-hood, he had done all that could be expected of him in the matter.

He had not. Mrs Drassilis expected a great deal more of him, the non-receipt of which had spoiled her temper, her looks, and the peace of mind of all who had anything much to do with her.

It used to irritate me when I overheard people, as I occasion-ally have done, speak of Cynthia as hard. I never found her so myself, though heaven knows she had enough to make her so. To me she was always a sympathetic, charming friend.

Ours was a friendship almost untouched by sex. Our minds fitted so smoothly into one another that I had no inclination to fall in love. I knew her too well. I had no discoveries to make about her. Her honest, simple soul had always been open to me to read. There was none of that curiosity, that sense of some-thing beyond that makes for love. We had reached a point of comradeship beyond which neither of us desired to pass.

Yet at the Fletchers' ball I asked Cynthia to marry me, and she consented.

Looking back, I can see that, though the determining cause was Mr Tankerville Gifford, it was Audrey who was re-sponsible. She had made me human, capable of sympathy, and it was sympathy, primarily, that led me to say what I said that night.

But the immediate cause was certainly young Mr Gifford.

I arrived at Marlow Square, where I was to pick up Cynthia and her mother, a little late, and found Mrs Drassilis, florid and overdressed, in the drawing-room with a sleek-haired, pale

young man known to me as Tankerville Gifford – to his inti-
mates, of whom I was not one, and in the personal paragraphs
of the coloured sporting weeklies, as 'Tanky'. I had seen him
frequently at restaurants. Once, at the Empire, somebody had
introduced me to him; but, as he had not been sober at the
moment, he had missed any intellectual pleasure my acquaintanceship might have afforded him. Like everybody else who
moves about in London, I knew all bout him. To sum him up,
he was a most unspeakable little cad, and, if the drawing-room
had not been Mrs Drassilis's, I should have wondered at finding
him in it.

Mrs Drassilis introduced us.

'I think we have already met,' I said.

He stared glassily.

'Don't remember.'

I was not surprised.

At this moment Cynthia came in. Out of the corner of my eye
I observed a look of fuddled displeasure come into Tanky's
face at her frank pleasure at seeing me.

I had never seen her looking better. She is a tall girl, who
carries herself magnificently. The simplicity of her dress gained
an added dignity from comparison with the rank glitter of her
mother's. She wore unrelieved black, a colour which set off to
wonderful advantage the clear white of her skin and her pale-
gold hair.

'You're late, Peter,' she said, looking at the clock.

'I know. I'm sorry.'

'Better be pushing, what?' suggested Tanky.

'My cab's waiting.'

'Will you ring the bell, Mr Gifford?' said Mrs Drassilis. 'I will
tell Parker to whistle for another.'

'Take me in yours,' I heard a voice whisper in my ear.

I looked at Cynthia. Her expression had not changed. Then I
looked at Tanky Gifford, and I understood. I had seen that
stuffed-fish look on his face before – on the occasion when I had
been introduced to him at the Empire.

'If you and Mr Gifford will take my cab,' I said to Mrs
Drassilis, 'we will follow.'

Mrs Drassilis blocked the motion. I imagine that the sharp note in her voice was lost on Tanky, but it rang out like a clarion to me.

'I am in no hurry,' she said. 'Mr Gifford, will you take Cynthia? I will follow with Mr Burns. You will meet Parker on the stairs. Tell him to call another cab.'

As the door closed behind them, she turned on me like a many-coloured snake.

'How *can* you be so extraordinarily tactless, Peter?' she cried. 'You're a perfect fool. Have you no eyes?'

'I'm sorry,' I said.

'He's devoted to her.'

'I'm sorry.'

'What do you mean?'

'Sorry for her.'

She seemed to draw herself together inside her dress. Her eyes glittered. My mouth felt very dry, and my heart was beginning to thump. We were both furiously angry. It was a moment that had been coming for years, and we both knew it. For my part I was glad that it had come. On subjects on which one feels deeply it is a relief to speak one's mind.

'Oh!' she said at last. Her voice quivered. She was clutching at her self-control as it slipped from her. 'Oh! And what is my daughter to you, Mr Burns!'

'A great friend.'

'And I suppose you think it friendly to try to spoil her chances?'

'If Mr Gifford is a sample of them – yes.'

'What do you mean?'

She choked.

'I see. I understand. I am going to put a stop to this once and for all. Do you hear? I have noticed it for a long time. Because I have given you the run of the house, and allowed you to come in and out as you pleased, like a tame cat, you presume – '

'Presume – ' I prompted.

'You come here and stand in Cynthia's way. You trade on the fact that you have known us all this time to monopolize her attention. You spoil her chances. You – '

The invaluable Parker entered to say that the cab was at the door.

We drove to the Fletchers' house in silence. The spell had been broken. Neither of us could recapture that first, fine, careless rapture which had carried us through the opening stages of the conflict, and discussion of the subject on a less exalted plane was impossible. It was that blessed period of calm, the rest between rounds, and we observed it to the full.

When I reached the ballroom a waltz was just finishing. Cynthia, a statue in black, was dancing with Tanky Gifford. They were opposite me when the music stopped, and she caught sight of me over his shoulder.

She disengaged herself and moved quickly towards me.

'Take me away,' she said under her breath. 'Anywhere. Quick.'

It was no time to consider the etiquette of the ballroom. Tanky, startled at his sudden loneliness, seemed by his expression to be endeavouring to bring his mind to bear on the matter. A couple making for the door cut us off from him, and following them, we passed out.

Neither of us spoke till we had reached the little room where I had meditated.

She sat down. She was looking pale and tired.

'Oh, dear!' she said.

I understood. I seemed to see that journey in the cab, those dances, those terrible between-dances . . .

It was very sudden.

I took her hand. She turned to me with a tired smile. There were tears in her eyes . . .

I heard myself speaking . . .

She was looking at me, her eyes shining. All the weariness seemed to have gone out of them.

I looked at her.

There was something missing. I had felt it when I was speaking. To me my voice had had no ring of conviction. And then I saw what it was. There was no mystery. We knew each other too well. Friendship kills love.

She put my thought into words.

'We have always been brother and sister,' she said doubt-fully.

'Till tonight.'

'You have changed tonight? You really want me?'

Did I? I tried to put the question to myself and answer it honestly. Yes, in a sense, I had changed tonight. There was an added appreciation of her fineness, a quickening of that blend of admiration and pity which I had always felt for her. I wanted with all my heart to help her, to take her away from her dread-ful surroundings, to make her happy. But did I want her in the sense in which she had used the word? Did I want her as I had wanted Audrey Blake? I winced away from the question. Audrey belonged to the dead past, but it hurt to think of her.

Was it merely because I was five years older now than when I had wanted Audrey that the fire had gone out of me?

I shut my mind against my doubts.

'I have changed tonight,' I said.

And I bent down and kissed her.

I was conscious of being defiant against somebody. And then I knew that the somebody was myself.

I poured myself out a cup of hot coffee from the flask which Smith, my man, had filled against my return. It put life into me. The oppression lifted.

And yet there remained something that made for uneasiness, a sort of foreboding at the back of my mind.

I had taken a step in the dark, and I was afraid for Cynthia. I had undertaken to give her happiness. Was I certain that I could succeed? The glow of chivalry had left me, and I began to doubt.

Audrey had taken from me something that I could not re-cover – poetry was as near as I could get to a definition of it. Yes, poetry. With Cynthia my feet would always be on the solid earth. To the end of the chapter we should be friends and nothing more.

I found myself pitying Cynthia intensely. I saw her future a series of years of intolerable dullness. She was too good to be tied for life to a battered hulk like myself.

I drank more coffee and my mood changed. Even in the grey of a winter morning a man of thirty, in excellent health, cannot pose to himself for long as a piece of human junk, especially if he comforts himself with hot coffee.

My mind resumed its balance. I laughed at myself as a sentimental fraud. Of course I could make her happy. No man and woman had ever been more admirably suited to each other. As for that first disaster, which I had been magnifying into a life-tragedy, what of it? An incident of my boyhood. A ridiculous episode which – I rose with the intention of doing so at once – I should now proceed to eliminate from my life.

I went quickly to my desk, unlocked it, and took out a photograph.

And then – undoubtedly four o'clock in the morning is no time for a man to try to be single-minded and decisive – I wavered. I had intended to tear the thing in pieces without a glance, and fling it into the wastepaper-basket. But I took the glance and I hesitated.

The girl in the photograph was small and slight, and she looked straight out of the picture with large eyes that met and challenged mine. How well I remembered them, those Irish-blue eyes under their expressive, rather heavy brows. How exactly the photographer had caught that half-wistful, half-impudent look, the chin tilted, the mouth curving into a smile.

In a wave all my doubts had surged back upon me. Was this mere sentimentalism, a four-in-the-morning tribute to the pathos of the flying years, or did she really fill my soul and stand guard over it so that no successor could enter in and usurp her place?

I had no answer, unless the fact that I replaced the photograph in its drawer was one. I felt that this thing could not be decided now. It was more difficult than I had thought.

All my gloom had returned by the time I was in bed. Hours seemed to pass while I tossed restlessly aching for sleep.

When I woke my last coherent thought was still clear in my mind. It was a passionate vow that, come what might, if those

Irish eyes were to haunt me till my death, I would play the game loyally with Cynthia.

II

The telephone bell rang just as I was getting ready to call at Marlow Square and inform Mrs Drassilis of the position of affairs. Cynthia, I imagined, would have broken the news already, which would mitigate the embarrassment of the interview to some extent; but the recollection of my last night's encounter with Mrs Drassilis prevented me from looking forward with any joy to the prospect of meeting her again.

Cynthia's voice greeted me as I unhooked the receiver.

'Hullo, Peter! Is that you? I want you to come round here at once.'

'I was just starting,' I said.

'I don't mean Marlow Square. I'm not there. I'm at the Guelph. Ask for Mrs Ford's suite. It's very important. I'll tell you all about it when you get here. Come as soon as you can.'

My rooms were conveniently situated for visits to the Hotel Guelph. A walk of a couple of minutes took me there. Mrs Ford's suite was on the third floor. I rang the bell and Cynthia opened the door to me.

'Come in,' she said. 'You're a dear to be so quick.'

'My rooms are only just round the corner.'

She shut the door, and for the first time we looked at one another. I could not say that I was nervous, but there was certainly, to me, a something strange in the atmosphere. Last night seemed a long way off and somehow a little unreal. I suppose I must have shown this in my manner, for she suddenly broke what had amounted to a distinct pause by giving a little laugh.

'Peter,' she said, 'you're embarrassed.'

I denied the charge warmly, but without real conviction. I *was* embarrassed.

'Then you ought to be,' she said. 'Last night, when I was looking my very best in a lovely dress, you asked me to marry you. Now you see me again in cold blood, and you're wondering how you can back out of it without hurting my feelings.'

I smiled. She did not. I ceased to smile. She was looking at me in a very peculiar manner.

'Peter,' she said, 'are you sure?'

'My dear old Cynthia,' I said, 'what's the matter with you?'

'You *are* sure?' she persisted.

'Absolutely, entirely sure.' I had a vision of two large eyes looking at me out of a photograph. It came and went in a flash.

I kissed Cynthia.

'What quantities of hair you have,' I said. 'It's a shame to cover it up.' She was not responsive. 'You're in a very queer mood today, Cynthia,' I went on. 'What's the matter?'

'I've been thinking.'

'Out with it. Something has gone wrong.' An idea flashed upon me. 'Er – has your mother – is your mother very angry about – '

'Mother's delighted. She always liked you, Peter.'

I had the self-restraint to check a grin.

'Then what is it?' I said. 'Tired after the dance?'

'Nothing as simple as that.'

'Tell me.'

'It's so difficult to put it into words.'

'Try.'

She was playing with the papers on the table, her face turned away. For a moment she did not speak.

'I've been worrying myself, Peter,' she said at last. 'You are so chivalrous and unselfish. You're quixotic. It's that that is troubling me. Are you marrying me just because you're sorry for me? Don't speak. I can tell you now if you will just let me say straight out what's in my mind. We have known each other for two years now. You know all about me. You know how – how unhappy I am at home. Are you marrying me just because you pity me and want to take me out of all that?'

'My dear girl!'

'You haven't answered my question.'

'I answered it two minutes ago when you asked me if – '

'You do love me?'

'Yes.'

All this time she had been keeping her face averted, but now she turned and looked into my eyes with an abrupt intensity which, I confess, startled me. Her words startled me more.

'Peter, do you love me as much as you loved Audrey Blake?'

In the instant which divided her words from my reply my mind flew hither and thither, trying to recall an occasion when I could have mentioned Audrey to her. I was convinced that I had not done so. I never mentioned Audrey to anyone.

There is a grain of superstition in the most level-headed man. I am not particularly level-headed, and I have more than a grain in me. I was shaken. Ever since I had asked Cynthia to marry me, it seemed as if the ghost of Audrey had come back into my life.

'Good Lord!' I cried. 'What do you know of Audrey Blake?'

She turned her face away again.

'Her name seems to affect you very strongly,' she said quietly.

I recovered myself.

'If you ask an old soldier,' I said, 'he will tell you that a wound, long after it has healed, is apt to give you an occasional twinge.'

'Not if it has really healed.'

'Yes, when it has really healed – when you can hardly remember how you were fool enough to get it.'

She said nothing.

'How did you hear about – it?' I asked.

'When I first met you, or soon after, a friend of yours – we happened to be talking about you – told me that you had been engaged to be married to a girl named Audrey Blake. He was to have been your best man, he said, but one day you wrote and told him there would be no wedding, and then you disappeared; and nobody saw you again for three years.'

'Yes,' I said: 'that is all quite true.'

'It seems to have been a serious affair, Peter. I mean – the sort of thing a man would find it hard to forget.'

I tried to smile, but I knew that I was not doing it well. It was hurting me extraordinarily, this discussion of Audrey.

'A man would find it almost impossible,' I said, 'unless he had a remarkably poor memory.'

'I didn't mean that. You know what I mean by forget.'

'Yes,' I said, 'I do.'

She came quickly to me and took me by the shoulders, looking into my face.

'Peter, can you honestly say you have forgotten her – in the sense I mean?'

'Yes,' I said.

Again that feeling swept over me – that curious sensation of being defiant against myself.

'She does not stand between us?'

'No,' I said.

I could feel the effort behind the word. It was as if some subconscious part of me were working to keep it back.

'Peter!'

There was a soft smile on her face; as she raised it to mine I put my arms around her.

She drew away with a little laugh. Her whole manner had changed. She was a different being from the girl who had looked so gravely into my eyes a moment before.

'Oh, my dear boy, how terribly muscular you are! You've crushed me. I expect you used to be splendid at football, like Mr Broster.'

I did not reply at once. I cannot wrap up the deeper emotions and put them back on their shelf directly I have no further immediate use for them. I slowly adjusted myself to the new key of the conversation.

'Who's Broster?' I asked at length.

'He used to be tutor to' – she turned me round and pointed – 'to *that.*'

I had seen a picture standing on one of the chairs when I entered the room but had taken no particular notice of it. I now gave it a closer glance. It was a portrait, very crudely done, of a singularly repulsive child of about ten or eleven years old.

'*Was* he, poor chap! Well, we all have our troubles, don't we! Who *is* this young thug! Not a friend of yours, I hope?'

'That is Ogden, Mrs Ford's son. It's a tragedy – '

'Perhaps it doesn't do him justice. Does he really squint like that, or is it just the artist's imagination?'

'Don't make fun of it. It's the loss of that boy that is breaking Nesta's heart.'

I was shocked.

'Is he dead? I'm awfully sorry. I wouldn't for the world – '

'No, no. He is alive and well. But he is dead to her. The court gave him into the custody of his father.'

'The court?'

'Mrs Ford was the wife of Elmer Ford, the American millionaire. They were divorced a year ago.'

'I see.'

Cynthia was gazing at the portrait.

'This boy is quite a celebrity in his way,' she said. 'They call him "The Little Nugget" in America.'

'Oh! Why is that?'

'It's a nickname the kidnappers have for him. Ever so many attempts have been made to steal him.'

She stopped and looked at me oddly.

'I made one today, Peter,' she said. 'I went down to the country, where the boy was, and kidnapped him.'

'Cynthia! What on earth do you mean?'

'Don't you understand? I did it for Nesta's sake. She was breaking her heart about not being able to see him, so I slipped down and stole him away, and brought him back here.'

I do not know if I was looking as amazed as I felt. I hope not, for I felt as if my brain were giving way. The perfect calmness with which she spoke of this extraordinary freak added to my confusion.

'You're joking!'

'No; I stole him.'

'But, good heavens! The law! It's a penal offence, you know!'

'Well, I did it. Men like Elmer Ford aren't fit to have charge of a child. You don't know him, but he's just an unscrupulous financier, without a thought above money. To think of a boy growing up in that tainted atmosphere – at his most impressionable age. It means death to any good there is in him.'

My mind was still grappling feebly with the legal aspect of the affair.

'But, Cynthia, kidnapping's kidnapping, you know! The law doesn't take any notice of motives. If you're caught – '

She cut through my babble.

'Would you have been afraid to do it, Peter?'

'Well – ' I began. I had not considered the point before.

'I don't believe you would. If I asked you to do it for my sake – '

'But, Cynthia, kidnapping, you know! It's such an infernally low-down game.'

'I played it. Do you despise *me*?'

I perspired. I could think of no other reply.

'Peter,' she said, 'I understand your scruples. I know exactly how you feel. But can't you see that this is quite different from the sort of kidnapping you naturally look on as horrible? It's just taking a boy away from surroundings that must harm him, back to his mother, who worships him. It's not wrong. It's splendid.'

She paused.

'You *will* do it for me, Peter?' she said.

'I don't understand,' I said feebly. 'It's done. You've kidnapped him yourself.'

'They tracked him and took him back. And now I want *you* to try.' She came closer to me. 'Peter, don't you see what it will mean to me if you agree to try? I'm only human, I can't help, at the bottom of my heart, still being a little jealous of this Audrey Blake. No, don't say anything. Words can't cure me; but if you do this thing for me, I shall be satisfied. I shall *know*.'

She was close beside me, holding my arm and looking into my face. That sense of the unreality of things which had haunted me since that moment at the dance came over me with renewed intensity. Life had ceased to be a rather grey, orderly business in which day succeeded day calmly and without event.

Its steady stream had broken up into rapids, and I was being whirled away on them.

'Will you do it, Peter? Say you will.'

A voice, presumably mine, answered 'Yes'.

'My dear old boy!'

She pushed me into a chair, and, sitting on the arm of it, laid her hand on mine and became of a sudden wondrously business-like.

'Listen,' she said, 'I'll tell you what we have arranged.'

It was borne in upon me, as she began to do so, that she appeared from the very beginning to have been extremely confident that that essential part of her plans, my consent to the scheme, could be relied upon as something of a certainty. Women have these intuitions.

III

Looking back, I think I can fix the point at which this insane venture I had undertaken ceased to be a distorted dream, from which I vaguely hoped that I might shortly waken, and took shape as a reality of the immediate future. That moment came when I met Mr Arnold Abney by appointment at his club.

Till then the whole enterprise had been visionary. I gathered from Cynthia that the boy Ogden was shortly to be sent to a preparatory school, and that I was to insinuate myself into this school and, watching my opportunity, to remove him; but it seemed to me that the obstacles to this comparatively lucid scheme were insuperable. In the first place, how were we to discover which of England's million preparatory schools Mr Ford, or Mr Mennick for him, would choose? Secondly, the plot which was to carry me triumphantly into this school when – or if – found, struck me as extremely thin. I was to pose, Cynthia told me, as a young man of private means, anxious to learn the business, with a view to setting up a school of his own. The objection to that was, I held, that I obviously did not want to do anything of the sort. I had not the appearance of a man with such an ambition. I had none of the conversation of such a man.

I put it to Cynthia.

'They would find me out in a day,' I assured her. 'A man who wants to set up a school has got to be a pretty brainy sort of fellow. I don't know anything.'

'You got your degree.'

'*A* degree. At any rate, I've forgotten all I knew.'

'That doesn't matter. You have the money. Anybody with money can start a school, even if he doesn't know a thing. Nobody would think it strange.'

It struck me as a monstrous slur on our educational system, but reflection told me it was true. The proprietor of a preparatory school, if he is a man of wealth, need not be able to teach, any more than an impresario need be able to write plays.

'Well, we'll pass that for the moment,' I said. 'Here's the real difficulty. How are you going to find out the school Mr Ford has chosen?'

'I have found it out already – or Nesta has. She set a detective to work. It was perfectly easy. Ogden's going to Mr Abney's. Sanstead House is the name of the place. It's in Hampshire somewhere. Quite a small school, but full of little dukes and earls and things. Lord Mountry's younger brother, Augustus Beckford, is there.'

I had known Lord Mountry and his family well some years ago. I remembered Augustus dimly.

'Mountry? Do you know him? He was up at Oxford with me.'

She seemed interested.

'What kind of a man is he?' she asked.

'Oh, quite a good sort. Rather an ass. I haven't seen him for years.'

'He's a friend of Nesta's. I've only met him once. He is going to be your reference.'

'My what?'

'You will need a reference. At least, I suppose you will. And, anyhow, if you say you know Lord Mountry it will make it simpler for you with Mr Abney, the brother being at the school.'

'Does Mountry know about this business? Have you told him why I want to go to Abney's?'

'Nesta told him. He thought it was very sporting of you. He will tell Mr Abney anything we like. By the way, Peter, you will have to pay a premium or something, I suppose. But Nesta will look after all expenses, of course.'

On this point I made my only stand of the afternoon.

'No,' I said; 'it's very kind of her, but this is going to be entirely an amateur performance. I'm doing this for you, and I'll stand the racket. Good heavens! Fancy taking money for a job of this kind!'

She looked at me rather oddly.

'That is very sweet of you, Peter,' she said, after a slight pause. 'Now let's get to work.'

And together we composed the letter which led to my sitting, two days later, in stately conference at his club with Mr Arnold Abney, M.A., of Sanstead House, Hampshire.

Mr Abney proved to be a long, suave, benevolent man with an Oxford manner, a high forehead, thin white hands, a cooing intonation, and a general air of hushed importance, as of one in constant communication with the Great. There was in his bearing something of the family solicitor in whom dukes confide, and something of the private chaplain at the Castle.

He gave me the key-note to his character in the first minute of our acquaintanceship. We had seated ourselves at a table in the smoking-room when an elderly gentleman shuffled past, giving a nod in transit. My companion sprang to his feet almost convulsively, returned the salutation, and subsided slowly into his chair again.

'The Duke of Devizes,' he said in an undertone. 'A most able man. Most able. His nephew, Lord Ronald Stokeshaye, was one of my pupils. A charming boy.'

I gathered that the old feudal spirit still glowed to some extent in Mr Abney's bosom.

We came to business.

'So you wish to be one of us, Mr Burns, to enter the scholastic profession?'

I tried to look as if I did.

'Well, in certain circumstances, the circumstances in which I – ah – myself, I may say, am situated, there is no more delightful occupation. The work is interesting. There is the constant fascination of seeing these fresh young lives develop – and of helping them to develop – under one's eyes; in any case, I may say, there is the exceptional interest of being in a position to mould the growing minds of lads who will some day take their place among the country's hereditary legislators, that little knot of devoted men who, despite the vulgar attacks of loud-mouthed demagogues, still do their share, and more, in the guidance of England's fortunes. Yes.'

He paused. I said I thought so, too.

'You are an Oxford man, Mr Burns, I think you told me? Ah, I have your letter here. Just so. You were at – ah, yes. A fine college. The Dean is a lifelong friend of mine. Perhaps you knew my late pupil, Lord Rollo? – no, he would have been since your time. A delightful boy. Quite delightful ... And you took your degree? Exactly. *And* represented the university at both cricket and Rugby football? Excellent. *Mens sana in* – ah – *corpore*, in fact, *sano*, yes!'

He folded the letter carefully and replaced it in his pocket.

'Your primary object in coming to me, Mr Burns, is, I gather, to learn the – ah – the ropes, the business? You have had little or no previous experience of school-mastering?'

'None whatever.'

'Then your best plan would undoubtedly be to consider yourself and work for a time simply as an ordinary assistant-master. You would thus get a sound knowledge of the intricacies of the profession which would stand you in good stead when you decide to set up your own school. School-mastering is a profession, which cannot be taught adequately except in practice. "Only those who – ah – brave its dangers comprehend its mystery." Yes, I would certainly recommend you to begin at the foot of the ladder and go, at least for a time, through the mill.'

'Certainly,' I said. 'Of course.'

My ready acquiescence pleased him. I could see that he was

50

relieved. I think he had expected me to jib at the prospect of actual work.

'As it happens,' he said, 'my classical master left me at the end of last term. I was about to go to the Agency for a successor when your letter arrived. Would you consider – '

I had to think this over. Feeling kindly disposed towards Mr Arnold Abney, I wished to do him as little harm as possible. I was going to rob him of a boy, who, while no moulding of his growing mind could make him into a hereditary legislator, did undoubtedly represent a portion of Mr Abney's annual income; and I did not want to increase my offence by being a useless assistant-master. Then I reflected that, if I was no Jowett, at least I knew enough Latin and Greek to teach the rudiments of those languages to small boys. My conscience was satisfied.

'I should be delighted,' I said.

'Excellent. Then let us consider that as – ah – settled,' said Mr Abney.

There was a pause. My companion began to fiddle a little uncomfortably with an ash-tray. I wondered what was the matter, and then it came to me. We were about to become sordid. The discussion of terms was upon us.

And as I realized this, I saw simultaneously how I could throw one more sop to my exigent conscience. After all, the whole thing was really a question of hard cash. By kidnapping Ogden I should be taking money from Mr Abney. By paying my premium I should be giving it back to him.

I considered the circumstances. Ogden was now about thirteen years old. The preparatory-school age limit may be estimated roughly at fourteen. That is to say, in any event Sanstead House could only harbour him for one year. Mr Abney's fees I had to guess at. To be on the safe side, I fixed my premium at an outside figure, and, getting to the point at once, I named it.

It was entirely satisfactory. My mental arithmetic had done me credit. Mr Abney beamed upon me. Over tea and muffins we became very friendly. In half an hour I heard more of the theory of school-mastering than I had dreamed existed.

We said good-bye at the club front door. He smiled down at me benevolently from the top of the steps.

'Good-bye, Mr Burns, good-bye,' he said. 'We shall meet at –
ah – Philippi.'

When I reached my rooms, I rang for Smith.

'Smith,' I said, 'I want you to get some books for me first
thing tomorrow. You had better take a note of them.'

He moistened his pencil.

'A Latin Grammar.'

'Yes, sir.'

'A Greek Grammar.'

'Yes, sir.'

'Brodley Arnold's *Easy Prose Sentences*.'

'Yes, sir.'

'And Caesar's *Gallic Wars*.'

'What name, sir?'

'Caesar.'

'Thank you, sir. Anything else, sir?'

'No, that will be all.'

'Very good, sir.'

He shimmered from the room.

Thank goodness, Smith always has thought me mad, and is
consequently never surprised at anything I ask him to do.

Chapter 2

Sanstead House was an imposing building in the Georgian style. It stood, foursquare, in the midst of about nine acres of land. For the greater part of its existence, I learned later, it had been the private home of a family of the name of Boone, and in its early days the estate had been considerable. But the progress of the years had brought changes to the Boones. Money losses had necessitated the sale of land. New roads had come into being, cutting off portions of the estate from their centre. New facilities for travel had drawn members of the family away from home. The old fixed life of the country had changed, and in the end the latest Boone had come to the conclusion that to keep up so large and expensive a house was not worth his while.

That the place should have become a school was the natural process of evolution. It was too large for the ordinary purchaser, and the estate had been so whittled down in the course of time that it was inadequate for the wealthy. Colonel Boone had been glad to let it to Mr Abney, and the school had started its career.

It had all the necessary qualifications for a school. It was isolated. The village was two miles from its gates. It was near the sea. There were fields for cricket and football, and inside the house a number of rooms of every size, suitable for classrooms and dormitories.

The household, when I arrived, consisted, besides Mr Abney, myself, another master named Glossop, and the matron, of twenty-four boys, the butler, the cook, the odd-job-man, two housemaids, a scullery-maid, and a parlour-maid. It was a little colony, cut off from the outer world.

With the exception of Mr Abney and Glossop, a dismal man of nerves and mannerisms, the only person with whom I exchanged speech on my first evening was White, the butler. There are some men one likes at sight. White was one of them. Even for a butler he was a man of remarkably smooth manners, but he lacked that quality of austere aloofness which I have noticed in other butlers.

He helped me unpack my box, and we chatted during the process. He was a man of medium height, square and muscular, with something, some quality of springiness, as it were, that seemed unusual in a butler. From one or two things he said, I gathered that he had travelled a good deal. Altogether he interested me. He had humour, and the half-hour which I had spent with Glossop made me set a premium on humour. I found that he, like myself, was a new-comer. His predecessor had left at short notice during the holidays, and he had secured the vacancy at about the same time that I was securing mine. We agreed that it was a pretty place. White, I gathered, regarded its isolation as a merit. He was not fond of village society.

On the following morning, at eight o'clock, my work began.

My first day had the effect of entirely revolutionizing what ideas I possessed of the lot of the private-school assistant-master.

My view, till then, had been that the assistant-master had an easy time. I had only studied him from the outside. My opinion was based on observations made as a boy at my own private school, when masters were an enviable race who went to bed when they liked, had no preparation to do, and couldn't be caned. It seemed to me then that those three facts, especially the last, formed a pretty good basis on which to build up the Perfect Life.

I had not been at Sanstead House two days before doubts began to creep in on this point. What the boy, observing the assistant-master standing about in apparently magnificent idleness, does not realize is that the unfortunate is really putting in a spell of exceedingly hard work. He is 'taking duty'. And 'taking duty' is a thing to be remembered, especially by a man who, like myself, has lived a life of fatted ease, protected from all the minor annoyances of life by a substantial income.

Sanstead House educated me. It startled me. It showed me a hundred ways in which I had allowed myself to become soft and inefficient, without being aware of it. There may be other professions which call for a fiercer display of energy, but for the man with a private income who has loitered through life at his own pace, a little school-mastering is brisk enough to be a wonderful tonic.

I needed it, and I got it.

It was almost as if Mr Abney had realized intuitively how excellent the discipline of work was for my soul, for the kindly man allowed me to do not only my own, but most of his as well. I have talked with assistant-masters since, and I have gathered from them that headmasters of private schools are divided into two classes: the workers and the runners-up-to-London. Mr Abney belonged to the latter class. Indeed, I doubt if a finer representative of the class could have been found in the length and breadth of southern England. London drew him like a magnet.

After breakfast he would take me aside. The formula was always the same.

'Ah – Mr Burns.'

Myself (apprehensively, scenting disaster, 'like some wild creature caught within a trap, who sees the trapper coming through the wood'). 'Yes? Er – yes?'

'I am afraid I shall be obliged to run up to London today. I have received an important letter from – ' And then he would name some parent or some prospective parent. (By 'prospective' I mean one who was thinking of sending his son to Sanstead House. You may have twenty children, but unless you send them to his school, a schoolmaster will refuse to dignify you with the name of parent.)

Then, 'He wishes – ah – to see me,' or, in the case of titled parents, 'He wishes – ah – to talk things over with me.' The distinction is subtle, but he always made it.

And presently the cab would roll away down the long drive, and my work would begin, and with it that soul-discipline to which I have alluded.

'Taking duty' makes certain definite calls upon a man. He has to answer questions; break up fights; stop big boys bullying small boys; prevent small boys bullying smaller boys; check stone-throwing, going-on-the-wet-grass, worrying-the-cook, teasing-the-dog, making-too-much-noise, and, in particular, discourage all forms of *hara-kiri* such as tree-climbing, water-spout-scaling, leaning-too-far-out-of-the-window, sliding-down-the-banisters, pencil-swallowing, and ink-drinking-because-somebody-dared-me-to.

At intervals throughout the day there are further feats to perform. Carving the joint, helping the pudding, playing football, reading prayers, teaching, herding stragglers in for meals, and going round the dormitories to see that the lights are out, are a few of them.

I wanted to oblige Cynthia, if I could, but there were moments during the first day or so when I wondered how on earth I was going to snatch the necessary time to combine kidnapping with my other duties. Of all the learned professions it seemed to me that that of the kidnapper most urgently demanded certain intervals for leisured thought, in which schemes and plots might be matured.

Schools vary. Sanstead House belonged to the more difficult class. Mr Abney's constant flittings did much to add to the burdens of his assistants, and his peculiar reverence for the aristocracy did even more. His endeavour to make Sanstead House a place where the delicately nurtured scions of the governing class might feel as little as possible the temporary loss of titled mothers led him into a benevolent tolerance which would have unsettled angels.

Success or failure for an assistant-master is, I consider, very much a matter of luck. My colleague, Glossop, had most of the qualities that make for success, but no luck. Properly backed up by Mr Abney, he might have kept order. As it was, his class-room was a bear-garden, and, when he took duty, chaos reigned.

I, on the other hand, had luck. For some reason the boys agreed to accept me. Quite early in my sojourn I enjoyed that sweetest triumph of the assistant-master's life, the spectacle of one boy smacking another boy's head because the latter persisted in making a noise after I had told him to stop. I doubt if a man can experience so keenly in any other way that thrill which comes from the knowledge that the populace is his friend. Political orators must have the same sort of feeling when their audience clamours for the ejection of a heckler, but it cannot be so keen. One is so helpless with boys, unless they decide that they like one.

It was a week from the beginning of the term before I made the acquaintance of the Little Nugget.

I had kept my eyes open for him from the beginning, and, when I discovered that he was not at school, I had felt alarmed. Had Cynthia sent me down here, to work as I had never worked before, on a wild-goose chase?

Then, one morning, Mr Abney drew me aside after breakfast.

'Ah – Mr Burns.'

It was the first time that I had heard those soon-to-be-familiar words.

'I fear I shall be compelled to run up to London today. I have an important appointment with the father of a boy who is coming to the school. He wishes – ah – to see me.'

This might be the Little Nugget at last.

I was right. During the interval before school, Augustus Beckford approached me. Lord Mountry's brother was a stolid boy with freckles. He had two claims to popular fame. He could hold his breath longer than any other boy in the school, and he always got hold of any piece of gossip first.

'There's a new kid coming tonight, sir,' he said – 'an American kid. I heard him talking about it to the matron. The kid's name's Ford. I believe the kid's father's awfully rich. Would you like to be rich, sir? I wish I was rich. If I was rich, I'd buy all sorts of things. I believe I'm going to be rich when I grow up. I heard father talking to a lawyer about it. There's a new parlour-maid coming soon, sir. I heard cook telling Emily. I'm blowed if I'd like to be a parlour-maid, would you, sir? I'd much rather be a cook.'

He pondered the point for a moment. When he spoke again, it was to touch on a still more profound problem.

'If you wanted a halfpenny to make up twopence to buy a lizard, what would you do, sir?'

He got it.

Ogden Ford, the El Dorado of the kidnapping industry, entered Sanstead House at a quarter past nine that evening. He was preceded by a Worried Look, Mr Arnold Abney, a cabman bearing a large box, and the odd-job man carrying two suitcases. I have given precedence to the Worried Look because it was a thing by itself. To say that Mr Abney wore it would be to create a wrong impression. Mr Abney simply followed in its wake. He was concealed behind it much as Macbeth's army was concealed behind the woods of Dunsinane.

I only caught a glimpse of Ogden as Mr Abney showed him into his study. He seemed a self-possessed boy, very like but, if anything, uglier than the portrait of him which I had seen at the Hotel Guelph.

A moment later the door opened, and my employer came out. He appeared relieved at seeing me.

'Ah, Mr Burns, I was about to go in search of you. Can you spare me a moment? Let us go into the dining-room.'

'That is a boy called Ford, Mr Burns,' he said, when he had closed the door. 'A rather – er – remarkable boy. He is an American, the son of a Mr Elmer Ford. As he will be to a great extent in your charge, I should like to prepare you for his – ah – peculiarities.'

'Is he peculiar?'

A faint spasm disturbed Mr Abney's face. He applied a silk handkerchief to his forehead before he replied.

'In many ways, judged by the standard of the lads who have passed through my hands – boys, of course, who, it is only fair to add, have enjoyed the advantages of a singularly refined home-life – he may be said to be – ah – somewhat peculiar. While I have no doubt that *au fond* ... *au fond* he is a charming boy, quite charming, at present he is – shall I say? – peculiar. I am disposed to imagine that he has been, from childhood up, systematically indulged. There has been in his life, I suspect, little or no discipline. The result has been to make him curiously unboylike. There is a complete absence of that diffidence, that childish capacity for surprise, which I for one find so charming in our English boys. Little Ford appears to be completely blasé. He has tastes and ideas which are precocious, and – unusual in a boy of his age ... He expresses himself in a curious manner sometimes ... He seems to have little or no reverence for – ah – constituted authority.'

He paused while he passed his handkerchief once more over his forehead.

'Mr Ford, the boy's father, who struck me as a man of great ability, a typical American merchant prince, was singularly frank with me about his domestic affairs as they concerned his son. I cannot recall his exact words, but the gist of what he said was that, until now, Mrs Ford had had sole charge of the boy's upbringing, and – Mr Ford was singularly outspoken – was too indulgent, in fact – ah – spoilt him. Indeed – you will, of course, respect my confidence – that was the real reason for the divorce which – ah – has unhappily come about. Mr Ford regards this school as in a measure – shall I say? – an antidote. He wishes there to be no lack of wholesome discipline. So that I shall expect you, Mr Burns, to check firmly, though, of course, kindly, such habits of his as – ah – cigarette-smoking. On our journey down he smoked incessantly. I found it impossible – without physical violence – to induce him to stop. But, of course, now that he is actually at the school, and subject to the discipline of the school ...'

'Exactly,' I said.

'That was all I wished to say. Perhaps it would be as well if you saw him now, Mr Burns. You will find him in the study.'

He drifted away, and I went to the study to introduce myself.

A cloud of tobacco-smoke rising above the back of an easy-chair greeted me as I opened the door. Moving into the room, I perceived a pair of boots resting on the grate. I stepped to the right, and the remainder of the Little Nugget came into view.

He was lying almost at full length in the chair, his eyes fixed in dreamy abstraction upon the ceiling. As I came towards him, he drew at the cigarette between his fingers, glanced at me, looked away again, and expelled another mouthful of smoke. He was not interested in me.

Perhaps this indifference piqued me, and I saw him with prejudiced eyes. At any rate, he seemed to me a singularly unprepossessing youth. That portrait had flattered him. He had a stout body and a round, unwholesome face. His eyes were dull, and his mouth dropped discontentedly. He had the air of one who is surfeited with life.

I am disposed to imagine, as Mr Abney would have said, that my manner in addressing him was brisker and more incisive than Mr Abney's own. I was irritated by his supercilious detachment.

'Throw away that cigarette,' I said.

To my amazement, he did, promptly. I was beginning to wonder whether I had not been too abrupt – he gave me a curious sensation of being a man of my own age – when he produced a silver case from his pocket and opened it. I saw that the cigarette in the fender was a stump.

I took the case from his hand and threw it on to a table. For the first time he seemed really to notice my existence.

'You've got a hell of a nerve,' he said.

He was certainly exhibiting his various gifts in rapid order. This, I took it, was what Mr Abney had called 'expressing himself in a curious manner'.

'And don't swear,' I said.

We eyed each other narrowly for the space of some seconds.

'Who are you?' he demanded.

I introduced myself.

'What do you want to come butting in for?'

'I am paid to butt in. It's the main duty of an assistant-master.'

'Oh, you're the assistant-master, are you?'

'One of them. And, in passing – it's a small technical point – you're supposed to call me "sir" during these invigorating little chats of ours.'

'Call you what? Up an alley!'

'I beg your pardon?'

60

'Fade away. Take a walk.'

I gathered that he was meaning to convey that he had considered my proposition, but regretted his inability to entertain it.

'Didn't you call your tutor "sir" when you were at home?'

'Me? Don't make me laugh. I've got a cracked lip.'

'I gather you haven't an overwhelming respect for those set in authority over you.'

'If you mean my tutors, I should say nix.'

'You use the plural. Had you a tutor before Mr Broster?'

He laughed.

'Had I? Only about ten million.'

'Poor devils!' I said.

'Who's swearing now?'

The point was well taken. I corrected myself.

'Poor brutes! What happened to them? Did they commit suicide?'

'Oh, they quit. And I don't blame them. I'm a pretty tough proposition, and you don't want to forget it.'

He reached out for the cigarette-case. I pocketed it.

'You make me tired,' he said.

'The sensation's mutual.'

'Do you think you can swell around, stopping me doing things?'

'You've defined my job exactly.'

'Guess again. I know all about this joint. The hot-air merchant was telling me about it on the train.'

I took the allusion to be to Mr Arnold Abney, and thought it rather a happy one.

'He's the boss, and nobody but him is allowed to hit the fellows. If you tried it, you'd lose your job. And he ain't going to, because the Dad's paying double fees, and he's scared stiff he'll lose me if there's any trouble.'

'You seem to have a grasp of the position.'

'Bet your life I have.'

I looked at him as he sprawled in the chair.

'You're a funny kid,' I said.

He stiffened, outraged. His little eyes gleamed.

'Say, it looks to me as if you wanted making a head shorter. You're a darned sight too fresh. Who do you think you are, anyway?'

'I'm your guardian angel,' I replied. 'I'm the fellow who's going to take you in hand and make you a little ray of sunshine about the home. I know your type backwards. I've been in America and studied it on its native asphalt. You superfatted millionaire kids are all the same. If Dad doesn't jerk you into the office before you're out of knickerbockers, you just run to seed. You get to think you're the only thing on earth, and you go on thinking it till one day somebody comes along and shows you you're not, and then you get what's coming to you – good and hard.'

He began to speak, but I was on my favourite theme, one I had studied and brooded upon since the evening when I had received a certain letter at my club.

'I knew a man,' I said, 'who started out just like you. He always had all the money he wanted: never worked: grew to think himself a sort of young prince. What happened?'

He yawned.

'I'm afraid I'm boring you,' I said.

'Go on. Enjoy yourself,' said the Little Nugget.

'Well, it's a long story, so I'll spare you it. But the moral of it was that a boy who is going to have money needs to be taken in hand and taught sense while he's young.'

He stretched himself.

'You talk a lot. What do you reckon you're going to do?'

I eyed him thoughtfully.

'Well, everything's got to have a beginning,' I said. 'What you seem to me to want most is exercise. I'll take you for a run every day. You won't know yourself at the end of a week.'

'Say, if you think you're going to get *me* to run – '

'When I grab your little hand, and start running, you'll find you'll soon be running too. And, years hence, when you win the Marathon at the Olympic Games, you'll come to me with tears in your eyes, and you'll say – '

'Oh, slush!'

'I shouldn't wonder.' I looked at my watch. 'Meanwhile, you had better go to bed. It's past your proper time.'

He stared at me in open-eyed amazement.

'Bed!'

'Bed.'

He seemed more amused than annoyed.

'Say, what time do you think I usually go to bed?'

'I know what time you go here. Nine o'clock.'

As if to support my words, the door opened, and Mrs Attwell, the matron, entered.

'I think it's time he came to bed, Mr Burns.'

'Just what I was saying, Mrs Attwell.'

'You're crazy,' observed the Little Nugget. 'Bed nothing!'

Mrs Attwell looked at me despairingly.

'I never saw such a boy!'

The whole machinery of the school was being held up by this legal infant. Any vacillation now, and Authority would suffer a set-back from which it would be hard put to it to recover. It seemed to me a situation that called for action.

I bent down, scooped the Little Nugget out of his chair like an oyster, and made for the door. Outside he screamed incessantly. He kicked me in the stomach and then on the knee. He continued to scream. He screamed all the way upstairs. He was screaming when we reached his room.

Half an hour later I sat in the study, smoking thoughtfully. Reports from the seat of war told of a sullen and probably only temporary acquiescence with Fate on the part of the enemy. He was in bed, and seemed to have made up his mind to submit to the position. An air of restrained jubilation prevailed among the elder members of the establishment. Mr Abney was friendly and Mrs Attwell openly congratulatory. I was something like the hero of the hour.

But was I jubilant? No, I was inclined to moodiness. Unforeseen difficulties had arisen in my path. Till now, I had regarded this kidnapping as something abstract. Personality had not entered into the matter. If I had had any picture in my mind's eye, it was of myself stealing away softly into the night with a docile child, his little hand laid trustfully in mine. From what I had seen and heard of Ogden Ford in moments of emotion, it seemed to me that whoever wanted to kidnap him with any approach to stealth would need to use chloroform.

Things were getting very complex.

Chapter 3

I have never kept a diary, and I have found it, in consequence, somewhat difficult, in telling this narrative, to arrange the minor incidents of my story in their proper sequence. I am writing by the light of an imperfect memory; and the work is complicated by the fact that the early days of my sojourn at Sanstead House are a blur, a confused welter like a Futurist picture, from which emerge haphazard the figures of boys – boys working, boys eating, boys playing football, boys whispering, shouting, asking questions, banging doors, jumping on beds, and clattering upstairs and along passages, the whole picture faintly scented with a composite aroma consisting of roast beef, ink, chalk, and that curious classroom smell which is like nothing else on earth.

I cannot arrange the incidents. I can see Mr Abney, furrowed as to the brow and drooping at the jaw, trying to separate Ogden Ford from a half-smoked cigar-stump. I can hear Glossop, feverishly angry, bellowing at an amused class. A dozen other pictures come back to me, but I cannot place them in their order; and perhaps, after all, their sequence is unimportant. This story deals with affairs which were outside the ordinary school life.

With the war between the Little Nugget and Authority, for instance, the narrative has little to do. It is a subject for an epic, but it lies apart from the main channel of the story, and must be avoided. To tell of his gradual taming, of the chaos his advent caused until we became able to cope with him, would be to turn this story into a treatise on education. It is enough to say that the process of moulding his character and exorcising the devil which seemed to possess him was slow.

It was Ogden who introduced tobacco-chewing into the school, with fearful effects one Saturday night on the aristocratic interiors of Lords Gartridge and Windhall and Honourables Edwin Bellamy and Hildebrand Kyne. It was the ingenious gambling-game imported by Ogden which was rapidly undermining the moral sense of twenty-four innocent English boys when it was pounced upon by Glossop. It was Ogden who, on the one occasion when Mr Abney reluctantly resorted to the cane, and administered four mild taps with it, relieved his feelings by going upstairs and breaking all the windows in all the bedrooms.

We had some difficult young charges at Sanstead House. Mr Abney's policy of benevolent toleration ensured that. But Ogden Ford stood alone.

I have said that it is difficult for me to place the lesser events of my narrative in their proper order. I except three, however, which I will call the Affair of the Strange American, the Adventure of the Sprinting Butler, and the Episode of the Genial Visitor.

I will describe them singly, as they happened.

It was the custom at Sanstead House for each of the assistant-masters to take half of one day in every week as a holiday. The allowance was not liberal, and in most schools, I believe, it is increased; but Mr Abney was a man with peculiar views on other people's holidays, and Glossop and I were accordingly restricted.

My day was Wednesday; and on the Wednesday of which I write I strolled towards the village. I had in my mind a game of billiards at the local inn. Sanstead House and its neighbourhood were lacking in the fiercer metropolitan excitements, and billiards at the 'Feathers' constituted for the pleasure-seeker the beginning and end of the Gay Whirl.

There was a local etiquette governing the game of billiards at the 'Feathers'. You played the marker a hundred up, then you took him into the bar-parlour and bought him refreshment. He raised his glass, said, 'To you, sir', and drained it at a gulp.

After that you could, if you wished, play another game, or go home, as your fancy dictated.

There was only one other occupant of the bar-parlour when we adjourned thither, and a glance at him told me that he was not ostentatiously sober. He was lying back in a chair, with his feet on the side-table, and crooning slowly, in a melancholy voice, the following words:

> *'I don't care – if he wears – a crown,*
> *He – can't – keep kicking my – dawg aroun'.'*

He was a tough, clean-shaven man, with a broken nose, over which was tilted a soft felt hat. His wiry limbs were clad in what I put down as a mail-order suit. I could have placed him by his appearance, if I had not already done so by his voice, as an East-side New Yorker. And what an East-side New Yorker could be doing in Sanstead it was beyond me to explain.

We had hardly seated ourselves when he rose and lurched out. I saw him pass the window, and his assertion that no crowned head should molest his dog came faintly to my ears as he went down the street.

'American!' said Miss Benjafield, the stately barmaid, with strong disapproval. 'They're all alike.'

I never contradict Miss Benjafield – one would as soon contradict the Statue of Liberty – so I merely breathed sympathetically.

'What's he here for I'd like to know?'

It occurred to me that I also should like to know. In another thirty hours I was to find out.

I shall lay myself open to a charge of denseness such as even Doctor Watson would have scorned when I say that, though I thought of the matter a good deal on my way back to the school, I did not arrive at the obvious solution. Much teaching and taking of duty had dulled my wits, and the presence at Sanstead House of the Little Nugget did not even occur to me as a reason why strange Americans should be prowling in the village.

We now come to the remarkable activity of White, the butler.

It happened that same evening.

It was not late when I started on my way back to the house, but the short January day was over, and it was very dark as I turned in at the big gate of the school and made my way up the drive. The drive at Sanstead House was a fine curving stretch of gravel, about two hundred yards in length, flanked on either side by fir trees and rhododendrons. I stepped out briskly, for it had begun to freeze. Just as I caught sight through the trees of the lights of the windows, there came to me the sound of running feet.

I stopped. The noise grew louder. There seemed to be two runners, one moving with short, quick steps, the other, the one in front, taking a longer stride.

I drew aside instinctively. In another moment, making a great clatter on the frozen gravel, the first of the pair passed me; and as he did so, there was a sharp crack, and something sang through the darkness like a large mosquito.

The effect of the sound on the man who had been running was immediate. He stopped in his stride and dived into the bushes. His footsteps thudded faintly on the turf.

The whole incident had lasted only a few seconds, and I was still standing there when I was aware of the other man approaching. He had apparently given up the pursuit, for he was walking quite slowly. He stopped within a few feet of me and I heard him swearing softly to himself.

'Who's that?' I cried sharply. The crack of the pistol had given a flick to my nerves. Mine had been a sheltered life, into which hitherto revolver-shots had not entered, and I was resenting this abrupt introduction of them. I felt jumpy and irritated.

It gave me a malicious pleasure to see that I had startled the unknown dispenser of shocks quite as much as he had startled me. The movement he made as he faced towards my direction was almost a leap; and it suddenly flashed upon me that I had better at once establish my identity as a noncombatant. I appeared to have wandered inadvertently into the midst of a private quarrel, one party to which – the one standing a couple of yards from me with a loaded revolver in his hand – was evidently a man of impulse, the sort of man who would shoot first and inquire afterwards.

'I'm Mr Burns,' I said. 'I'm one of the assistant-masters. Who are you?'

'Mr Burns?'

Surely that rich voice was familiar.

'White?' I said.

'Yes, sir.'

'What on earth do you think you're doing? Have you gone mad? Who was that man?'

'I wish I could tell you, sir. A very doubtful character. I found him prowling at the back of the house very suspiciously. He took to his heels and I followed him.'

'But' – I spoke querulously, my orderly nature was shocked – 'you can't go shooting at people like that just because you find them at the back of the house. He might have been a tradesman.'

'I think not, sir.'

'Well, so do I, if it comes to that. He didn't behave like one. But, all the same – '

'I take your point, sir. But I was merely intending to frighten him.'

'You succeeded all right. He went through those bushes like a cannon-ball.'

I heard him chuckle.

'I think I may have scared him a little, sir.'

'We must phone to the police-station. Could you describe the man?'

'I think not, sir. It was very dark. And, if I may make the suggestion, it would be better not to inform the police. I have a very poor opinion of these country constables.'

'But we can't have men prowling – '

'If you will permit me, sir. I say – let them prowl. It's the only way to catch them.'

'If you think this sort of thing is likely to happen again I must tell Mr Abney.'

'Pardon me, sir, I think it would be better not. He impresses me as a somewhat nervous gentleman, and it would only disturb him.'

At this moment it suddenly struck me that, in my interest in the mysterious fugitive, I had omitted to notice what was really the most remarkable point in the whole affair. How did White happen to have a revolver at all? I have met many butlers who behaved unexpectedly in their spare time. One I knew played the fiddle; another preached Socialism in Hyde Park. But I had never yet come across a butler who fired pistols.

'What were you doing with a revolver?' I asked.

He hesitated.

'May I ask you to keep it to yourself, sir, if I tell you something?' he said at last.

'What do you mean?'

'I'm a detective.'

'What!'

'A Pinkerton's man, Mr Burns.'

I felt like one who sees the 'danger' board over thin ice. But for this information, who knew what rash move I might not have made, under the assumption that the Little Nugget was unguarded? At the same time, I could not help reflecting that, if things had been complex before, they had become far more so in the light of this discovery. To spirit Ogden away had never struck me, since his arrival at the school, as an easy task. It seemed more difficult now than ever.

I had the sense to affect astonishment. I made my imitation of an innocent assistant-master astounded by the news that the butler is a detective in disguise as realistic as I was able. It appeared to be satisfactory, for he began to explain.

'I am employed by Mr Elmer Ford to guard his son. There are several parties after that boy, Mr Burns. Naturally he is a considerable prize. Mr Ford would pay a large sum to get back his only son if he were kidnapped. So it stands to reason he takes precautions.'

'Does Mr Abney know what you are?'

'No, sir. Mr Abney thinks I am an ordinary butler. You are the only person who knows, and I have only told you because

70

you have happened to catch me in a rather queer position for a butler to be in. You will keep it to yourself, sir? It doesn't do for it to get about. These things have to be done quietly. It would be bad for the school if my presence here were advertised. The other parents wouldn't like it. They would think that their sons were in danger, you see. It would be disturbing for them. So if you will just forget what I've been telling you, Mr Burns – '

I assured him that I would. But I was very far from meaning it. If there was one thing which I intended to bear in mind, it was the fact that watchful eyes besides mine were upon that Little Nugget.

The third and last of this chain of occurrences, the Episode of the Genial Visitor, took place on the following day, and may be passed over briefly. All that happened was that a well-dressed man, who gave his name as Arthur Gordon, of Philadelphia, dropped in unexpectedly to inspect the school. He apologized for not having written to make an appointment, but explained that he was leaving England almost immediately. He was looking for a school for his sister's son, and, happening to meet his business acquaintance, Mr Elmer Ford, in London, he had been recommended to Mr Abney. He made himself exceedingly pleasant. He was a breezy, genial man, who joked with Mr Abney, chaffed the boys, prodded the Little Nugget in the ribs, to that overfed youth's discomfort, made a rollicking tour of the house, in the course of which he inspected Ogden's bedroom – in order, he told Mr Abney, to be able to report conscientiously to his friend Ford that the son and heir was not being pampered too much, and departed in a whirl of good-humour, leaving every one enthusiastic over his charming personality. His last words were that everything was thoroughly satisfactory, and that he had learned all he wanted to know.

Which, as was proved that same night, was the simple truth.

Chapter 4

I

I owed it to my colleague Glossop that I was in the centre of the surprising things that occurred that night. By sheer weight of boredom, Glossop drove me from the house, so that it came about that, at half past nine, the time at which the affair began, I was patrolling the gravel in front of the porch.

It was the practice of the staff of Sanstead House School to assemble after dinner in Mr Abney's study for coffee. The room was called the study, but it was really more of a master's common room. Mr Abney had a smaller sanctum of his own, reserved exclusively for himself.

On this particular night he went there early, leaving me alone with Glossop.

It is one of the drawbacks of the desert-island atmosphere of a private school that everybody is always meeting everybody else. To avoid a man for long is impossible. I had been avoiding Glossop as long as I could, for I knew that he wanted to corner me with a view to a heart-to-heart talk on Life Insurance.

These amateur Life Insurance agents are a curious band. The world is full of them. I have met them at country-houses, at seaside hotels, on ships, everywhere; and it has always amazed me that they should find the game worth the candle. What they add to their incomes I do not know, but it cannot be very much, and the trouble they have to take is colossal. Nobody loves them, and they must see it; yet they persevere. Glossop, for instance, had been trying to buttonhole me every time there was a five minutes' break in the day's work.

He had his chance now, and he did not mean to waste it. Mr Abney had scarcely left the room when he began to exude pamphlets and booklets at every pocket.

I eyed him sourly, as he droned on about 'reactionable endowment', 'surrender-value', and 'interest accumulating on the tontine policy', and tried, as I did so, to analyse the loathing I felt for him. I came to the conclusion that it was partly due to his pose of doing the whole thing from purely altruistic motives, entirely for my good, and partly because he forced me to face the fact that I was not always going to be young. In an abstract fashion I had already realized that I should in time cease to be thirty, but the way in which Glossop spoke of my sixty-fifth birthday made me feel as if it was due tomorrow. He was a man with a manner suggestive of a funeral mute suffering from suppressed jaundice, and I had never before been so weighed down with a sense of the inevitability of decay and the remorseless passage of time. I could feel my hair whitening.

A need for solitude became imperative; and, murmuring something about thinking it over, I escaped from the room.

Except for my bedroom, whither he was quite capable of following me, I had no refuge but the grounds. I unbolted the front door and went out.

It was still freezing, and, though the stars shone, the trees grew so closely about the house that it was too dark for me to see more than a few feet in front of me.

I began to stroll up and down. The night was wonderfully still. I could hear somebody walking up the drive – one of the maids, I supposed, returning from her evening out. I could even hear a bird rustling in the ivy on the walls of the stables.

I fell into a train of thought. I think my mind must still have been under Glossop's gloom-breeding spell, for I was filled with a sense of the infinite pathos of Life. What was the good of it all? Why was a man given chances of happiness without the sense to realize and use them? If Nature had made me so self-satisfied that I had lost Audrey because of my self-satisfaction why had she not made me so self-satisfied that I could lose her without a pang? Audrey! It annoyed me that, whenever I was free for a moment from active work, my thoughts should keep turning to her. It frightened me, too. Engaged to Cynthia, I had no right to have such thoughts.

Perhaps it was the mystery which hung about her that kept her in my mind. I did not know where she was. I did not know how she fared. I did not know what sort of a man it was whom she had preferred to me. That, it struck me, was the crux of the matter. She had vanished absolutely with another man whom I had never seen and whose very name I did not know. I had been beaten by an unseen foe.

I was deep in a very slough of despond when suddenly things began to happen. I might have known that Sanstead House would never permit solitary brooding on Life for long. It was a place of incident, not of abstract speculation.

I had reached the end of my 'beat', and had stopped to relight my pipe, when drama broke loose with the swift unexpectedness which was characteristic of the place. The stillness of the night was split by a sound which I could have heard in a gale and recognized among a hundred conflicting noises. It was a scream, a shrill, piercing squeal that did not rise to a crescendo, but started at its maximum and held the note; a squeal which could only proceed from one throat: the deafening war-cry of the Little Nugget.

I had grown accustomed, since my arrival at Sanstead House, to a certain quickening of the pace of life, but tonight events succeeded one another with a rapidity which surprised me. A whole cinematograph-drama was enacted during the space of time it takes for a wooden match to burn.

At the moment when the Little Nugget gave tongue, I had just struck one, and I stood, startled into rigidity, holding it in the air as if I had decided to constitute myself a sort of limelight man to the performance.

It cannot have been more than a few seconds later before some person unknown nearly destroyed me.

I was standing, holding my match and listening to the sounds of confusion indoors, when this person, rounding the angle of the house in a desperate hurry, emerged from the bushes and rammed me squarely.

He was a short man, or he must have crouched as he ran, for his shoulder – a hard, bony shoulder – was precisely the same distance from the ground as my solar plexus. In the brief impact which ensued between the two, the shoulder had the advantage of being in motion, while the solar plexus was

74

stationary, and there was no room for any shadow of doubt as to which had the worst of it.

That the mysterious unknown was not unshaken by the encounter was made clear by a sharp yelp of surprise and pain. He staggered. What happened to him after that was not a matter of interest to me. I gather that he escaped into the night. But I was too occupied with my own affairs to follow his movements.

Of all cures for melancholy introspection a violent blow in the solar plexus is the most immediate. If Mr Corbett had any abstract worries that day at Carson City, I fancy they ceased to occupy his mind from the moment when Mr Fitzsimmons administered that historic left jab. In my case the cure was instantaneous. I can remember reeling across the gravel and falling in a heap and trying to breathe and knowing that I should never again be able to, and then for some minutes all interest in the affairs of this world left me.

How long it was before my breath returned, hesitatingly, like some timid Prodigal Son trying to muster up courage to enter the old home, I do not know; but it cannot have been many minutes, for the house was only just beginning to disgorge its occupants as I sat up. Disconnected cries and questions filled the air. Dim forms moved about in the darkness.

I had started to struggle to my feet, feeling very sick and boneless, when it was borne in upon me that the sensations of this remarkable night were not yet over. As I reached a sitting position, and paused before adventuring further, to allow a wave of nausea to pass, a hand was placed on my shoulder and a voice behind me said, 'Don't move!'

II

I was not in a condition to argue. Beyond a fleeting feeling that a liberty was being taken with me and that I was being treated unjustly, I do not remember resenting the command. I had no notion who the speaker might be, and no curiosity. Breathing just then had all the glamour of a difficult feat cleverly performed. I concentrated my whole attention upon it. I was pleased, and surprised, to find myself getting on so well. I

75

remember having much the same sensation when I first learned to ride a bicycle – a kind of dazed feeling that I seemed to be doing it, but Heaven alone knew how.

A minute or so later, when I had leisure to observe outside matters, I perceived that among the other actors in the drama confusion still reigned. There was much scuttering about and much meaningless shouting. Mr Abney's reedy tenor voice was issuing directions, each of which reached a dizzier height of futility than the last. Glossop was repeating over and over again the words, 'Shall I telephone for the police?' to which nobody appeared to pay the least attention. One or two boys were darting about like rabbits and squealing unintelligibly. A female voice – I think Mrs Attwell's – was saying, 'Can you see him?'

Up to this point, my match, long since extinguished, had been the only illumination the affair had received; but now somebody, who proved to be White, the butler, came from the direction of the stable-yard with a carriage-lamp. Every one seemed calmer and happier for it. The boys stopped squealing, Mrs Attwell and Glossop subsided, and Mr Abney said 'Ah!' in a self-satisfied voice, as if he had directed this move and was congratulating himself on the success with which it had been carried out.

The whole strength of the company gathered round the light.

'Thank you, White,' said Mr Abney. 'Excellent. I fear the scoundrel has escaped.'

'I suspect so, sir.'

'This is a very remarkable occurrence, White.'

'Yes, sir.'

'The man was actually in Master Ford's bedroom.'

'Indeed, sir?'

A shrill voice spoke. I recognized it as that of Augustus Beckford, always to be counted upon to be in the centre of things gathering information.

'Sir, please, sir, what was up? Who was it, sir? Sir, was it a burglar, sir? Have you ever met a burglar, sir? My father took me to see Raffles in the holidays, sir. Do you think this chap was like Raffles, sir? Sir – '

'It was undoubtedly – ' Mr Abney was beginning, when the identity of the questioner dawned upon him, and for the first time he realized that the drive was full of boys actively engaged in catching their deaths of cold. His all-friends-here-let-us-discuss-this-interesting-episode-fully manner changed. He became the outraged schoolmaster. Never before had I heard him speak so sharply to boys, many of whom, though breaking rules, were still titled.

'What are you boys doing out of bed? Go back to bed instantly. I shall punish you most severely. I – '

'Shall I telephone for the police?' asked Glossop. Disregarded.

'I will not have this conduct. You will catch cold. This is disgraceful. Ten bad marks! I shall punish you most severely if you do not instantly – '

A calm voice interrupted him.

'Say!'

The Little Nugget strolled easily into the circle of light. He was wearing a dressing-gown, and in his hand was a smouldering cigarette, from which he proceeded, before continuing his remarks, to blow a cloud of smoke.

'Say, I guess you're wrong. That wasn't any ordinary porch-climber.'

The spectacle of his *bête noire* wreathed in smoke, coming on top of the emotions of the night, was almost too much for Mr Abney. He gesticulated for a moment in impassioned silence, his arms throwing grotesque shadows on the gravel.

'How *dare* you smoke, boy! How *dare* you smoke that cigarette!'

'It's the only one I've got,' responded the Little Nugget amiably.

'I have spoken to you – I have warned you – Ten bad marks! – I will not have – Fifteen bad marks!'

The Little Nugget ignored the painful scene. He was smiling quietly.

'If you ask *me*,' he said, 'that guy was after something better than plated spoons. Yes, sir! If you want my opinion, it was Buck MacGinnis, or Chicago Ed., or one of those guys, and what he was trailing was me. They're always at it. Buck had a try for me in the fall of '07, and Ed. – '

'Do you hear me? Will you return instantly – '

'If you don't believe me I can show you the piece there was about it in the papers. I've got a press-clipping album in my box. Whenever there's a piece about me in the papers, I cut it out and paste it into my album. If you'll come right along, I'll show you the story about Buck now. It happened in Chicago, and he'd have got away with me if it hadn't been – '

'Twenty bad marks!'

'Mr Abney!'

It was the person standing behind me who spoke. Till now he or she had remained a silent spectator, waiting, I suppose, for a lull in the conversation.

They jumped, all together, like a well-trained chorus.

'Who is that?' cried Mr Abney. I could tell by the sound of his voice that his nerves were on wires. 'Who was that who spoke?'

'Shall I telephone for the police?' asked Glossop. Ignored.

'I am Mrs Sheridan, Mr Abney. You were expecting me to-night.'

'Mrs Sheridan? Mrs Sher – I expected you in a cab. I expected you in – ah – in fact, a cab.'

'I walked.'

I had a curious sensation of having heard the voice before. When she had told me not to move, she had spoken in a whisper – or, to me, in my dazed state, it had sounded like a whisper – but now she was raising her voice, and there was a note in it that seemed familiar. It stirred some chord in my memory, and I waited to hear it again.

When it came it brought the same sensation, but nothing more definite. It left me groping for the clue.

'Here is one of the men, Mr Abney.'

There was a profound sensation. Boys who had ceased to squeal, squealed with fresh vigour. Glossop made his suggestion about the telephone with a new ring of hope in his voice. Mrs Attwell shrieked. They made for us in a body, boys and all,

White leading with the lantern. I was almost sorry for being compelled to provide an anticlimax.

Augustus Beckford was the first to recognize me, and I expect he was about to ask me if I liked sitting on the gravel on a frosty night, or what gravel was made of, when Mr Abney spoke.

'Mr Burns! What – dear me! – *what* are you doing there?'

'Perhaps Mr Burns can give us some information as to where the man went, sir,' suggested White.

'On everything except that,' I said, 'I'm a mine of information. I haven't the least idea where he went. All I know about him is that he has a shoulder like the ram of a battleship, and that he charged me with it.'

As I was speaking, I thought I heard a little gasp behind me. I turned. I wanted to see this woman who stirred my memory with her voice. But the rays of the lantern did not fall on her, and she was a shapeless blur in the darkness. Somehow I felt that she was looking intently at me.

I resumed my narrative.

'I was lighting my pipe when I heard a scream – ' A chuckle came from the group behind the lantern.

'I screamed,' said the Little Nugget. 'You bet I screamed! What would *you* do if you woke up in the dark and found a strong-armed roughneck prising you out of bed as if you were a clam? He tried to get his hand over my mouth, but he only connected with my forehead, and I'd got going before he could switch. I guess I threw a scare into that gink!'

He chuckled again, reminiscently, and drew at his cigarette.

'How dare you smoke! Throw away that cigarette!' cried Mr Abney, roused afresh by the red glow.

'Forget it!' advised the Little Nugget tersely.

'And then,' I said, 'somebody whizzed out from nowhere and hit me. And after that I didn't seem to care much about him or anything else.' I spoke in the direction of my captor. She was still standing outside the circle of light. 'I expect you can tell us what happened, Mrs Sheridan?'

I did not think that her information was likely to be of any practical use, but I wanted to make her speak again.

Her first words were enough. I wondered how I could ever have been in doubt. I knew the voice now. It was one which I had not heard for five years, but one which I could never forget if I lived for ever.

'Somebody ran past me.' I hardly heard her. My heart was pounding, and a curious dizziness had come over me. I was grappling with the incredible. 'I think he went into the bushes.'

I heard Glossop speak, and gathered from Mr Abney's reply that he had made his suggestion about the telephone once more.

'I think that will be – ah – unnecessary, Mr Glossop. The man has undoubtedly – ah – made good his escape. I think we had all better return to the house.' He turned to the dim figure beside me. 'Ah, Mrs Sheridan, you must be tired after your journey and the – ah – unusual excitement. Mrs Attwell will show you where you – in fact, your room.'

In the general movement White must have raised the lamp or stepped forward, for the rays shifted. The figure beside me was no longer dim, but stood out sharp and clear in the yellow light.

I was aware of two large eyes looking into mine as, in the grey London morning two weeks before, they had looked from a faded photograph.

Chapter 5

Of all the emotions which kept me awake that night, a vague discomfort and a feeling of resentment against Fate more than against any individual, were the two that remained with me next morning. Astonishment does not last. The fact of Audrey and myself being under the same roof after all these years had ceased to amaze me. It was a minor point, and my mind shelved it in order to deal with the one thing that really mattered, the fact that she had come back into my life just when I had definitely, as I thought, put her out of it.

My resentment deepened. Fate had played me a wanton trick. Cynthia trusted me. If I were weak, I should not be the only one to suffer. And something told me that I should be weak. How could I hope to be strong, tortured by the thousand memories which the sight of her would bring back to me?

But I would fight, I told myself. I would not yield easily. I promised that to my self-respect, and was rewarded with a certain glow of excitement. I felt defiant. I wanted to test myself at once.

My opportunity came after breakfast. She was standing on the gravel in front of the house, almost, in fact, on the spot where we had met the night before. She looked up as she heard my step, and I saw that her chin had that determined tilt which, in the days of our engagement, I had noticed often without attaching any particular significance to it. Heavens, what a ghastly lump of complacency I must have been in those days! A child, I thought, if he were not wrapped up in the contemplation of his own magnificence, could read its meaning.

It meant war, and I was glad of it. I wanted war.

'Good morning,' I said.

'Good morning.'

There was a pause. I took the opportunity to collect my thoughts.

I looked at her curiously. Five years had left their mark on her, but entirely for the good. She had an air of quiet strength which I had never noticed in her before. It may have been there in the old days, but I did not think so. It was, I felt certain, a later development. She gave the impression of having been through much and of being sure of herself.

In appearance she had changed amazingly little. She looked as small and slight and trim as ever she had done. She was a little paler, I thought, and the Irish eyes were older and a shade harder; but that was all.

I awoke with a start to the fact that I was staring at her. A slight flush had crept into her pale cheeks.

'Don't!' she said suddenly, with a little gesture of irritation.

The word and the gesture killed, as if they had been a blow, a kind of sentimental tenderness which had been stealing over me.

'What are you doing here?' I asked.

She was silent.

'Please don't think I want to pry into your affairs,' I said viciously. 'I was only interested in the coincidence that we should meet here like this.'

She turned to me impulsively. Her face had lost its hard look.

'Oh, Peter,' she said, 'I'm sorry. I *am* sorry.'

It was my chance, and I snatched at it with a lack of chivalry which I regretted almost immediately. But I was feeling bitter, and bitterness makes a man do cheap things.

'Sorry?' I said, politely puzzled. 'Why?'

She looked taken aback, as I hoped she would.

'For – for what happened.'

'My dear Audrey! Anybody would have made the same mistake. I don't wonder you took me for a burglar.'

'I didn't mean that. I meant – five years ago.'

I laughed. I was not feeling like laughter at the moment, but I did my best, and had the satisfaction of seeing that it jarred upon her.

'Surely you're not worrying yourself about that?' I said. I laughed again. Very jovial and debonair I was that winter morning.

The brief moment in which we might have softened towards each other was over. There was a glitter in her blue eyes which told me that it was once more war between us.

'I thought you would get over it,' she said.

'Well,' I said, 'I was only twenty-five. One's heart doesn't break at twenty-five.'

'I don't think yours would ever be likely to break, Peter.'

'Is that a compliment, or otherwise?'

'You would probably think it a compliment. I meant that you were not human enough to be heart-broken.'

'So that's your idea of a compliment!'

'I said I thought it was probably yours.'

'I must have been a curious sort of man five years ago, if I gave you that impression.'

'You were.'

She spoke in a meditative voice, as if, across the years, she were idly inspecting some strange species of insect. The attitude annoyed me. I could look, myself, with a detached eye at the man I had once been, but I still retained a sort of affection for him, and I felt piqued.

'I suppose you looked on me as a kind of ogre in those days?' I said.

'I suppose I did.'

There was a pause.

'I didn't mean to hurt your feelings,' she said. And that was the most galling part of it. Mine was an attitude of studied offensiveness. I did want to hurt her feelings. But hers, it seemed to me, was no pose. She really had had – and, I suppose, still retained – a genuine horror of me. The struggle was unequal.

'You were very kind,' she went on, 'sometimes – when you happened to think of it.'

Considered as the best she could find to say of me, it was not an eulogy.

'Well,' I said, 'we needn't discuss what I was or did five years ago. Whatever I was or did, you escaped. Let's think of the present. What are we going to do about this?'

'You think the situation's embarrassing?'

'I do.'

'One of us ought to go, I suppose,' she said doubtfully.

'Exactly.'

'Well, I can't go.'

'Nor can I.'

'I have business here.'

'Obviously, so have I.'

'It's absolutely necessary that I should be here.'

'And that I should.'

She considered me for a moment.

'Mrs Attwell told me that you were one of the assistant-masters at the school.'

'I am acting as assistant-master. I am supposed to be learning the business.'

She hesitated.

'Why?' she said.

'Why not?'

'But – but – you used to be very well off.'

'I'm better off now. I'm working.'

She was silent for a moment.

'Of course it's impossible for you to leave. You couldn't, could you?'

'No.'

'I can't either.'

'Then I suppose we must face the embarrassment.'

'But why must it be embarrassing? You said yourself you had – got over it.'

'Absolutely. I am engaged to be married.'

She gave a little start. She drew a pattern on the gravel with her foot before she spoke.

'I congratulate you,' she said at last.

'Thank you.'

'I hope you will be very happy.'

'I'm sure I shall.'

She relapsed into silence. It occurred to me that, having

posted her thoroughly in my affairs, I was entitled to ask about hers.

'How in the world did you come to be here?' I said.

'It's rather a long story. After my husband died – '

'Oh!' I exclaimed, startled.

'Yes; he died three years ago.'

She spoke in a level voice, with a ring of hardness in it, for which I was to learn the true reason later. At the time it seemed to me due to resentment at having to speak of the man she had loved to me, whom she disliked, and my bitterness increased.

'I have been looking after myself for a long time.'

'In England?'

'In America. We went to New York directly we – directly I had written to you. I have been in America ever since. I only returned to England a few weeks ago.'

'But what brought you to Sanstead?'

'Some years ago I got to know Mr Ford, the father of the little boy who is at the school. He recommended me to Mr Abney, who wanted somebody to help with the school.'

'And you are dependent on your work? I mean – forgive me if I am personal – Mr Sheridan did not – '

'He left no money at all.'

'Who was he?' I burst out. I felt that the subject of the dead man was one which it was painful for her to talk about, at any rate to me; but the Sheridan mystery had vexed me for five years, and I thirsted to know something of this man who had dynamited my life without ever appearing in it.

'He was an artist, a friend of my father.'

I wanted to hear more. I wanted to know what he looked like, how he spoke, how he compared with me in a thousand ways; but it was plain that she would not willingly be communicative about him; and, with a feeling of resentment, I gave her her way and suppressed my curiosity.

'So your work here is all you have?' I said.

'Absolutely all. And, if it's the same with you, well, here we are!'

'Here we are!' I echoed. 'Exactly.'

'We must try and make it as easy for each other as we can,' she said.

'Of course.'

She looked at me in that curious, wide-eyed way of hers.

'You have got thinner, Peter,' she said.

'Have I?' I said. 'Suffering, I suppose, or exercise.'

Her eyes left my face. I saw her bite her lip.

'You hate me,' she said abruptly. 'You've been hating me all these years. Well, I don't wonder.'

She turned and began to walk slowly away, and as she did so a sense of the littleness of the part I was playing came over me. Ever since our talk had begun I had been trying to hurt her, trying to take a petty revenge on her – for what? All that had happened five years ago had been my fault. I could not let her go like this. I felt unutterably mean.

'Audrey!' I called.

She stopped. I went to her.

'Audrey!' I said, 'you're wrong. If there's anybody I hate, it's myself. I just want to tell you I understand.'

Her lips parted, but she did not speak.

'I understand just what made you do it,' I went on. 'I can see now the sort of man I was in those days.'

'You're saying that to – to help me,' she said in a low voice.

'No. I have felt like that about it for years.'

'I treated you shamefully.'

'Nothing of the kind. There's a certain sort of man who badly needs a – jolt, and he has to get it sooner or later. It happened that you gave me mine, but that wasn't your fault. I was bound to get it – somehow.' I laughed. 'Fate was waiting for me round the corner. Fate wanted something to hit me with. You happened to be the nearest thing handy.'

'I'm sorry, Peter.'

'Nonsense. You knocked some sense into me. That's all you did. Every man needs education. Most men get theirs in small doses, so that they hardly know they are getting it at all. My money kept me from getting mine that way. By the time I met you there was a great heap of back education due to me, and I got it in a lump. That's all.'

'You're generous.'

'Nothing of the kind. It's only that I see things clearer than I did. I was a pig in those days.'

'You weren't!'

'I was. Well, we won't quarrel about it.'

Inside the house the bell rang for breakfast. We turned. As I drew back to let her go in, she stopped.

'Peter,' she said.

She began to speak quickly.

'Peter, let's be sensible. Why should we let this embarrass us, this being together here? Can't we just pretend that we're two old friends who parted through a misunderstanding, and have come together again, with all the misunderstanding cleared away – friends again? Shall we?'

She held out her hand. She was smiling, but her eyes were grave.

'Old friends, Peter?'

I took her hand.

'Old friends,' I said.

And we went in to breakfast. On the table, beside my plate, was lying a letter from Cynthia.

Chapter 6

I

I give the letter in full. It was written from the s.y. *Mermaid*, lying in Monaco Harbour.

MY DEAR PETER, Where is Ogden? We have been expecting him every day. Mrs Ford is worrying herself to death. She keeps asking me if I have any news, and it is very tiresome to have to keep telling her that I have not heard from you. Surely, with the opportunities you must get every day, you can manage to kidnap him. Do be quick. We are relying on you. – In haste,

CYNTHIA.

I read this brief and business-like communication several times during the day; and after dinner that night, in order to meditate upon it in solitude, I left the house and wandered off in the direction of the village.

I was midway between house and village when I became aware that I was being followed. The night was dark, and the wind moving in the tree-tops emphasized the loneliness of the country road. Both time and place were such as made it peculiarly unpleasant to hear stealthy footsteps on the road behind me.

Uncertainty in such cases is the unnerving thing. I turned sharply, and began to walk back on tiptoe in the direction from which I had come.

I had not been mistaken. A moment later a dark figure loomed up out of the darkness, and the exclamation which greeted me, as I made my presence known, showed that I had taken him by surprise.

There was a momentary pause. I expected the man, whoever he might be, to run, but he held his ground. Indeed, he edged forward.

'Get back!' I said, and allowed my stick to rasp suggestively on the road before raising it in readiness for any sudden development. It was as well that he should know it was there.

The hint seemed to wound rather than frighten him.

'Aw, cut out the rough stuff, bo,' he said reproachfully in a cautious, husky undertone. 'I ain't goin' to start anything.'

I had an impression that I had heard the voice before, but I could not place it.

'What are you following me for?' I demanded. 'Who are you?'

'Say, I want a talk wit youse. I took a slant at youse under de lamp-post back dere, an' I seen it was you, so I tagged along. Say, I'm wise to your game, sport.'

I had identified him by this time. Unless there were two men in the neighbourhood of Sanstead who hailed from the Bowery, this must be the man I had seen at the 'Feathers' who had incurred the disapproval of Miss Benjafield.

'I haven't the faintest idea what you mean,' I said. 'What is my game?'

His voice became reproachful again.

'Ah chee!' he protested. 'Quit yer kiddin'! What was youse rubberin' around de house for last night if you wasn't trailin' de kid?'

'Was it you who ran into me last night?' I asked.

'Gee! I t'ought it was a tree. I came near takin' de count.'

'I did take it. You seemed in a great hurry.'

'Hell!' said the man simply, and expectorated.

'Say,' he resumed, having delivered this criticism on that stirring episode, 'dat's a great kid, dat Nugget. I t'ought it was a Black Hand soup explosion when he cut loose. But, say, let's don't waste time. We gotta get together about dat kid.'

'Certainly, if you wish it. What do you happen to mean?'

'Aw, quit yer kiddin'!' He expectorated again. He seemed to be a man who could express the whole gamut of emotions by this simple means. 'I know you!'

'Then you have the advantage of me, though I believe I remember seeing you before. Weren't you at the "Feathers" one Wednesday evening, singing something about a dog?'

'Sure. Dat was me.'

'What do you mean by saying that you know me?'

'Aw, quit yer kiddin', Sam!'

There was, it seemed to me, a reluctantly admiring note in his voice.

'Tell me, who do you think I am?' I asked patiently.

'Ahr ghee! You can't string me, sport. Smooth Sam Fisher, is who you are, bo. I know you.'

I was too surprised to speak. Verily, some have greatness thrust upon them.

'I hain't never seen youse, Sam,' he continued, 'but I know it's you. And I'll tell youse how I doped it out. To begin with, there ain't but you and your bunch and me and my bunch dat knows de Little Nugget's on dis side at all. Dey sneaked him out of New York mighty slick. And I heard that you had come here after him. So when I runs into a guy dat's trailin' de kid down here, well, who's it going to be if it ain't youse? And when dat guy talks like a dude, like they all say you do, well, who's it going to be if it ain't youse? So quit yer kiddin', Sam, and let's get down to business.'

'Have I the pleasure of addressing Mr Buck MacGinnis?' I said. I felt convinced that this could be no other than that celebrity.

'Dat's right. Dere's no need to keep up anyt'ing wit me, Sam. We're bote on de same trail, so let's get down to it.'

'One moment,' I said. 'Would it surprise you to hear that my name is Burns, and that I am a master at the school?'

He expectorated admirably.

'Hell, no!' he said. 'Gee, it's just what you would be, Sam. I always heard youse had been one of dese rah-rah boys oncest. Say, it's mighty smart of youse to be a perfessor. You're right in on de ground floor.'

His voice became appealing.

'Say, Sam, don't be a hawg. Let's go fifty-fifty in dis deal. My bunch and me has come a hell of a number of miles on dis proposition, and dere ain't no need for us to fall scrappin' over it. Dere's plenty for all of us. Old man Ford'll cough up enough for every one, and dere won't be any fuss. Let's sit in togedder on dis nuggett'ing. It ain't like as if it was an ornery two-by-four deal. I wouldn't ask youse if it wasn't big enough fir de whole bunch of us.'

As I said nothing, he proceeded.

'It ain't square, Sam, to take advantage of your having education. If it was a square fight, and us bote wit de same chance, I wouldn't say; but you bein' a dude perfessor and gettin' right into de place like dat ain't right. Say, don't be a hawg, Sam. Don't swipe it all. Fifty-fifty! Does dat go?'

'I don't know,' I said. 'You had better ask the real Sam. Good night.'

I walked past him and made for the school gates at my best pace. He trotted after me, pleading.

'Sam, give us a quarter, then.'

I walked on.

'Sam, don't be a hawg!'

He broke into a run.

'Sam!' His voice lost its pleading tone and rasped menacingly.

'Gee, if I had me canister, youse wouldn't be so flip! Listen here, you big cheese! You t'ink youse is de only t'ing in sight, huh? Well, we ain't done yet. You'll see yet. We'll fix you! Youse had best watch out.'

I stopped and turned on him.

'Look here, you fool,' I cried. 'I tell you I am not Sam Fisher. Can't you understand that you have got hold of the wrong man? My name is Burns – *Burns*.'

He expectorated – scornfully this time. He was a man slow by nature to receive ideas, but slower to rid himself of one that had contrived to force its way into what he probably called his brain. He had decided on the evidence that I was Smooth Sam Fisher, and no denials on my part were going to shake his belief. He looked on them merely as so many unsportsmanlike quibbles prompted by greed.

'Tell it to Sweeney!' was the form in which he crystallized his scepticism.

'May be you'll say youse ain't trailin' de Nugget, huh?'

It was a home-thrust. If truth-telling has become a habit, one gets slowly off the mark when the moment arrives for the

91

prudent lie. Quite against my will, I hesitated. Observant Mr MacGinnis perceived my hesitation and expectorated triumphantly.

'Ah ghee!' he remarked. And then with a sudden return to ferocity, 'All right, you Sam, you wait! We'll fix you, and fix you good! See? Dat goes. You t'ink youse kin put it across us, huh? All right, you'll get yours. You wait!'

And with these words he slid off into the night. From somewhere in the murky middle distance came a scornful 'Hawg!' and he was gone, leaving me with a settled conviction that, while I had frequently had occasion, since my expedition to Sanstead began, to describe affairs as complex, their complexity had now reached its height. With a watchful Pinkerton's man within, and a vengeful gang of rivals without, Sanstead House seemed likely to become an unrestful place for a young kidnapper with no previous experience.

The need for swift action had become imperative.

II

White, the butler, looking singularly unlike a detective – which, I suppose, is how a detective wants to look – was taking the air on the football field when I left the house next morning for a before-breakfast stroll. The sight of him filled me with a desire for first-hand information on the subject of the man Mr MacGinnis supposed me to be and also of Mr MacGinnis himself. I wanted to be assured that my friend Buck, despite appearances, was a placid person whose bark was worse than his bite.

White's manner, at our first conversational exchanges, was entirely that of the butler. From what I came to know of him later, I think he took an artistic pride in throwing himself into whatever role he had to assume.

At the mention of Smooth Sam Fisher, however, his manner peeled off him like a skin, and he began to talk as himself, a racy and vigorous self vastly different from the episcopal person he thought it necessary to be when on duty.

'White,' I said, 'do you know anything of Smooth Sam Fisher?'

He stared at me. I suppose the question, led up to by no previous remark, was unusual.

'I met a gentleman of the name of Buck MacGinnis – he was our visitor that night, by the way – and he was full of Sam. Do you know him?'

'Buck?'

'Either of them.'

'Well, I've never seen Buck, but I know all about him. There's pepper to Buck.'

'So I should imagine. And Sam?'

'You may take it from me that there's more pepper to Sam's little finger than there is to Buck's whole body. Sam could make Buck look like the last run of shad, if it came to a showdown. Buck's just a common roughneck. Sam's an educated man. He's got brains.'

'So I gathered. Well, I'm glad to hear you speak so well of him, because that's who I'm supposed to be.'

'How's that?'

'Buck MacGinnis insists that I am Smooth Sam Fisher. Nothing I can say will shift him.'

White stared. He had very bright humorous brown eyes. Then he began to laugh.

'Well, what do you know about that?' he exclaimed. 'Wouldn't that jar you!'

'It would. I may say it did. He called me a hog for wanting to keep the Little Nugget to myself, and left threatening to "fix me". What would you say the verb "to fix" signified in Mr MacGinnis's vocabulary?'

White was still chuckling quietly to himself.

'He's a wonder!' he observed. 'Can you beat it? Taking you for Smooth Sam!'

'He said he had never seen Smooth Sam. Have you?'

'Lord, yes.'

'Does he look like me?'

'Not a bit.'

'Do you think he's over here in England?'

'Sam? I know he is.'

'Then Buck MacGinnis was right?'

'Dead right, as far as Sam being on the trail goes. Sam's after the Nugget to get him this time. He's tried often enough before, but we've been too smart for him. This time he allows he's going to bring it off.'

'Then why haven't we seen anything of him? Buck Mac-Ginnis seems to be monopolizing the kidnapping industry in these parts.'

'Oh, Sam'll show up when he feels good and ready. You can take it from me that Sam knows what he is doing. Sam's a special pet of mine. I don't give a flip for Buck MacGinnis.'

'I wish I had your cheery disposition! To me Buck Mac-Ginnis seems a pretty important citizen. I wonder what he meant by "fix"?'

White, however, declined to leave the subject of Buck's more gifted rival.

'Sam's a college man, you know. That gives him a pull. He has brains, and can use them.'

'That was one of the points on which Buck MacGinnis reproached me. He said it was not fair to use my superior education.'

He laughed.

'Buck's got no sense. That's why you find him carrying on like a porch-climber. It's his only notion of how to behave when he wants to do a job. And that's why there's only one man to keep your eye on in this thing of the Little Nugget, and that's Sam. I wish you could get to know Sam. You'd like him.'

'You seem to look on him as a personal friend. I certainly don't like Buck.'

'Oh, Buck!' said White scornfully.

We turned towards the house as the sound of the bell came to us across the field.

'Then you think we may count on Sam's arrival, sooner or later, as a certainty?' I said.

'Surest thing you know.'

'You will have a busy time.'

'All in the day's work.'

'I suppose I ought to look at it in that way. But I do wish I knew exactly what Buck meant by "fix".'

White at last condescended to give his mind to the trivial point.

'I guess he'll try to put one over on you with a sand-bag,' he said carelessly. He seemed to face the prospect with calm.

'A sand-bag, eh?' I said. 'It sounds exciting.'

'And feels it. I know. I've had some.'

I parted from him at the door. As a comforter he had failed to qualify. He had not eased my mind to the slightest extent.

Chapter 7

Looking at it now I can see that the days which followed Audrey's arrival at Sanstead marked the true beginning of our acquaintanceship. Before, during our engagement, we had been strangers, artificially tied together, and she had struggled against the chain. But now, for the first time, we were beginning to know each other, and were discovering that, after all, we had much in common.

It did not alarm me, this growing feeling of comradeship. Keenly on the alert as I was for the least sign that would show that I was in danger of weakening in my loyalty to Cynthia, I did not detect one in my friendliness for Audrey. On the contrary, I was hugely relieved, for it seemed to me that the danger was past. I had not imagined it possible that I could ever experience towards her such a tranquil emotion as this easy friendliness. For the last five years my imagination had been playing round her memory, until I suppose I had built up in my mind some almost superhuman image, some goddess. What I was passing through now, of course, though I was unaware of it, was the natural reaction from that state of mind. Instead of the goddess, I had found a companionable human being, and I imagined that I had effected the change myself, and by sheer force of will brought Audrey into a reasonable relation to the scheme of things.

I suppose a not too intelligent moth has much the same views with regard to the lamp. His last thought, as he enters the flame, is probably one of self-congratulation that he has arranged his dealings with it on such a satisfactory commonsense basis.

And then, when I was feeling particularly safe and complacent, disaster came.

The day was Wednesday, and my 'afternoon off', but the rain was driving against the windows, and the attractions of billiards with the marker at the 'Feathers' had not proved sufficient to make me face the two-mile walk in the storm. I had settled myself in the study. There was a noble fire burning in the grate, and the darkness lit by the glow of the coals, the dripping of the rain, the good behaviour of my pipe, and the reflection that, as I sat there, Glossop was engaged downstairs in wrestling with my class, combined to steep me in a meditative peace. Audrey was playing the piano in the drawing-room. The sound came to me faintly through the closed doors. I recognized what she was playing. I wondered if the melody had the same associations for her that it had for me.

The music stopped. I heard the drawing-room door open. She came into the study.

'I didn't know there was anyone here,' she said. 'I'm frozen. The drawing-room fire's out.'

'Come and sit down,' I said. 'You don't mind the smoke?'

I drew a chair up to the fire for her, feeling, as I did so, a certain pride. Here I was, alone with her in the fire-light, and my pulse was regular and my brain cool. I had a momentary vision of myself as the Strong Man, the strong, quiet man with the iron grip on his emotions. I was pleased with myself.

She sat for some minutes, gazing into the fire. Little spurts of flame whistled comfortably in the heart of the black-red coals. Outside the storm shrieked faintly, and flurries of rain dashed themselves against the window.

'It's very nice in here,' she said at last.

'Peaceful.'

I filled my pipe and re-lit it. Her eyes, seen for an instant in the light of the match, looked dreamy.

'I've been sitting here listening to you,' I said. 'I liked that last thing you played.'

'You always did.'

'You remember that? Do you remember one evening – no, you wouldn't.'

'Which evening?'

'Oh, you wouldn't remember. It's only one particular evening when you played that thing. It sticks in my mind. It was at your father's studio.'

She looked up quickly.

'We went out afterwards and sat in the park.'

I sat up thrilled.

'A man came by with a dog,' I said.

'Two dogs.'

'One surely!'

'Two. A bull-dog and a fox-terrier.'

'I remember the bull-dog, but – by Jove, you're right. A fox-terrier with a black patch over his left eye.'

'Right eye.'

'Right eye. They came up to us, and you – '

'Gave them chocolates.'

I sank back slowly in my chair.

'You've got a wonderful memory,' I said.

She bent over the fire without speaking. The rain rattled on the window.

'So you still like my playing, Peter?'

'I like it better than ever; there's something in it now that I don't believe there used to be. I can't describe it – something –'

'I think it's knowledge, Peter,' she said quietly. 'Experience. I'm five years older than I was when I used to play to you before, and I've seen a good deal in those five years. It may not be altogether pleasant seeing life, but – well, it makes you play the piano better. Experience goes in at the heart and comes out at the finger-tips.'

It seemed to me that she spoke a little bitterly.

'Have you had a bad time, Audrey, these last years?' I said.

'Pretty bad.'

'I'm sorry.'

'I'm not – altogether. I've learned a lot.'

She was silent again, her eyes fixed on the fire.

'What are you thinking about?' I said.

'Oh, a great many things.'

'Pleasant?'

'Mixed. The last thing I thought about was pleasant. That

was, that I am very lucky to be doing the work I am doing now.
Compared with some of the things I have done – '

She shivered.

'I wish you would tell me about those years, Audrey,' I said.
'What were some of the things you did?'

She leaned back in her chair and shaded her face from the fire
with a newspaper. Her eyes were in the shadow.

'Well, let me see. I was a nurse for some time at the Lafayette
Hospital in New York.'

'That's hard work?'

'Horribly hard. I had to give it up after a while. But – it
teaches you ... You learn ... You learn – all sorts of things.
Realities. How much of your own trouble is imagination. You
get real trouble in a hospital. You get it thrown at you.'

I said nothing. I was feeling – I don't know why – a little
uncomfortable, a little at a disadvantage, as one feels in the
presence of some one bigger than oneself.

'Then I was a waitress.'

'A waitress?'

'I tell you I did everything. I was a waitress, and a very bad
one. I broke plates. I muddled orders. Finally I was very rude to
a customer and I went on to try something else. I forget what
came next. I think it was the stage. I travelled for a year with a
touring company. That was hard work, too, but I liked it. After
that came dressmaking, which was harder and which I hated.
And then I had my first stroke of real luck.'

'What was that?'

'I met Mr Ford.'

'How did that happen?'

'You wouldn't remember a Miss Vanderley, an American girl
who was over in London five or six years ago? My father taught
her painting. She was very rich, but she was wild at that time to
be Bohemian. I think that's why she chose Father as a teacher.
Well, she was always at the studio, and we became great
friends, and one day, after all these things I have been telling
you of, I thought I would write to her, and see if she could not
find me something to do. She was a *dear*.' Her voice trembled,
and she lowered the newspaper till her whole face was hidden.

'She wanted me to come to their home and live on her for ever, but I couldn't have that. I told her I must work. So she sent me to Mr Ford, whom the Vanderleys knew very well, and I became Ogden's governess.'

'Great Scott!' I cried. 'What!'

She laughed rather shakily.

'I don't think I was a very good governess. I knew next to nothing. I ought to have been having a governess myself. But I managed somehow.'

'But Ogden?' I said. 'That little fiend, didn't he worry the life out of you?'

'Oh, I had luck there again. He happened to take a mild liking to me, and he was as good as gold – for him; that's to say, if I didn't interfere with him too much, and I didn't. I was horribly weak; he let me alone. It was the happiest time I had had for ages.'

'And when he came here, you came too, as a sort of ex-governess, to continue exerting your moral influence over him?'

She laughed.

'More or less that.'

We sat in silence for a while, and then she put into words the thought which was in both our minds.

'How odd it seems, you and I sitting together chatting like this, Peter, after all – all these years.'

'Like a dream!'

'Just like a dream ... I'm so glad ... You don't know how I've hated myself sometimes for – for – '

'Audrey! You mustn't talk like that. Don't let's think of it. Besides, it was my fault.'

She shook her head.

'Well, put it that we didn't understand one another.'

She nodded slowly.

'No, we didn't understand one another.'

'But we do now,' I said. 'We're friends, Audrey.'

She did not answer. For a long time we sat in silence. And then – the newspaper must have moved – a gleam from the fire fell upon her face, lighting up her eyes; and at the sight something in me began to throb, like a drum warning a city against danger. The next moment the shadow had covered them again.

I sat there, tense, gripping the arms of my chair. I was tingling. Something was happening to me. I had a curious sensation of being on the threshold of something wonderful and perilous.

From downstairs there came the sound of boys' voices. Work was over, and with it this talk by the firelight. In a few minutes somebody, Glossop, or Mr Abney, would be breaking in on our retreat.

We both rose, and then – it happened. She must have tripped in the darkness. She stumbled forward, her hand caught at my coat, and she was in my arms.

It was a thing of an instant. She recovered herself, moved to the door, and was gone.

But I stood where I was, motionless, aghast at the revelation which had come to me in that brief moment. It was the physical contact, the feel of her, warm and alive, that had shattered for ever that flimsy structure of friendship which I had fancied so strong. I had said to Love, 'Thus far, and no farther', and Love had swept over me, the more powerful for being checked. The time of self-deception was over. I knew myself.

Chapter 8

That Buck MacGinnis was not the man to let the grass grow under his feet in a situation like the present one, I would have gathered from White's remarks if I had not already done so from personal observation. The world is divided into dreamers and men of action. From what little I had seen of him I placed Buck MacGinnis in the latter class. Every day I expected him to act, and was agreeably surprised as each twenty-four hours passed and left me still unfixed. But I knew the hour would come, and it did.

I looked for frontal attack from Buck, not subtlety; but, when the attack came, it was so excessively frontal that my chief emotion was a sort of paralysed amazement. It seemed incredible that such peculiarly Wild Western events could happen in peaceful England, even in so isolated a spot as Sanstead House.

It had been one of those interminable days which occur only at schools. A school, more than any other institution, is dependent on the weather. Every small boy rises from his bed of a morning charged with a definite quantity of devilry; and this, if he is to sleep the sound sleep of health, he has got to work off somehow before bedtime. That is why the summer term is the one a master longs for, when the intervals between classes can be spent in the open. There is no pleasanter sight for an assistant-master at a private school than that of a number of boys expending their venom harmlessly in the sunshine.

On this particular day, snow had begun to fall early in the morning, and, while his pupils would have been only too delighted to go out and roll in it by the hour, they were prevented from doing so by Mr Abney's strict orders. No schoolmaster enjoys seeing his pupils running risks of catching cold, and just then Mr Abney was especially definite on the subject. The Saturnalia which had followed Mr MacGinnis' nocturnal visit to the school had had the effect of giving violent colds to three lords, a baronet, and the younger son of an honourable. And, in addition to that, Mr Abney himself, his penetrating tenor changed to a guttural croak, was in his bed looking on the world with watering eyes. His views, therefore, on playing in the snow as an occupation for boys were naturally prejudiced.

The result was that Glossop and I had to try and keep order among a mob of small boys, none of whom had had any chance of working off his superfluous energy. How Glossop fared I can only imagine. Judging by the fact that I, who usually kept fair order without excessive effort, was almost overwhelmed, I should fancy he fared badly. His classroom was on the opposite side of the hall from mine, and at frequent intervals his voice would penetrate my door, raised to a frenzied fortissimo.

Little by little, however, we had won through the day, and the boys had subsided into comparative quiet over their evening preparation, when from outside the front door there sounded the purring of the engine of a large automobile. The bell rang.

I did not, I remember, pay much attention to this at the moment. I supposed that somebody from one of the big houses in the neighbourhood had called, or, taking the lateness of the hour into consideration, that a motoring party had come, as they did sometimes – Sanstead House standing some miles from anywhere in the middle of an intricate system of by-roads – to inquire the way to Portsmouth or London. If my class had allowed me, I would have ignored the sound. But for them it supplied just that break in the monotony of things which they had needed. They welcomed it vociferously.

A voice: 'Sir, please, sir, there's a motor outside.'

Myself (austerely): 'I know there's a motor outside. Get on with your work.'

Various voices: 'Sir, have you ever ridden in a motor?'

'Sir, my father let me help drive our motor last Easter, sir.'

'Sir, who do you think it is?'

An isolated genius (imitating the engine): 'Pr-prr! Pr-prr! Pr-prr!'

I was on the point of distributing bad marks (the school-master's stand-by) broadcast, when a curious sound checked me. It followed directly upon the opening of the front door. I heard White's footsteps crossing the hall, then the click of the latch, and then – a sound that I could not define. The closed door of the classroom deadened it, but for all that it was audible. It resembled the thud of a falling body, but I knew it could not be that, for in peaceful England butlers opening front doors did not fall with thuds.

My class, eager listeners, found fresh material in the sound for friendly conversation.

'Sir, what was that, sir?'

'Did you hear that, sir?'

'What do you think's happened, sir?'

'Be quiet,' I shouted. 'Will you be – '

There was a quick footstep outside, the door flew open, and on the threshold stood a short, sturdy man in a motoring coat and cap. The upper part of his face was covered by a strip of white linen, with holes for the eyes, and there was a Browning pistol in his hand.

It is my belief that, if assistant-masters were allowed to wear white masks and carry automatic pistols, keeping order in a school would become child's play. A silence such as no threat of bad marks had ever been able to produce fell instantaneously upon the classroom. Out of the corner of my eye, as I turned to face our visitor, I could see small boys goggling rapturously at this miraculous realization of all the dreams induced by juvenile adventure fiction. As far as I could ascertain, on subsequent inquiry, not one of them felt a tremor of fear. It was all too tremendously exciting for that. For their exclusive benefit an illustration from a weekly paper for boys had come to life, and they had no time to waste in being frightened.

As for me, I was dazed. Motor bandits may terrorize France, and desperadoes hold up trains in America, but this was peaceful England. The fact that Buck MacGinnis was at large in the neighbourhood did not make the thing any the less incredible. I had looked on my affair with Buck as a thing of the open air and the darkness. I had figured him lying in wait in lonely roads, possibly, even, lurking about the grounds; but in my most apprehensive moments I had not imagined him calling at the front door and holding me up with a revolver in my own classroom.

And yet it was the simple, even the obvious, thing for him to do. Given an automobile, success was certain. Sanstead House stood absolutely alone. There was not even a cottage within half a mile. A train broken down in the middle of the Bad Lands was not more cut off.

Consider, too, the peculiar helplessness of a school in such a case. A school lives on the confidence of parents, a nebulous foundation which the slightest breath can destroy. Everything connected with it must be done with exaggerated discretion. I do not suppose Mr MacGinnis had thought the thing out in all its bearings, but he could not have made a sounder move if he had been a Napoleon. Where the owner of an ordinary country-house raided by masked men can raise the countryside in pursuit, a schoolmaster must do precisely the opposite. From his point of view, the fewer people that know of the affair the better. Parents are a jumpy race. A man may be the ideal schoolmaster, yet will a connection with melodrama damn him in the eyes of parents. They do not inquire. They are too panic-stricken for that. Golden-haired Willie may be receiving the finest education conceivable, yet if men with Browning pistols are familiar objects at his shrine of learning they will remove him. Fortunately for schoolmasters it is seldom that such visitors call upon them. Indeed, I imagine Mr MacGinnis's effort to have been the first of its kind.

I do not, as I say, suppose that Buck, whose forte was action rather than brain-work, had thought all this out. He had trusted to luck, and luck had stood by him. There would be no raising of the countryside in his case. On the contrary, I could see Mr Abney becoming one of the busiest persons on record in his endeavour to hush the thing up and prevent it getting into the papers.

The man with the pistol spoke. He sighted me – I was standing with my back to the mantelpiece, parallel with the door – made a sharp turn, and raised his weapon.

'Put 'em up, sport,' he said.

It was not the voice of Buck MacGinnis. I put my hands up.

'Say, which of dese is de Nugget?'

He half turned his head to the class.

'Which of youse kids is Ogden Ford?'

The class was beyond speech. The silence continued.

'Ogden Ford is not here,' I said.

Our visitor had not that simple faith which is so much better than Norman blood. He did not believe me. Without moving his head he gave a long whistle. Steps sounded outside. Another short, sturdy form, entered the room.

'He ain't in de odder room,' observed the newcomer. 'I been rubberin'!'

This was friend Buck beyond question. I could have recognized his voice anywhere!

'Well dis guy,' said the man with the pistol, indicating me, 'says he ain't here. What's de answer?'

'Why, it's Sam!' said Buck. 'Howdy, Sam? Pleased to see us, huh? We're in on de ground floor, too, dis time, all right, all right.'

His words had a marked effect on his colleague.

'Is dat Sam? Hell! Let me blow de head off'n him!' he said, with simple fervour; and, advancing a step nearer, he waved his disengaged fist truculently. In my role of Sam I had plainly made myself very unpopular. I have never heard so much emotion packed into a few words.

Buck, to my relief, opposed the motion. I thought this decent of Buck.

'Cheese it,' he said curtly.

The other cheesed it. The operation took the form of lowering the fist. The pistol he kept in position.

Mr MacGinnis resumed the conduct of affairs.

'Now den, Sam,' he said, 'come across! Where's de Nugget?'

'My name is not Sam,' I said. 'May I put my hands down?'

'Yep, if you want the top of your damn head blown off.'

Such was not my desire. I kept them up.

'Now den, you Sam,' said Mr MacGinnis again, 'we ain't got time to burn. Out with it. Where's dat Nugget?'

Some reply was obviously required. It was useless to keep protesting that I was not Sam.

'At this time in the evening he is generally working with Mr Glossop.'

'Who's Glossop? Dat dough-faced dub in de room over dere?'

'Exactly. You have described him perfectly.'

'Well, he ain't dere. I bin rubberin'. Aw, quit yer foolin', Sam, where is he?'

'I couldn't tell you just where he is at the present moment,' I said precisely.

'Ahr chee! Let me swot him one!' begged the man with the pistol; a most unlovable person. I could never have made a friend of him.

'Cheese it, you!' said Mr MacGinnis.

The other cheesed it once more, regretfully.

'You got him hidden away somewheres, Sam,' said Mr MacGinnis. 'You can't fool me. I'm com' t'roo dis joint wit a fine-tooth comb till I find him.'

'By all means,' I said. 'Don't let me stop you.'

'You? You're coming wit me.'

'If you wish it. I shall be delighted.'

'An' cut out dat dam' sissy way of talking, you rummy,' bellowed Buck, with a sudden lapse into ferocity. 'Spiel like a regular guy! Standin' dere, pullin' dat dude stuff on me! Cut it out!'

'Say, why *mayn't* I hand him one?' demanded the pistol-bearer pathetically. 'What's your kick against pushin' his face in?'

I thought the question in poor taste. Buck ignored it.

'Gimme dat canister,' he said, taking the Browning pistol from him. 'Now den, Sam, are youse goin' to be good, and come across, or ain't you – which?'

'I'd be delighted to do anything you wished, Mr MacGinnis,' I said, 'but – '

'Aw, hire a hall!' said Buck disgustedly. 'Step lively, den, an' we'll go t'roo de joint. I t'ought youse 'ud have had more sense, Sam, dan to play dis fool game when you know you're beat. You – '

Shooting pains in my shoulders caused me to interrupt him.

'One moment,' I said. 'I'm going to put my hands down. I'm getting cramp.'

'I'll blow a hole in you if you do!'

'Just as you please. But I'm not armed.'

'Lefty,' he said to the other man, 'feel around to see if he's carryin' anyt'ing.'

Lefty advanced and began to tap me scientifically in the neighbourhood of my pockets. He grunted morosely the while. I suppose, at this close range, the temptation to 'hand me one' was almost more than he could bear.

'He ain't got no gun,' he announced gloomily.

'Den youse can put 'em down,' said Mr MacGinnis.

'Thanks,' I said.

'Lefty, youse stay here and look after dese kids. Get a move on, Sam.'

We left the room, a little procession of two, myself leading, Buck in my immediate rear administering occasional cautionary prods with the faithful 'canister'.

II

The first thing that met my eyes as we entered the hall was the body of a man lying by the front door. The light of the lamp fell on his face and I saw that it was White. His hands and feet were tied. As I looked at him, he moved, as if straining against his bonds, and I was conscious of a feeling of relief. That sound that had reached me in the classroom, that thud of a falling body, had become, in the light of what had happened later, very sinister. It was good to know that he was still alive. I gathered – correctly, as I discovered subsequently – that in his case the sand-bag had been utilized. He had been struck down and stunned the instant he opened the door.

There was a masked man leaning against the wall by

Glossop's classroom. He was short and sturdy. The Buck Mac-Ginnis gang seemed to have been turned out on a pattern. Externally, they might all have been twins. This man, to give him a semblance of individuality, had a ragged red moustache. He was smoking a cigar with the air of the warrior taking his rest.

'Hello!' he said, as we appeared. He jerked a thumb towards the classroom. 'I've locked dem in. What's doin', Buck?' he asked, indicating me with a languid nod.

'We're going t'roo de joint,' explained Mr MacGinnis. 'De kid ain't in dere. Hump yourself, Sam!'

His colleague's languor disappeared with magic swiftness.

'Sam! Is dat Sam? Here, let me beat de block off'n him!'

Few points in this episode struck me as more remarkable than the similarity of taste which prevailed, as concerned myself, among the members of Mr MacGinnis's gang. Men, doubtless of varying opinions on other subjects, on this one point they were unanimous. They all wanted to assault me.

Buck, however, had other uses for me. For the present, I was necessary as a guide, and my value as such would be impaired were the block to be beaten off me. Though feeling no friendlier towards me than did his assistants, he declined to allow sentiment to interfere with business. He concentrated his attention on the upward journey with all the earnestness of the young gentleman who carried the banner with the strange device in the poem.

Briefly requesting his ally to cheese it – which he did – he urged me on with the nozzle of the pistol. The red-moustached man sank back against the wall again with an air of dejection, sucking his cigar now like one who has had disappointments in life, while we passed on up the stairs and began to draw the rooms on the first floor.

These consisted of Mr Abney's study and two dormitories. The study was empty, and the only occupants of the dormitories were the three boys who had been stricken down with colds on the occasion of Mr MacGinnis's last visit. They squeaked with surprise at the sight of the assistant-master in such questionable company.

Buck eyed them disappointedly. I waited with something of

109

the feelings of a drummer taking a buyer round the sample room.

'Get on,' said Buck.

'Won't one of those do?'

'Hump yourself, Sam.'

'Call me Sammy,' I urged. 'We're old friends now.'

'Don't get fresh,' he said austerely. And we moved on.

The top floor was even more deserted than the first. There was no one in the dormitories. The only other room was Mr Abney's; and, as we came opposite it, a sneeze from within told of the sufferings of its occupant.

The sound stirred Buck to his depths. He 'pointed' at the door like a smell-dog.

'Who's in dere?' he demanded.

'Only Mr Abney. Better not disturb him. He has a bad cold.'

He placed a wrong construction on my solicitude for my employer. His manner became excited.

'Open dat door, you,' he cried.

'It'll give him a nasty shock.'

'G'wan! Open it!'

No one who is digging a Browning pistol into the small of my back will ever find me disobliging. I opened the door – knocking first, as a mild concession to the conventions – and the procession passed in.

My stricken employer was lying on his back, staring at the ceiling, and our entrance did not at first cause him to change this position.

'Yes?' he said thickly, and disappeared beneath a huge pocket-handkerchief. Muffled sounds, as of distant explosions of dynamite, together with earthquake shudderings of the bed-clothes, told of another sneezing-fit.

'I'm sorry to disturb you,' I began, when Buck, ever the man of action, with a scorn of palaver, strode past me, and, having prodded with the pistol that part of the bedclothes beneath which a rough calculation suggested that Mr Abney's lower ribs were concealed, uttered the one word, 'Sa-a-ay!'

110

Mr Abney sat up like a Jack-in-the-box. One might almost say that he shot up. And then he saw Buck.

I cannot even faintly imagine what were Mr Abney's emotions at that moment. He was a man who, from boyhood up, had led a quiet and regular life. Things like Buck had appeared to him hitherto, if they appeared at all, only in dreams after injudicious suppers. Even in the ordinary costume of the Bowery gentleman, without such adventitious extras as masks and pistols, Buck was no beauty. With that hideous strip of dingy white linen on his face, he was a walking nightmare.

Mr Abney's eyebrows had risen and his jaw had fallen to their uttermost limits. His hair, disturbed by contact with the pillow, gave the impression of standing on end. His eyes seemed to bulge like a snail's. He stared at Buck, fascinated.

'Say, you, quit rubberin'. Youse ain't in a dime museum. Where's dat Ford kid, huh?'

I have set down all Mr MacGinnis's remarks as if they had been uttered in a bell-like voice with a clear and crisp enunciation; but, in doing so, I have flattered him. In reality, his mode of speech suggested that he had something large and unwieldy permanently stuck in his mouth; and it was not easy for a stranger to follow him. Mr Abney signally failed to do so. He continued to gape helplessly till the tension was broken by a sneeze.

One cannot interrogate a sneezing man with any satisfaction to oneself. Buck stood by the bedside in moody silence, waiting for the paroxysm to spend itself.

I, meanwhile, had remained where I stood, close to the door. And, as I waited for Mr Abney to finish sneezing, for the first time since Buck's colleague Lefty had entered the classroom the idea of action occurred to me. Until this moment, I suppose, the strangeness and unexpectedness of these happenings had numbed my brain. To precede Buck meekly upstairs and to wait with equal meekness while he interviewed Mr Abney had seemed the only course open to me. To one whose life has lain apart from such things, the hypnotic influence of a Browning pistol is irresistible.

But now, freed temporarily from this influence, I began to

think; and, my mind making up for its previous inaction by working with unwonted swiftness, I formed a plan of action at once.

It was simple, but I had an idea that it would be effective. My strength lay in my acquaintance with the geography of Sanstead House and Buck's ignorance of it. Let me but get an adequate start, and he might find pursuit vain. It was this start which I saw my way to achieving.

To Buck it had not yet occurred that it was a tactical error to leave me between the door and himself. I supposed he relied too implicitly on the mesmeric pistol. He was not even looking at me.

The next moment my fingers were on the switch of the electric light, and the room was in darkness.

There was a chair by the door. I seized it and swung it into the space between us. Then, springing back, I banged the door and ran.

I did not run without a goal in view. My objective was the study. This, as I have explained, was on the first floor. Its window looked out on to a strip of lawn at the side of the house ending in a shrubbery. The drop would not be pleasant, but I seemed to remember a waterspout that ran up the wall close to the window, and, in any case, I was not in a position to be deterred by the prospect of a bruise or two. I had not failed to realize that my position was one of extreme peril. When Buck, concluding the tour of the house, found that the Little Nugget was not there – as I had reason to know that he would – there was no room for doubt that he would withdraw the protection which he had extended to me up to the present in my capacity of guide. On me the disappointed fury of the raiders would fall. No prudent consideration for their own safety would restrain them. If ever the future was revealed to man, I saw mine. My only chance was to get out into the grounds, where the darkness would make pursuit an impossibility.

It was an affair which must be settled one way or the other in a few seconds, and I calculated that it would take Buck just those few seconds to win his way past the chair and find the door-handle.

I was right. Just as I reached the study, the door of the bed-room flew open, and the house rang with shouts and the noise of feet on the uncarpeted landing. From the hall below came answering shouts, but with an interrogatory note in them. The assistants were willing, but puzzled. They did not like to leave their posts without specific instructions, and Buck, shouting as he clattered over the bare boards, was unintelligible.

I was in the study, the door locked behind me, before they could arrive at an understanding. I sprang to the window.

The handle rattled. Voices shouted. A panel splintered be-neath a kick, and the door shook on its hinges.

And then, for the first time, I think, in my life, panic gripped me, the sheer, blind fear which destroys the reason. It swept over me in a wave, that numbing terror which comes to one in dreams. Indeed, the thing had become dream-like. I seemed to be standing outside myself, looking on at myself, watching myself heave and strain with bruised fingers at a window that would not open.

III

The arm-chair critic, reviewing a situation calmly and at his ease, is apt to make too small allowances for the effect of hurry and excitement on the human mind. He is cool and detached. He sees exactly what ought to have been done, and by what simple means catastrophe might have been averted.

He would have made short work of my present difficulty, I feel certain. It was ridiculously simple. But I had lost my head, and had ceased for the moment to be a reasoning creature. In the end, indeed, it was no presence of mind but pure good luck which saved me. Just as the door, which had held out gallantly, gave way beneath the attack from outside, my fingers, slipping, struck against the catch of the window, and I understood why I had failed to raise it.

I snapped the catch back, and flung up the sash. An icy wind swept into the room, bearing particles of snow. I scrambled on to the window-sill, and a crash from behind me told of the falling of the door.

The packed snow on the sill was drenching my knees as I worked my way out and prepared to drop. There was a deafening explosion inside the room, and simultaneously something seared my shoulder like a hot iron. I cried out with the pain of it, and, losing my balance, fell from the sill.

There was, fortunately for me, a laurel bush immediately below the window, or I should have been undone. I fell into it, all arms and legs, in a way which would have meant broken bones if I had struck the hard turf. I was on my feet in an instant, shaken and scratched and, incidentally, in a worse temper than ever in my life before. The idea of flight, which had obsessed me a moment before, to the exclusion of all other mundane affairs, had vanished absolutely. I was full of fight, I might say overflowing with it. I remember standing there, with the snow trickling in chilly rivulets down my face and neck, and shaking my fist at the window. Two of my pursuers were leaning out of it, while a third dodged behind them, like a small man on the outskirts of a crowd. So far from being thankful for my escape, I was conscious only of a feeling of regret that there was no immediate way of getting at them.

They made no move towards travelling the quick but trying route which had commended itself to me. They seemed to be waiting for something to happen. It was not long before I was made aware of what this something was. From the direction of the front door came the sound of one running. A sudden diminution of the noise of his feet told me that he had left the gravel and was on the turf. I drew back a pace or two and waited.

It was pitch dark, and I had no fear that I should be seen. I was standing well outside the light from the window.

The man stopped just in front of me. A short parley followed.

'Can'tja see him?'

The voice was not Buck's. It was Buck who answered. And when I realized that this man in front of me, within easy reach, on whose back I was shortly about to spring, and whose neck I proposed, under Providence, to twist into the shape of a corkscrew, was no mere underling, but Mr MacGinnis himself, I

114

was filled with a joy which I found it hard to contain in silence.

Looking back, I am a little sorry for Mr MacGinnis. He was not a good man. His mode of speech was not pleasant, and his manners were worse than his speech. But, though he undoubtedly deserved all that was coming to him, it was nevertheless bad luck for him to be standing just there at just that moment. The reactions after my panic, added to the pain of my shoulder, the scratches on my face, and the general misery of being wet and cold, had given me a reckless fury and a determination to do somebody, whoever happened to come along, grievous bodily hurt, such as seldom invades the bosoms of the normally peaceful. To put it crisply, I was fighting mad, and I looked on Buck as something sent by Heaven.

He had got as far, in his reply, as 'Naw, I can't – ' when I sprang.

I have read of the spring of the jaguar, and I have seen some very creditable flying-tackles made on the football field. My leap combined the outstanding qualities of both. I connected with Mr MacGinnis in the region of the waist, and the howl he gave as we crashed to the ground was music to my ears.

But how true is the old Roman saying, '*Surgit amari aliquid*'. Our pleasures are never perfect. There is always something. In the programme which I had hastily mapped out, the upsetting of Mr MacGinnis was but a small item, a mere preliminary. There were a number of things which I had wished to do to him, once upset. But it was not to be. Even as I reached for his throat I perceived that the light of the window was undergoing an eclipse. A compact form had wriggled out on to the sill, as I had done, and I heard the grating of his shoes on the wall as he lowered himself for the drop.

There is a moment when the pleasantest functions must come to an end. I was loath to part from Mr MacGinnis just when I was beginning, as it were, to do myself justice; but it was unavoidable. In another moment his ally would descend upon us, like some Homeric god swooping from a cloud, and I was not prepared to continue the battle against odds.

I disengaged myself – Mr MacGinnis strangely quiescent during the process – and was on my feet in the safety of the darkness just as the reinforcement touched earth. This time I did not wait. My hunger for fight had been appeased to some extent by my brush with Buck, and I was satisfied to have achieved safety with honour.

Making a wide detour I crossed the drive and worked my way through the bushes to within a few yards of where the automobile stood, filling the night with the soft purring of its engines. I was interested to see what would be the enemy's next move. It was improbable that they would attempt to draw the grounds in search of me. I imagined that they would recognize failure and retire whence they had come.

I was right. I had not been watching long, before a little group advanced into the light of the automobile's lamps. There were four of them. Three were walking, the fourth, cursing with the vigour and breadth that marks the expert, lying on their arms, of which they had made something resembling a stretcher.

The driver of the car, who had been sitting woodenly in his seat, turned at the sound.

'Ja get him?' he inquired.

'Get nothing!' replied one of the three moodily. 'De Nugget ain't dere, an' we was chasin' Sam to fix him, an' he laid for us, an' what he did to Buck was plenty.'

They placed their valuable burden in the tonneau, where he lay repeating himself, and two of them climbed in after him. The third seated himself beside the driver.

'Buck's leg's broke,' he announced.

'Hell!' said the chauffeur.

No young actor, receiving his first round of applause, could have felt a keener thrill of gratification than I did at those words. Life may have nobler triumphs than the breaking of a kidnapper's leg, but I did not think so then. It was with an effort that I stopped myself from cheering.

'Let her go,' said the man in the front seat.

The purring rose to a roar. The car turned and began to move with increasing speed down the drive. Its drone grew fainter, and ceased. I brushed the snow from my coat and walked to the front door.

My first act on entering the house, was to release White. He was still lying where I had seen him last. He appeared to have made no headway with the cords on his wrists and ankles. I came to his help with a rather blunt pocket-knife, and he rose stiffly and began to chafe the injured arms in silence.

'They've gone,' I said.

He nodded.

'Did they hit you with a sand-bag?'

He nodded again.

'I broke Buck's leg,' I said, with modest pride.

He looked up incredulously. I related my experiences as briefly as possible, and when I came to the part where I made my flying tackle, the gloom was swept from his face by a joyful smile. Buck's injury may have given its recipient pain, but it was certainly the cause of pleasure to others. White's manner was one of the utmost enthusiasm as I described the scene.

'That'll hold Buck for a while,' was his comment. 'I guess we shan't hear from *him* for a week or two. That's the best cure for the headache I've ever struck.'

He rubbed the lump that just showed beneath his hair. I did not wonder at his emotion. Whoever had wielded the sand-bag had done his work well, in a manner to cause hard feelings on the part of the victim.

I had been vaguely conscious during this conversation of an intermittent noise like distant thunder. I now perceived that it came from Glossop's classroom, and was caused by the beating of hands on the door-panels. I remembered that the red-moustached man had locked Glossop and his young charges in. It seemed to me that he had done well. There would be plenty of confusion without their assistance.

I was turning towards my own classroom when I saw Audrey on the stairs and went to meet her.

'It's all right,' I said. 'They've gone.'

'Who was it? What did they want?'

'It was a gentleman named MacGinnis and some friends. They came after Ogden Ford, but they didn't get him.'

'Where is he? Where is Ogden?'

Before I could reply, babel broke loose. While we had been talking, White had injudiciously turned the key of Glossop's classroom which now disgorged its occupants, headed by my colleague, in a turbulent stream. At the same moment my own classroom began to empty itself. The hall was packed with boys, and the din became deafening. Every one had something to say, and they all said it at once.

Glossop was at my side, semaphoring violently.

'We must telephone,' he bellowed in my ear, 'for the police.'

Somebody tugged at my arm. It was Audrey. She was saying something which was drowned in the uproar. I drew her towards the stairs, and we found comparative quiet on the first landing.

'What were you saying?' I asked.

'He isn't there.'

'Who?'

'Ogden Ford. Where is he? He is not in his room. They must have taken him.'

Glossop came up at a gallop, springing from stair to stair like the chamois of the Alps.

'We must telephone for the police!' he cried.

'I have telephoned,' said Audrey, 'ten minutes ago. They are sending some men at once. Mr Glossop, was Ogden Ford in your classroom?'

'No, Mrs Sheridan. I thought he was with you, Burns.'

I shook my head.

'Those men came to kidnap him, Mr Glossop,' said Audrey.

'Undoubtedly the gang of scoundrels to which that man the other night belonged! This is preposterous. My nerves will not stand these repeated outrages. We must have police protection. The villains must be brought to justice. I never heard of such a thing! In an English school!'

Glossop's eyes gleamed agitatedly behind their spectacles. Macbeth's deportment when confronted with Banquo's ghost was stolid by comparison. There was no doubt that Buck's visit had upset the smooth peace of our happy little community to quite a considerable extent.

The noise in the hall had increased rather than subsided. A belated sense of professional duty returned to Glossop and myself. We descended the stairs and began to do our best, in our respective styles, to produce order. It was not an easy task. Small boys are always prone to make a noise, even without provocation. When they get a genuine excuse like the incursion of men in white masks, who prod assistant-masters in the small of the back with Browning pistols, they tend to eclipse themselves. I doubt whether we should ever have quieted them, had it not been that the hour of Buck's visit had chanced to fall within a short time of that set apart for the boys' tea, and that the kitchen had lain outside the sphere of our visitors' operations. As in many English country houses, the kitchen at Sanstead House was at the end of a long corridor, shut off by doors through which even pistol-shots penetrated but faintly. Our excellent cook had, moreover, the misfortune to be somewhat deaf, with the result that, throughout all the storm and stress in our part of the house, she, like the lady in Goethe's poem, had gone on cutting bread and butter; till now, when it seemed that nothing could quell the uproar, there rose above it the ringing of the bell.

If there is anything exciting enough to keep the Englishman or the English boy from his tea, it has yet to be discovered. The shouting ceased on the instant. The general feeling seemed to be that inquiries could be postponed till a more suitable occasion, but not tea. There was a general movement in the direction of the dining-room.

Glossop had already gone with the crowd, and I was about to follow, when there was another ring at the front-door bell.

I gathered that this must be the police, and waited. In the impending inquiry I was by way of being a star witness. If any one had been in the thick of things from the beginning it was myself.

White opened the door. I caught a glimpse of blue uniforms, and came forward to do the honours.

There were two of them, no more. In response to our urgent appeal for assistance against armed bandits, the Majesty of the Law had materialized itself in the shape of a stout inspector and a long, lean constable. I thought, as I came to meet them, that they were fortunate to have arrived late. I could see Lefty and the red-moustached man, thwarted in their designs on me, making dreadful havoc among the official force, as here represented.

White, the simple butler once more, introduced us.

'This is Mr Burns, one of the masters at the school,' he said, and removed himself from the scene. There never was a man like White for knowing his place when he played the butler.

The inspector looked at me sharply. The constable gazed into space.

'H'm!' said the inspector.

Mentally I had named them Bones and Johnson. I do not know why, except that they seemed to deserve it.

'You telephoned for us,' said Bones accusingly.

'We did.'

'What's the trouble? What – got your notebook? – has been happening?'

Johnson removed his gaze from the middle distance and produced a notebook.

'At about half past five – ' I began.

Johnson moistened his pencil.

'At about half past five an automobile drove up to the front door. In it were five masked men with revolvers.'

I interested them. There was no doubt of that. Bones's healthy colour deepened, and his eyes grew round. Johnson's pencil raced over the page, wobbling with emotion.

'Masked men?' echoed Bones.

'With revolvers,' I said. 'Now aren't you glad you didn't go to the circus? They rang the front-door bell; when White opened it, they stunned him with a sand-bag. Then – '

Bones held up a large hand.

'Wait!'

I waited.

'Who is White?'

'The butler.'

'I will take his statement. Fetch the butler.'

Johnson trotted off obediently.

Left alone with me, Bones became friendlier and less official.

'This is as queer a start as ever I heard of, Mr Burns,' he said. 'Twenty years I've been in the force, and nothing like this has transpired. It beats cock-fighting. What in the world do you suppose men with masks and revolvers was after? First idea I had was that you were making fun of me.'

I was shocked at the idea. I hastened to give further details.

'They were a gang of American crooks who had come over to kidnap Mr Elmer Ford's son, who is a pupil at the school. You have heard of Mr Ford? He is an American millionaire, and there have been several attempts during the past few years to kidnap Ogden.'

At this point Johnson returned with White. White told his story briefly, exhibited his bruise, showed the marks of the cords on his wrists, and was dismissed. I suggested that further conversation had better take place in the presence of Mr Abney, who, I imagined, would have something to say on the subject of hushing the thing up.

We went upstairs. The broken door of the study delayed us a while and led to a fresh spasm of activity on the part of Johnson's pencil. Having disposed of this, we proceeded to Mr Abney's room.

Bones's authoritative rap upon the door produced an agitated 'Who's that?' from the occupant. I explained the nature of the visitation through the keyhole and there came from within the sound of moving furniture. His one brief interview with Buck had evidently caused my employer to ensure against a second by barricading himself in with everything he could find suitable for the purpose. It was some moments before the way was clear for our entrance.

'Cub id,' said a voice at last.

Mr Abney was sitting up in bed, the blankets wrapped tightly about him. His appearance was still disordered. The furniture of the room was in great confusion, and a poker on the floor by the dressing-table showed that he had been prepared to sell his life dearly.

'I ab glad to see you, Idspector,' he said. 'Bister Burds, what is the expladation of this extraordinary affair?'

It took some time to explain matters to Mr Abney, and more to convince Bones and his colleague that, so far from wanting a hue and cry raised over the countryside and columns about the affair in the papers, publicity was the thing we were anxious to avoid. They were visibly disappointed when they grasped the position of affairs. The thing, properly advertised, would have been the biggest that had ever happened to the neighbourhood, and their eager eyes could see glory within easy reach. Mention of a cold snack and a drop of beer, however, to be found in the kitchen, served to cast a gleam of brightness on their gloom, and they vanished in search of it with something approaching cheeriness, Johnson taking notes to the last.

They had hardly gone when Glossop whirled into the room in a state of effervescing agitation.

'Mr Abney, Ogden Ford is nowhere to be found!'

Mr Abney greeted the information with a prodigious sneeze.

'What do you bead?' he demanded, when the paroxysm was over. He turned to me. 'Bister Burds, I understood you to – ah – say that the scou'drels took their departure without the boy Ford.'

'They certainly did. I watched them go.'

'I have searched the house thoroughly,' said Glossop, 'and there are no signs of him. And not only that, the Boy Beckford cannot be found.'

Mr Abney clasped his head in his hands. Poor man, he was in no condition to bear up with easy fortitude against this succession of shocks. He was like one who, having survived an earthquake, is hit by an automobile. He had partly adjusted his mind to the quiet contemplation of Mr MacGinnis and friends when he was called upon to face this fresh disaster. And he had a cold in the head, which unmans the stoutest. Napoleon would have won Waterloo if Wellington had had a cold in the head.

'Augustus Beckford caddot be fou'd?' he echoed feebly.

'They must have run away together,' said Glossop.

Mr Abney sat up, galvanized.

'Such a thing has never happened id the school before!' he cried. 'It has aldways beed my – ah – codstant endeavour to make my boys look upod Sadstead House as a happy hobe. I have systebatically edcouraged a spirit of cheerful codtedment. I caddot seriously credit the fact that Augustus Beckford, one of the bost charbig boys it has ever beed by good fortude to have id by charge, has deliberately rud away.'

'He must have been persuaded by that boy Ford,' said Glossop, 'who,' he added morosely, 'I believe, is the devil in disguise.'

Mr Abney did not rebuke the strength of his language. Probably the theory struck him as eminently sound. To me there certainly seemed something in it.

'Subbthig bust be done at once!' Mr Abney exclaimed. 'It is – ah – ibperative that we take ibbediate steps. They bust have gone to Londod. Bister Burds, you bust go to Londod by the next traid. I caddot go byself with this cold.'

It was the irony of fate that, on the one occasion when duty really summoned that champion popper-up-to-London to the Metropolis, he should be unable to answer the call.

'Very well,' I said. 'I'll go and look out a train.'

'Bister Glossop, you will be in charge of the school. Perhaps you had better go back to the boys dow.'

White was in the hall when I got there.

'White,' I said, 'do you know anything about the trains to London?'

'Are you going to London?' he asked, in his more conversational manner. I thought he looked at me curiously as he spoke.

'Yes. Ogden Ford and Lord Beckford cannot be found. Mr Abney thinks they must have run away to London.'

'I shouldn't wonder,' said White dryly, it seemed to me. There was something distinctly odd in his manner. 'And you're going after them.'

'Yes. I must look up a train.'

'There is a fast train in an hour. You will have plenty of time.'

'Will you tell Mr Abney that, while I go and pack my bag? And telephone for a cab.'

'Sure,' said White, nodding.

I went up to my room and began to put a few things together in a suit-case. I felt happy, for several reasons. A visit to London, after my arduous weeks at Sanstead, was in the nature of an unexpected treat. My tastes are metropolitan, and the vision of an hour at a music-hall – I should be too late for the theatres – with supper to follow in some restaurant where there was an orchestra, appealed to me.

When I returned to the hall, carrying my bag, I found Audrey there.

'I'm being sent to London,' I announced.

'I know. White told me. Peter, bring him back.'

'That's why I'm being sent.'

'It means everything to me.'

I looked at her in surprise. There was a strained, anxious expression on her face, for which I could not account. I declined to believe that anybody could care what happened to the Little Nugget purely for that amiable youth's own sake. Besides, as he had gone to London willingly, the assumption was that he was enjoying himself.

'I don't understand,' I said. 'What do you mean?'

'I'll tell you. Mr Ford sent me here to be near Ogden, to guard him. He knew that there was always a danger of attempts being made to kidnap him, even though he was brought over to England very quietly. That is how I come to be here. I go wherever Ogden goes. I am responsible for him. And I have failed. If Ogden is not brought back, Mr Ford will have nothing more to do with me. He never forgives failures. It will mean going back to the old work again – the dressmaking, or the waiting, or whatever I can manage to find.' She gave a little shiver. 'Peter, I can't. All the pluck has gone out of me. I'm afraid. I couldn't face all that again. Bring him back. You must. You will. Say you will.'

I did not answer. I could find nothing to say; for it was I who was responsible for all her trouble. I had planned everything. I had given Ogden Ford the money that had taken him to London. And soon, unless I could reach London before it happened, and prevent him, he, with my valet Smith, would be in the Dover boat-train on his way to Monaco.

Chapter 9

I

It was only after many hours of thought that it had flashed upon me that the simplest and safest way of removing the Little Nugget was to induce him to remove himself. Once the idea had come, the rest was simple. The negotiations which had taken place that morning in the stable-yard had been brief. I suppose a boy in Ogden's position, with his record of narrow escapes from the kidnapper, comes to take things as a matter of course which would startle the ordinary boy. He assumed, I imagine, that I was the accredited agent of his mother, and that the money which I gave him for travelling expenses came from her. Perhaps he had been expecting something of the sort. At any rate, he grasped the essential points of the scheme with amazing promptitude. His little hand was extended to receive the cash almost before I had finished speaking.

The main outline of my plan was that he should slip away to London, during the afternoon, go to my rooms, where he would find Smith, and with Smith travel to his mother at Monaco. I had written to Smith, bidding him be in readiness for the expedition. There was no flaw in the scheme as I had mapped it out, and though Ogden had complicated it a little by gratuitously luring away Augustus Beckford to bear him company, he had not endangered its success.

But now an utterly unforeseen complication had arisen. My one desire now was to undo everything for which I had been plotting.

I stood there, looking at her dumbly, hating myself for being the cause of the anxiety in her eyes. If I had struck her, I could not have felt more despicable. In my misery I cursed Cynthia for leading me into this tangle.

I heard my name spoken, and turned to find White at my elbow.

'Mr Abney would like to see you, sir.'

I went upstairs, glad to escape. The tension of the situation had begun to tear at my nerves.

'Cub id, Bister Burds,' said my employer, swallowing a lozenge. His aspect was more dazed than ever. 'White has just bade an – ah – extraordinary cobbudicatiod to me. It seebs he is in reality a detective, an employee of Pidkertod's Agedcy, of which you have, of course – ah – heard.'

So White had revealed himself. On the whole, I was not surprised. Certainly his motive for concealment, the fear of making Mr Abney nervous, was removed. An inrush of Red Indians with tomahawks could hardly have added greatly to Mr Abney's nervousness at the present juncture.

'Sent here by Mr Ford, I suppose?' I said. I had to say something.

'Exactly. Ah – precisely.' He sneezed. 'Bister Ford, without codsulting me – I do not cobbedt on the good taste or wisdob of his actiod – dispatched White to apply for the post of butler at this – ah – house, his predecessor having left at a bobedt's dotice, bribed to do so, I strodgly suspect, by Bister Ford himself. I bay be wrodging Bister Ford, but I do dot thig so.'

I thought the reasoning sound.

'All thad, however,' resumed Mr Abney, removing his face from a jug of menthol at which he had been sniffing with the tense concentration of a dog at a rabbit-hole, 'is beside the poidt. I berely bedtiod it to explaid why White will accompady you to London.'

'What!'

The exclamation was forced from me by my dismay. This was appalling. If this infernal detective was to accompany me, my chance of bringing Ogden back was gone. It had been my intention to go straight to my rooms, in the hope of finding him not yet departed. But how was I to explain his presence there to White?

'I don't think it's necessary, Mr Abney,' I protested. 'I am sure I can manage this affair by myself.'

'Two heads are better thad wud,' said the invalid sententiously, burying his features in the jug once more.

'Too many cooks spoil the broth,' I replied. If the conversation was to consist of copybook maxims, I could match him as long as he pleased.

He did not keep up the intellectual level of the discussion.

'Dodseds!' he snapped, with the irritation of a man whose proverb has been capped by another. I had seldom heard him speak so sharply. White's revelation had evidently impressed him. He had all the ordinary peaceful man's reverence for the professional detective.

'White will accompany you, Bister Burds,' he said doggedly.

'Very well,' I said.

After all, it might be that I should get an opportunity of giving him the slip. London is a large city.

A few minutes later the cab arrived, and White and I set forth on our mission.

We did not talk much in the cab. I was too busy with my thoughts to volunteer remarks, and White, apparently, had meditations of his own to occupy him.

It was when we had settled ourselves in an empty compartment and the train had started that he found speech. I had provided myself with a book as a barrier against conversation, and began at once to make a pretence of reading, but he broke through my defences.

'Interesting book, Mr Burns?'

'Very,' I said.

'Life's more interesting than books.'

I made no comment on this profound observation. He was not discouraged.

'Mr Burns,' he said, after the silence had lasted a few moments.

'Yes?'

'Let's talk for a spell. These train-journeys are pretty slow.'

Again I seemed to detect that curious undercurrent of meaning in his voice which I had noticed in the course of our brief exchange of remarks in the hall. I glanced up and met his eye.

He was looking at me in a way that struck me as curious. There was something in those bright brown eyes of his which had the effect of making me vaguely uneasy. Something seemed to tell me that he had a definite motive in forcing his conversation on me.

'I guess I can interest you a heap more than that book, even if it's the darndest best seller that ever hatched.'

'Oh!'

He lit a cigarette.

'You didn't want me around on this trip, did you?'

'It seemed rather unnecessary for both of us to go,' I said indifferently. 'Still, perhaps two heads are better than one, as Mr Abney remarked. What do you propose to do when you get to London?'

He bent forward and tapped me on the knee.

'I propose to stick to you like a label on a bottle, sonny,' he said. 'That's what I propose to do.'

'What do you mean?'

I was finding it difficult, such is the effect of a guilty conscience, to meet his eye, and the fact irritated me.

'I want to find out that address you gave the Ford kid this morning out in the stable-yard.'

It is strange how really literal figurative expressions are. I had read stories in which some astonished character's heart leaped into his mouth. For an instant I could have supposed that mine had actually done so. The illusion of some solid object blocking up my throat was extraordinarily vivid, and there certainly seemed to be a vacuum in the spot where my heart should have been. Not for a substantial reward could I have uttered a word at that moment. I could not even breathe. The horrible unexpectedness of the blow had paralysed me.

White, however, was apparently prepared to continue the chat without my assistance.

'I guess you didn't know I was around, or you wouldn't have talked that way. Well, I was, and I heard every word you said. Here was the money, you said, and he was to take it and break for London, and go to the address on this card, and your pal Smith would look after him. I guess there had been some talk

129

before that, but I didn't arrive in time to hear it. But I heard all I wanted, except that address. And that's what I'm going to find out when we get to London.'

He gave out this appalling information in a rich and soothing voice, as if it were some ordinary commonplace. To me it seemed to end everything. I imagined I was already as good as under arrest. What a fool I had been to discuss such a matter in a place like a stable-yard, however apparently empty. I might have known that at a school there are no empty places.

'I must say it jarred me when I heard you pulling that stuff,' continued White. 'I haven't what you might call a childlike faith in my fellow-man as a rule, but it had never occurred to me for a moment that you could be playing that game. It only shows,' he added philosophically, 'that you've got to suspect everybody when it comes to a gilt-edged proposition like the Little Nugget.'

The train rattled on. I tried to reduce my mind to working order, to formulate some plan, but could not.

Beyond the realization that I was in the tightest corner of my life, I seemed to have lost the power of thought.

White resumed his monologue.

'You had me guessing,' he admitted. 'I couldn't figure you out. First thing, of course, I thought you must be working in with Buck MacGinnis and his crowd. Then all that happened tonight, and I saw that, whoever you might be working in with, it wasn't Buck. And now I've placed you. You're not in with any one. You're just playing it by yourself. I shouldn't mind betting this was your first job, and that you saw your chance of making a pile by holding up old man Ford, and thought it was better than schoolmastering, and grabbed it.'

He leaned forward and tapped me on the knee again. There was something indescribably irritating in the action. As one who has had experience, I can state that, while to be arrested at all is bad, to be arrested by a detective with a fatherly manner is maddening.

'See here,' he said, 'we must get together over this business.'

I suppose it was the recollection of the same words in the

mouth of Buck MacGinnis that made me sit up with a jerk and stare at him.

'We'll make a great team,' he said, still in that same cosy voice. 'If ever there was a case of fifty-fifty, this is it. You've got the kid, and I've got you. I can't get away with him without your help, and you can't get away with him unless you square me. It's a stand-off. The only thing is to sit in at the game together and share out. Does it go?'

He beamed kindly on my bewilderment during the space of time it takes to select a cigarette and light a match. Then, blowing a contented puff of smoke, he crossed his legs and leaned back.

'When I told you I was a Pinkerton's man, sonny,' he said, 'I missed the cold truth by about a mile. But you caught me shooting off guns in the grounds, and it was up to me to say something.'

He blew a smoke-ring and watched it dreamily till it melted in the draught from the ventilator.

'I'm Smooth Sam Fisher,' he said.

II

When two emotions clash, the weaker goes to the wall. Any surprise I might have felt was swallowed up in my relief. If I had been at liberty to be astonished, my companion's information would no doubt have astonished me. But I was not. I was so relieved that he was not a Pinkerton's man that I did not really care what else he might be.

'It's always been a habit of mine, in these little matters,' he went on, 'to let other folks do the rough work, and chip in myself when they've cleared the way. It saves trouble and expense. I don't travel with a gang, like that bone-headed Buck. What's the use of a gang? They only get tumbling over each other and spoiling everything. Look at Buck! Where is he? Down and out. While I – '

He smiled complacently. His manner annoyed me. I objected to being looked upon as a humble cat's paw by this bland scoundrel.

'While you – what?' I said.

He looked at me in mild surprise.

'Why, I come in with you, sonny, and take my share like a gentleman.'

'Do you!'

'Well, don't I?'

He looked at me in the half-reproachful half-affectionate manner of the kind old uncle who reasons with a headstrong nephew.

'Young man,' he said, 'you surely aren't thinking you can put one over on me in this business? Tell me, you don't take me for that sort of ivory-skulled boob? Do you imagine for one instant, sonny, that I'm not next to every move in this game? Are you deluding yourself with the idea that this thing isn't a perfect cinch for me? Let's hear what's troubling you. You seem to have gotten some foolish ideas in your head. Let's talk it over quietly.'

'If you have no objection,' I said, 'no. I don't want to talk to you, Mr Fisher. I don't like you, and I don't like your way of earning your living. Buck MacGinnis was bad enough, but at least he was a straightforward tough. There's no excuse for you.'

'Surely we are unusually righteous this p.m., are we not?' said Sam suavely.

I did not answer.

'Is this not mere professional jealousy?'

This was too much for me.

'Do you imagine for a moment that I'm doing this for money?'

'I did have that impression. Was I wrong? Do you kidnap the sons of millionaires for your health?'

'I promised that I would get this boy back to his mother. That is why I gave him the money to go to London. And that is why my valet was to have taken him to – to where Mrs Ford is.'

He did not reply in words, but if ever eyebrows spoke, his said, 'My dear sir, really!' I could not remain silent under their patent disbelief.

'That's the simple truth,' I said.

He shrugged his shoulders, as who would say, 'Have it your own way. Let us change the subject.'

'You say "was to have taken". Have you changed your plans?'

'Yes, I'm going to take the boy back to the school.'

He laughed – a rich, rolling laugh. His double chin shook comfortably.

'It won't do,' he said, shaking his head with humorous reproach. 'It won't do.'

'You don't believe me?'

'Frankly, I do not.'

'Very well,' I said, and began to read my book.

'If you want to give me the slip,' he chuckled, 'you must do better than that. I can see you bringing the Nugget back to the school.'

'You will, if you wait,' I said.

'I wonder what that address was that you gave him,' he mused. 'Well, I shall soon know.'

He lapsed into silence. The train rolled on. I looked at my watch. London was not far off now.

'The present arrangement of equal division,' said Sam, breaking a long silence, 'holds good, of course, only in the event of your quitting this fool game and doing the square thing by me. Let me put it plainly. We are either partners or competitors. It is for you to decide. If you will be sensible and tell me that address, I will pledge my word – '

'Your word!' I said scornfully.

'Honour among thieves!' replied Sam, with unruffled geniality. 'I wouldn't double-cross you for worlds. If, however, you think you can manage without my assistance, it will then be my melancholy duty to beat you to the kid, and collect him and the money entirely on my own account. Am I to take it,' he said, as I was silent, 'that you prefer war to an alliance?'

I turned a page of my book and went on reading.

'If Youth but knew!' he sighed. 'Young man, I am nearly twice your age, and I have, at a modest estimate, about ten times as much sense. Yet, in your overweening self-confidence, with your ungovernable gall, you fancy you can hand me a lemon. *Me!* I should smile!'

'Do,' I said. 'Do, while you can.'

He shook his head reprovingly.

'You will not be so fresh, sonny, in a few hours. You will be biting pieces out of yourself, I fear. And later on, when my automobile splashes you with mud in Piccadilly, you will taste the full bitterness of remorse. Well, Youth must buy its experience, I suppose!'

I looked across at him as he sat, plump and rosy and complacent, puffing at his cigarette, and my heart warmed to the old ruffian. It was impossible to maintain an attitude of righteous iciness with him. I might loathe his mode of life, and hate him as a representative – and a leading representative – of one of the most contemptible trades on earth, but there was a sunny charm about the man himself which made it hard to feel hostile to him as an individual.

I closed my book with a bang and burst out laughing.

'You're a wonder!' I said.

He beamed at what he took to be evidence that I was coming round to the friendly and sensible view of the matter.

'Then you think, on consideration – ' he said. 'Excellent! Now, my dear young man, all joking aside, you will take me with you to that address, will you not? You observe that I do not ask you to give it to me. Let there be not so much as the faintest odour of the double-cross about this business. All I ask is that you allow me to accompany you to where the Nugget is hidden, and then rely on my wider experience of this sort of game to get him safely away and open negotiations with the dad.'

'I suppose your experience has been wide?' I said.

'Quite tolerably – quite tolerably.'

'Doesn't it ever worry you the anxiety and misery you cause?'

'Purely temporary, both. And then, look at it in another way. Think of the joy and relief of the bereaved parents when sonny comes toddling home again! Surely it is worth some temporary distress to taste that supreme happiness? In a sense, you might call me a human benefactor. I teach parents to appreciate their children. You know what parents are. Father gets caught short in steel rails one morning. When he reaches home, what does he do? He eases his mind by snapping at little Willie. Mrs Van First-Family forgets to invite mother to her freak-dinner. What happens? Mother takes it out of William. They love him, maybe, but they are too used to him. They do not realize all he is to them. And then, one afternoon, he disappears. The agony! The remorse! "How could I ever have told our lost angel to stop his darned noise!" moans father. "I struck him!" sobs mother. "With this jewelled hand I spanked our vanished darling!" "We were not worthy to have him," they wail together. "But oh, if we could but get him back!" Well they do. They get him back as soon as ever they care to come across in unmarked hundred-dollar bills. And after that they think twice before working off their grouches on the poor kid. So I bring universal happiness into the home. I don't say father doesn't get a twinge every now and then when he catches sight of the hole in his bank balance, but, darn it, what's money for if it's not to spend?'

He snorted with altruistic fervour.

'What makes you so set on kidnapping Ogden Ford?' I asked. 'I know he is valuable, but you must have made your pile by this time. I gather that you have been practising your particular brand of philanthropy for a good many years. Why don't you retire?'

He sighed.

'It is the dream of my life to retire, young man. You may not believe me, but my instincts are thoroughly domestic. When I have the leisure to weave day-dreams, they centre around a cosy little home with a nice porch and stationary washtubs.'

He regarded me closely, as if to decide whether I was worthy of these confidences. There was something wistful in his brown eyes. I suppose the inspection must have been favourable, or he was in a mood when a man must unbosom himself to someone, for he proceeded to open his heart to me. A man in his particular line of business, I imagine, finds few confidants, and the strain probably becomes intolerable at times.

'Have you ever experienced the love of a good woman,

135

sonny? It's a wonderful thing.' He brooded sentimentally for a moment, then continued, and – to my mind – somewhat spoiled the impressiveness of his opening words. 'The love of a good woman,' he said, 'is about the darnedest wonderful lay-out that ever came down the pike. I know. I've had some.'

A spark from his cigarette fell on his hand. He swore a startled oath.

'We came from the same old town,' he resumed, having recovered from this interlude. 'Used to be kids at the same school ... Walked to school together ... me carrying her luncheon-basket and helping her over the fences ... Ah! ... Just the same when we grew up. Still pals. And that was twenty years ago ... The arrangement was that I should go out and make the money to buy the home, and then come back and marry her.'

'Then why the devil haven't you done it?' I said severely.

He shook his head.

'If you know anything about crooks, young man,' he said, 'you'll know that outside of their own line they are the easiest marks that ever happened. They fall for anything. At least, it's always been that way with me. No sooner did I get together a sort of pile and start out for the old town, when some smooth stranger would come along and steer me up against some skin-game, and back I'd have to go to work. That happened a few times, and when I did manage at last to get home with the dough I found she had married another guy. It's hard on women, you see,' he explained chivalrously. 'They get lonesome and Roving Rupert doesn't show up, so they have to marry Stay-at-Home Henry just to keep from getting the horrors.'

'So she's Mrs Stay-at-Home Henry now?' I said sympathetically.

'She was till a year ago. She's a widow now. Deceased had a misunderstanding with a hydrophobia skunk, so I'm informed. I believe he was a good man. Outside of licking him at school I didn't know him well. I saw her just before I left to come here. She's as fond of me as ever. It's all settled, if only I can connect with the mazuma. And she don't want much, either. Just enough to keep the home together.'

'I wish you happiness,' I said.

'You can do better than that. You can take me with you to that address.'

I avoided the subject.

'What does she say to your way of making money?' I asked.

'She doesn't know, and she ain't going to know. I don't see why a man has got to tell his wife every little thing in his past. She thinks I'm a drummer, travelling in England for a dry-goods firm. She wouldn't stand for the other thing, not for a minute. She's very particular. Always was. That's why I'm going to quit after I've won out over this thing of the Little Nugget.' He looked at me hopefully. 'So you *will* take me along, sonny, won't you?'

I shook my head.

'You won't?'

'I'm sorry to spoil a romance, but I can't. You must look around for some other home into which to bring happiness. The Fords' is barred.'

'You are very obstinate, young man,' he said, sadly, but without any apparent ill-feeling. 'I can't persuade you?'

'No.'

'Ah, well! So we are to be rivals, not allies. You will regret this, sonny. I may say you will regret it very bitterly. When you see me in my automo – '

'You mentioned your automobile before.'

'Ah! So I did.'

The train had stopped, as trains always do on English railways before entering a terminus. Presently it began to move forward hesitatingly, as if saying to itself, 'Now, am I really wanted here? Shall I be welcome?' Eventually, after a second halt, it glided slowly alongside the platform.

I sprang out and ran to the cab-rank. I was aboard a taxi, bowling out of the station before the train had stopped.

Peeping out of the window at the back, I was unable to see Sam. My adroit move, I took it, had baffled him. I had left him standing.

*

It was a quarter of an hour's drive to my rooms, but to me, in my anxiety, it seemed more. This was going to be a close thing, and success or failure a matter of minutes. If he followed my instructions Smith would be starting for the Continental boat-train tonight with his companion; and, working out the distances, I saw that, by the time I could arrive, he might already have left my rooms. Sam's supervision at Sanstead Station had made it impossible for me to send a telegram. I had had to trust to chance. Fortunately my train, by a miracle, had been up to time, and at my present rate of progress I ought to catch Smith a few minutes before he left the building.

The cab pulled up. I ran up the stairs and opened the door of my apartment.

'Smith!' I called.

A chair scraped along the floor and a door opened at the end of the passage. Smith came out.

'Thank goodness you have not started. I thought I should miss you. Where is the boy?'

'The boy, sir?'

'The boy I wrote to you about.'

'He has not arrived, sir.'

'Not arrived?'

'No, sir.'

I stared at him blankly.

'How long have you been here?'

'All day, sir.'

'You have not been out?'

'Not since the hour of two, sir.'

'I can't understand it,' I said.

'Perhaps the young gentleman changed his mind and never started, sir?'

'I know he started.'

Smith had no further suggestion to offer.

'Pending the young gentleman's arrival, sir, I remain in London?'

A fruity voice spoke at the door behind me.

'What! Hasn't he arrived?'

I turned. There, beaming and benevolent, stood Mr Fisher.

'It occurred to me to look your name out in the telephone directory,' he explained. 'I might have thought of that before.'

'Come in here,' I said, opening the door of the sitting-room. I did not want to discuss the thing with him before Smith.

He looked about the room admiringly.

'So these are your quarters,' he said. 'You do yourself pretty well, young man. So I understand that the Nugget has gone wrong in transit. He has altered his plans on the way?'

'I can't understand it.'

'I can! You gave him a certain amount of money?'

'Yes. Enough to get him to – where he was going.'

'Then, knowing the boy, I should say that he has found other uses for it. He's whooping it up in London, and, I should fancy, having the time of his young life.'

He got up.

'This of course,' he said, 'alters considerably any understanding we may have come to, sonny. All idea of a partnership is now out of the question. I wish you well, but I have no further use for you. Somewhere in this great city the Little Nugget is hiding, and I mean to find him – entirely on my own account. This is where our paths divide, Mr Burns. Good night.'

Chapter 10

When Sam had left, which he did rather in the manner of a heavy father in melodrama, shaking the dust of an erring son's threshold off his feet, I mixed myself a high-ball, and sat down to consider the position of affairs. It did not take me long to see that the infernal boy had double-crossed me with a smooth effectiveness which Mr Fisher himself might have envied. Somewhere in this great city, as Sam had observed, he was hiding. But where? London is a vague address.

I wondered what steps Sam was taking. Was there some underground secret service bureau to which persons of his profession had access? I doubted it. I imagined that he, as I proposed to do, was drawing the city at a venture in the hope of flushing the quarry by accident. Yet such was the impression he had made upon me as a man of resource and sagacity, that I did not relish the idea of his getting a start on me, even in a venture so uncertain as this. My imagination began to picture him miraculously inspired in the search, and such was the vividness of the vision that I jumped up from my chair, resolved to get on the trail at once. It was hopelessly late, however, and I did not anticipate that I should meet with any success.

Nor did I. For two hours and a half I tramped the streets, my spirits sinking more and more under the influence of failure and a blend of snow and sleet which had begun to fall; and then, tired out, I went back to my rooms, and climbed sorrowfully into bed.

It was odd to wake up and realize that I was in London. Years seemed to have passed since I had left it. Time is a thing of emotions, not of hours and minutes, and I had certainly packed a considerable number of emotional moments into my stay at Sanstead House. I lay in bed, reviewing the past, while

Smith, with a cheerful clatter of crockery, prepared my breakfast in the next room.

A curious lethargy had succeeded the feverish energy of the previous night. More than ever the impossibility of finding the needle in this human bundle of hay oppressed me. No one is optimistic before breakfast, and I regarded the future with dull resignation, turning my thoughts from it after a while to the past. But the past meant Audrey, and to think of Audrey hurt.

It seemed curious to me that in a life of thirty years I should have been able to find, among the hundreds of women I had met, only one capable of creating in me that disquieting welter of emotions which is called love, and hard that that one should reciprocate my feeling only to the extent of the mild liking which Audrey entertained for me.

I tried to analyse her qualifications for the place she held in my heart. I had known women who had attracted me more physically, and women who had attracted me more mentally. I had known wiser women, handsomer women, more amiable women, but none of them had affected me like Audrey. The problem was inexplicable. Any idea that we might be affinities, soul-mates destined for each other from the beginning of time, was disposed of by the fact that my attraction for her was apparently in inverse ratio to hers for me. For possibly the millionth time in the past five years I tried to picture in my mind the man Sheridan, that shadowy wooer to whom she had yielded so readily. What quality had he possessed that I did not? Wherein lay the magnetism that had brought about his triumph?

These were unprofitable speculations. I laid them aside until the next occasion when I should feel disposed for self-torture, and got out of bed. A bath and breakfast braced me up, and I left the house in a reasonably cheerful frame of mind.

To search at random for an individual unit among London's millions lends an undeniable attraction to a day in town. In a desultory way I pursued my investigations through the morning and afternoon, but neither of Ogden nor of his young friend Lord Beckford was I vouchsafed a glimpse. My consolation was that Smooth Sam was probably being equally unsuccessful.

Towards the evening there arose the question of return to Sanstead. I had not gathered whether Mr Abney had intended to set any time-limit on my wanderings, or whether I was not supposed to come back except with the deserters. I decided that I had better remain in London, at any rate for another night, and went to the nearest post office to send Mr Abney a telegram to that effect.

As I was writing it, the problem which had baffled me for twenty-four hours, solved itself in under a minute. Whether my powers of inductive reasoning had been under a cloud since I left Sanstead, or whether they were normally beneath contempt, I do not know. But the fact remains, that I had completely overlooked the obvious solution of my difficulty. I think I must have been thinking so exclusively of the Little Nugget that I had entirely forgotten the existence of Augustus Beckford. It occurred to me now that, by making inquiries at the latter's house, I should learn something to my advantage. A boy of the Augustus type does not run away from school without a reason. Probably some party was taking place tonight at the ancestral home, at which, tempted by the lawless Nugget, he had decided that his presence was necessary.

I knew the house well. There had been a time, when Lord Mountry and I were at Oxford, when I had spent frequent week-ends there. Since then, owing to being abroad, I had seen little of the family. Now was the moment to reintroduce myself. I hailed a cab.

Inductive reasoning had not played me false. There was a red carpet outside the house, and from within came the sounds of music.

Lady Wroxham, the mother of Mountry and the vanishing Augustus, was one of those women who take things as they come. She did not seem surprised at seeing me.

'How nice of you to come and see us,' she said. 'Somebody told me you were abroad. Ted is in the south of France in the yacht. Augustus is here. Mr Abney, his schoolmaster, let him come up for the night.'

I perceived that Augustus had been playing a bold game.

I saw the coaching of Ogden behind these dashing false-hoods.

'You will hardly remember Sybil. She was quite a baby when you were here last. She is having her birthday-party this evening.'

'May I go in and help?' I said.

'I wish you would. They would love it.'

I doubted it, but went in. A dance had just finished. Strolling towards me in his tightest Eton suit, his face shining with honest joy, was the errant Augustus, and close behind him, wearing the blasé air of one for whom custom has staled the pleasures of life, was the Little Nugget.

I think they both saw me at the same moment. The effect of my appearance on them was illustrative of their respective characters. Augustus turned a deep shade of purple and fixed me with a horrified stare. The Nugget winked. Augustus halted and shuffled his feet. The Nugget strolled up and accosted me like an old friend.

'Hello!' he said. 'How did you get here? Say, I was going to try and get you on the phone some old time and explain things. I've been pretty much on the jump since I hit London.'

'You little brute!'

My gleaming eye, travelling past him, met that of the Hon. Augustus Beckford, causing that youth to jump guiltily. The Nugget looked over his shoulder.

'I guess we don't want him around if we're to talk business,' he said. 'I'll go and tell him to beat it.'

'You'll do nothing of the kind. I don't propose to lose sight of either of you.'

'Oh, he's all right. You don't have to worry about him. He was going back to the school anyway tomorrow. He only ran away to go to this party. Why not let him enjoy himself while he's here? I'll go and make a date for you to meet at the end of the show.'

He approached his friend, and a short colloquy ensued, which ended in the latter shuffling off in the direction of the other revellers. Such is the buoyancy of youth that a moment later he was dancing a two-step with every appearance of careless

143

enjoyment. The future, with its storms, seemed to have slipped from his mind.

'That's all right,' said the Nugget, returning to me. 'He's promised he won't duck away. You'll find him somewhere around whenever you care to look for him. Now we can talk.'

'I hardly like to trespass on your valuable time,' I said. The airy way in which this demon boy handled what should have been – to him – an embarrassing situation irritated me. For all the authority I seemed to have over him I might have been the potted palm against which he was leaning.

'That's all right.' Everything appeared to be all right with him. 'This sort of thing does not appeal to me. Don't be afraid of spoiling my evening. I only came because Becky was so set on it. Dancing bores me pallid, so let's get somewhere where we can sit down and talk.'

I was beginning to feel that a children's party was the right place for me. Sam Fisher had treated me as a child, and so did the Little Nugget. That I was a responsible person, well on in my thirty-first year, with a narrow escape from death and a hopeless love-affair on my record, seemed to strike neither of them. I followed my companion to a secluded recess with the utmost meekness.

He leaned back and crossed his legs.

'Got a cigarette?'

'I have not got a cigarette, and, if I had, I wouldn't give it to you.'

He regarded me tolerantly.

'Got a grouch tonight, haven't you? You seem all flittered up about something. What's the trouble? Sore about my not showing up at your apartment? I'll explain that all right.'

'I shall be glad to listen.'

'It's like this. It suddenly occurred to me that a day or two one way or the other wasn't going to affect our deal and that, while I was about it, I might just as well see a bit of London before I left. I suggested it to Becky, and the idea made the biggest kind of a hit with him. I found he had only been in an automobile once in his life. Can you beat it? I've had one of my own ever since I was a kid. Well, naturally, it was up to me to blow him to a joy-ride, and that's where the money went.'

'Where the money went?'

'Sure. I've got two dollars left, and that's all. It wasn't altogether the automobiling. It was the meals that got away with my roll. Say, that kid Beckford is one swell feeder. He's wrapping himself around the eats all the time. I guess it's not smoking that does it. I haven't the appetite I used to have. Well, that's how it was, you see. But I'm through now. Cough up the fare and I'll make the trip tomorrow. Mother'll be tickled to death to see me.'

'She won't see you. We're going back to the school tomorrow.'

He looked at me incredulously.

'What's that? Going back to school?'

'I've altered my plans.'

'I'm not going back to any old school. You daren't take me. Where'll you be if I tell the hot-air merchant about our deal and you slipping me the money and all that?'

'Tell him what you like. He won't believe it.'

He thought this over, and its truth came home to him. The complacent expression left his face.

'What's the matter with you? Are you dippy, or what? You get me away up to London, and the first thing that happens when I'm here is that you want to take me back. You make me tired.'

It was borne in upon me that there was something in his point of view. My sudden change of mind must have seemed inexplicable to him. And, having by a miracle succeeded in finding him, I was in a mood to be generous. I unbent.

'Ogden, old sport,' I said cordially, 'I think we've both had all we want of this children's party. You're bored and if I stop on another half hour I may be called on to entertain these infants with comic songs. We men of the world are above this sort of thing. Get your hat and coat and I'll take you to a show. We can discuss business later over a bit of supper.'

The gloom of his countenance melted into a pleased smile.

'You said something that time!' he observed joyfully; and we slunk away to get our hats, the best of friends. A note for Augustus Beckford, requesting his presence at Waterloo Station at ten minutes past twelve on the following morning, I left with the butler. There was a certain informality about my methods which I doubt if Mr Abney would have approved, but I felt that I could rely on Augustus.

Much may be done by kindness. By the time the curtain fell on the musical comedy which we had attended all was peace between the Nugget and myself. Supper cemented our friendship, and we drove back to my rooms on excellent terms with one another. Half an hour later he was snoring in the spare room, while I smoked contentedly before the fire in the sitting-room.

I had not been there five minutes when the bell rang. Smith was in bed, so I went to the door myself and found Mr Fisher on the mat.

My feeling of benevolence towards all created things, the result of my successful handling of the Little Nugget, embraced Sam. I invited him in.

'Well,' I said, when I had given him a cigar and filled his glass, 'and how have you been getting on, Mr Fisher? Any luck?'

He shook his head at me reproachfully.

'Young man, you're deep. I've got to hand it to you. I underestimated you. You're very deep.'

'Approbation from Smooth Sam Fisher is praise indeed. But why these stately compliments?'

'You took me in, young man. I don't mind owning it. When you told me the Nugget had gone astray, I lapped it up like a babe. And all the time you were putting one over on me. Well, well!'

'But he had gone astray, Mr Fisher.'

He knocked the ash off his cigar. He wore a pained look.

'You needn't keep it up, sonny. I happened to be standing within three yards of you when you got into a cab with him in Shaftesbury Avenue.'

I laughed.

'Well, if that's the case, let there be no secrets between us. He's asleep in the next room.'

Sam leaned forward earnestly and tapped me on the knee.

'Young man, this is a critical moment. This is where, if you aren't careful, you may undo all the good work you have done by getting chesty and thinking that, because you've won out so far, you're the whole show. Believe me, the difficult part is to come, and it's right here that you need an experienced man to work in with you. Let me in on this and leave the negotiations with old man Ford to me. You would only make a mess of them. I've handled this kind of thing a dozen times, and I know just how to act. You won't regret taking me on as a partner. You won't lose a cent by it. I can work him for just double what you would get, even supposing you didn't make a mess of the deal and get nothing.'

'It's very good of you, but there won't be any negotiations with Mr Ford. I am taking the boy back to Sanstead, as I told you.' I caught his pained eye. 'I'm afraid you don't believe me.'

He drew at his cigar without replying.

It is a human weakness to wish to convince those who doubt us, even if their opinion is not intrinsically valuable. I remembered that I had Cynthia's letter in my pocket. I produced it as exhibit A in my evidence and read it to him.

Sam listened carefully.

'I see,' he said. 'Who wrote that?'

'Never mind. A friend of mine.'

I returned the letter to my pocket.

'I was going to have sent him over to Monaco, but I altered my plans. Something interfered.'

'What?'

'I might call it coincidence, if you know what that means.'

'And you are really going to take him back to the school?'

'I am.'

'We shall travel back together,' he said. 'I had hoped I had seen the last of the place. The English countryside may be delightful in the summer, but for winter give me London. However,' he sighed resignedly, and rose from his chair, 'I will say good-bye till tomorrow. What train do you catch?'

'Do you mean to say,' I demanded, 'that you have the nerve to come back to Sanstead after what you have told me about yourself?'

'You entertain some idea of exposing me to Mr Abney? Forget it, young man. We are both in glass houses. Don't let us throw stones. Besides, would he believe it? What proof have you?'

I had thought this argument tolerably sound when I had used it on the Nugget. Now that it was used on myself I realized its soundness even more thoroughly. My hands were tied.

'Yes,' said Sam, 'tomorrow, after our little jaunt to London, we shall all resume the quiet, rural life once more.'

He beamed expansively upon me from the doorway.

'However, even the quiet, rural life has its interest. I guess we shan't be dull!' he said.

I believed him.

Chapter 11

Considering the various handicaps under which he laboured – notably a cold in the head, a fear of the Little Nugget, and a reverence for the aristocracy – Mr Abney's handling of the situation, when the runaways returned to school, bordered on the masterly. Any sort of physical punishment being out of the question – especially in the case of the Nugget, who would certainly have retaliated with a bout of window-breaking – he had to fall back on oratory, and he did this to such effect that, when he had finished, Augustus wept openly and was so subdued that he did not ask a single question for nearly three days.

One result of the adventure was that Ogden's bed was moved to a sort of cubby-hole adjoining my room. In the house, as originally planned, this had evidently been a dressing-room. Under Mr Abney's rule it had come to be used as a general repository for lumber. My boxes were there, and a portmanteau of Glossop's. It was an excellent place in which to bestow a boy in quest of whom kidnappers might break in by night. The window was too small to allow a man to pass through, and the only means of entrance was by way of my room. By night, at any rate, the Nugget's safety seemed to be assured.

The curiosity of the small boy, fortunately, is not lasting. His active mind lives mainly in the present. It was not many days, therefore, before the excitement caused by Buck's raid and the Nugget's disappearance began to subside. Within a week both episodes had been shelved as subjects of conversation, and the school had settled down to its normal humdrum life.

To me, however, there had come a period of mental unrest more acute than I had ever experienced. My life, for the past five years, had run in so smooth a stream that, now that I found myself tossed about in the rapids, I was bewildered. It was a peculiar aggravation of the difficulty of my position that in my world, the little world of Sanstead House, there should be but one woman, and she the very one whom, if I wished to recover my peace of mind, it was necessary for me to avoid.

My feelings towards Cynthia at this time defied my powers of analysis. There were moments when I clung to the memory of her, when she seemed the only thing solid and safe in a world of chaos, and moments, again, when she was a burden crushing me. There were days when I would give up the struggle and let myself drift, and days when I would fight myself inch by inch. But every day found my position more hopeless than the last.

At night sometimes, as I lay awake, I would tell myself that if only I could see her or even hear from her the struggle would be easier. It was her total disappearance from my life that made it so hard for me. I had nothing to help me to fight.

And then, one morning, as if in answer to my thoughts her letter came.

The letter startled me. It was as if there had been some telepathic communion between us.

It was very short, almost formal:

'MY DEAR PETER – I want to ask you a question. I can put it quite shortly. It is this. Are your feelings towards me still the same? I don't tell you why I ask this. I simply ask it. Whatever your answer is, it cannot affect our friendship, so be quite candid. CYNTHIA.'

I sat down there and then to write my reply. The letter, coming when it did and saying what it said, had affected me profoundly. It was like an unexpected reinforcement in a losing battle. It filled me with a glow of self-confidence. I felt strong again, able to fight and win. My mood bore me away, and I poured out my whole heart to her. I told her that my feelings had not altered, that I loved her and nobody but her. It was a letter, I can see, looking back, born of fretted nerves; but at the time I had no such criticism to make. It seemed to me a true expression of my real feelings.

That the fight was not over because in my moment of exaltation I had imagined that I had conquered myself was made uncomfortably plain to me by the thrill that ran through me when, returning from posting my letter, I met Audrey. The sight of her reminded me that a reinforcement is only a reinforcement, a help towards victory, not victory itself.

For the first time I found myself feeling resentful towards her. There was no reason in my resentment. It would not have borne examination. But it was there, and its presence gave me support. I found myself combating the thrill the sight of her had caused, and looking at her with a critical and hostile eye. Who was she that she should enslave a man against his will? Fascination exists only in the imagination of the fascinated. If he have the strength to deny the fascination and convince himself that it does not exist, he is saved. It is purely a matter of willpower and calm reasonableness. There must have been sturdy, level-headed Egyptian citizens who could not understand what people saw to admire in Cleopatra.

Thus reasoning, I raised my hat, uttered a crisp 'Good morning', and passed on, the very picture of the brisk man of affairs.

'Peter!'

Even the brisk man of affairs must stop when spoken to. Otherwise, apart from any question of politeness, it looks as if he were running away.

Her face was still wearing the faint look of surprise which my manner had called forth.

'You're in a great hurry.'

I had no answer. She did not appear to expect one.

We moved towards the house in silence, to me oppressive silence. The force of her personality was beginning to beat against my defences, concerning the stability of which, under pressure, a certain uneasiness troubled my mind.

'Are you worried about anything, Peter?' she said at last.

'No,' I said. 'Why?'

'I was afraid you might be.'

I felt angry with myself. I was mismanaging this thing in the most idiotic way. Instead of this bovine silence, gay small-talk, the easy eloquence, in fact, of the brisk man of affairs should have been my policy. No wonder Smooth Sam Fisher treated me as a child. My whole bearing was that of a sulky school-boy.

The silence became more oppressive.

We reached the house. In the hall we parted, she to upper regions, I to my classroom. She did not look at me. Her face was cold and offended.

One is curiously inconsistent. Having created what in the circumstances was a most desirable coldness between Audrey and myself, I ought to have been satisfied. Reason told me that this was the best thing that could have happened. Yet joy was one of the few emotions which I did not feel during the days which followed. My brief moment of clear-headedness had passed, and with it the exhilaration that had produced the letter to Cynthia and the resentment which had helped me to reason calmly with myself on the intrinsic nature of fascination in woman. Once more Audrey became the centre of my world. But our friendship, that elusive thing which had contrived to exist side by side with my love, had vanished. There was a breach between us which widened daily. Soon we hardly spoke.

Nothing, in short, could have been more eminently satisfactory, and the fact that I regretted it is only a proof of the essential weakness of my character.

Chapter 12

I

In those grey days there was one thought, of the many that occupied my mind, which brought with it a certain measure of consolation. It was the reflection that this state of affairs could not last for ever. The school term was drawing to a close. Soon I should be free from the propinquity which paralysed my efforts to fight. I was resolved that the last day of term should end for ever my connection with Sanstead House and all that was in it. Mrs Ford must find some other minion. If her happiness depended on the recovery of the Little Nugget, she must learn to do without happiness, like the rest of the inhabitants of this horrible world.

Meanwhile, however, I held myself to be still on duty. By what tortuous processes of thought I had arrived at the conclusion I do not know, but I considered myself responsible to Audrey for the safeguarding of the Little Nugget, and no altered relations between us could affect my position. Perhaps mixed up with this attitude of mind, was the less altruistic wish to foil Smooth Sam. His continued presence at the school was a challenge to me.

Sam's behaviour puzzled me. I do not know exactly what I expected him to do, but I certainly did not expect him to do nothing. Yet day followed day, and still he made no move. He was the very model of a butler. But our dealings with one another in London had left me vigilant, and his inaction did not disarm me. It sprang from patience, not from any weakening of purpose or despair of success. Sooner or later I knew he would act, swiftly and suddenly, with a plan perfected in every detail.

But when he made his attack it was the very simplicity of his methods that tricked me, and only pure chance defeated him.

I have said that it was the custom of the staff of masters at Sanstead House School – in other words, of every male adult in the house except Mr Fisher himself – to assemble in Mr Abney's study after dinner of an evening to drink coffee. It was a ceremony, like most of the ceremonies at an establishment such as a school, where things are run on a schedule, which knew of no variation. Sometimes Mr Abney would leave us immediately after the ceremony, but he never omitted to take his part in it first.

On this particular evening, for the first time since the beginning of the term, I was seized with a prejudice against coffee. I had been sleeping badly for several nights, and I decided that abstention from coffee might remedy this.

I waited, for form's sake, till Glossop and Mr Abney had filled their cups, then went to my room, where I lay down in the dark to wrestle with a more than usually pronounced fit of depression which had descended upon me. Solitude and darkness struck me as the suitable setting for my thoughts.

At this moment Smooth Sam Fisher had no place in my meditations. My mind was not occupied with him at all. When, therefore, the door, which had been ajar, began to open slowly, I did not become instantly on the alert. Perhaps it was some sound, barely audible, that aroused me from my torpor and set my blood tingling with anticipation. Perhaps it was the way the door was opening. An honest draught does not move a door furtively, in jerks.

I sat up noiseless, tense, and alert. And then, very quietly, somebody entered the room.

There was only one person in Sanstead House who would enter a room like that. I was amused. The impudence of the thing tickled me. It seemed so foreign to Mr Fisher's usual cautious methods. This strolling in and helping oneself was certainly kidnapping *de luxe*. In the small hours I could have understood it; but at nine o'clock at night, with Glossop, Mr Abney and myself awake and liable to be met at any moment on the stairs, it was absurd. I marvelled at Smooth Sam's effrontery.

I lay still. I imagined that, being in, he would switch on the electric light. He did, and I greeted him pleasantly.

'And what can I do for *you*, Mr Fisher?'

For a man who had learned to control himself in difficult situations he took the shock badly. He uttered a startled exclamation and spun round, open-mouthed.

I could not help admiring the quickness with which he recovered himself. Almost immediately he was the suave, chatty Sam Fisher who had unbosomed his theories and dreams to me in the train to London.

'I quit,' he said pleasantly. 'The episode is closed. I am a man of peace, and I take it that you would not keep on lying quietly on that bed while I went into the other room and abstracted our young friend? Unless you have changed your mind again, would a fifty-fifty offer tempt you?'

'Not an inch.'

'Just so. I merely asked.'

'And how about Mr Abney, in any case? Suppose we met him on the stairs?'

'We should not meet him on the stairs,' said Sam confidently. 'You did not take coffee tonight, I gather?'

'I didn't – no. Why?'

He jerked his head resignedly.

'Can you beat it! I ask you, young man, could I have foreseen that, after drinking coffee every night regularly for two months, you would pass it up tonight of all nights? You certainly are my jinx, sonny. You have hung the Indian sign on me all right.'

His words had brought light to me.

'Did you drug the coffee?'

'Did I! I fixed it so that one sip would have an insomnia patient in dreamland before he had time to say "Good night". That stuff Rip Van Winkle drank had nothing on my coffee. And all wasted! Well, well!'

He turned towards the door.

'Shall I leave the light on, or would you prefer it off?'

'On please. I might fall asleep in the dark.'

'Not you! And, if you did, you would dream that I was there,

155

and wake up. There are moments, young man, when you bring me pretty near to quitting and taking to honest work.'

He paused.

'But not altogether. I have still a shot or two in my locker. We shall see what we shall see. I am not dead yet. Wait!'

'I will, and some day, when I am walking along Piccadilly, a passing automobile will splash me with mud. A heavily furred plutocrat will stare haughtily at me from the tonneau, and with a start of surprise I shall recognize – '

'Stranger things have happened. Be flip while you can, sonny. You win so far, but this hoodoo of mine can't last for ever.'

He passed from the room with a certain sad dignity. A moment later he reappeared.

'A thought strikes me,' he said. 'The fifty-fifty proposition does not impress you. Would it make things easier if I were to offer my cooperation for a mere quarter of the profit?'

'Not in the least.'

'It's a handsome offer.'

'Wonderfully. I'm afraid I'm not dealing on any terms.'

He left the room, only to return once more. His head appeared, staring at me round the door, in a disembodied way, like the Cheshire Cat.

'You won't say later on I didn't give you your chance?' he said anxiously.

He vanished again, permanently this time. I heard his steps passing down the stairs.

iI

We had now arrived at the last week of term, at the last days of the last week. The holiday spirit was abroad in the school. Among the boys it took the form of increased disorderliness. Boys who had hitherto only made Glossop bellow now made him perspire and tear his hair as well. Boys who had merely spilt ink now broke windows. The Little Nugget abandoned cigarettes in favour of an old clay pipe which he had found in the stables.

As for me, I felt like a spent swimmer who sees the shore

almost within his reach. Audrey avoided me when she could, and was frigidly polite when we met. But I suffered less now. A few more days, and I should have done with this phase of my life for ever, and Audrey would once more become a memory.

Complete quiescence marked the deportment of Mr Fisher during these days. He did not attempt to repeat his last effort. The coffee came to the study unmixed with alien drugs. Sam, like lightning, did not strike twice in the same place. He had the artist's soul, and disliked patching up bungled work. If he made another move, it would, I knew, be on entirely fresh lines.

Ignoring the fact that I had had all the luck, I was inclined to be self-satisfied when I thought of Sam. I had pitted my wits against his, and I had won. It was a praiseworthy performance for a man who had done hitherto nothing particular in his life.

If all the copybook maxims which had been drilled into me in my childhood and my early disaster with Audrey had not been sufficient, I ought to have been warned by Sam's advice not to take victory for granted till the fight was over. As Sam had said, his luck would turn sooner or later.

One realizes these truths in theory, but the practical application of them seldom fails to come as a shock. I received mine on the last morning but one of the term.

Shortly after breakfast a message was brought to me that Mr Abney would like to see me in his study. I went without any sense of disaster to come. Most of the business of the school was discussed in the study after breakfast, and I imagined that the matter had to do with some detail of the morrow's exodus.

I found Mr Abney pacing the room, a look of annoyance on his face. At the desk, her back to me, Audrey was writing. It was part of her work to take charge of the business correspondence of the establishment. She did not look round when I came in, nor when Mr Abney spoke my name, but went on writing as if I did not exist.

There was a touch of embarrassment in Mr Abney's manner, for which I could not at first account. He was stately, but with the rather defensive stateliness which marked his

157

announcements that he was about to pop up to London and leave me to do his work. He coughed once or twice before proceeding to the business of the moment.

'Ah, Mr Burns,' he said at length, 'might I ask if your plans for the holidays, the – ah – earlier part of the holidays are settled? No? ah – excellent.'

He produced a letter from the heap of papers on the desk.

'Ah – excellent. That simplifies matters considerably. I have no right to ask what I am about to – ah – in fact ask. I have no claim on your time in the holidays. But, in the circumstances, perhaps you may see your way to doing me a considerable service. I have received a letter from Mr Elmer Ford which puts me in a position of some difficulty. It is not my wish – indeed, it is foreign to my policy – to disoblige the parents of the boys who are entrusted to my – ah – care, and I should like, if possible, to do what Mr Ford asks. It appears that certain business matters call him to the north of England for a few days, this rendering it impossible for him to receive little Ogden tomorrow. It is not my custom to criticize parents who have paid me the compliment of placing their sons at the most malleable and important period of their lives, in my – ah – charge, but I must say that a little longer notice would have been a – in fact, a convenience. But Mr Ford, like so many of his countrymen, is what I believe is called a hustler. He does it now, as the expression is. In short, he wishes to leave little Ogden at the school for the first few days of the holidays, and I should be extremely obliged, Mr Burns, if you should find it possible to stay here and – ah – look after him.'

Audrey stopped writing and turned in her chair, the first intimation she had given that she had heard Mr Abney's remarks.

'It really won't be necessary to trouble Mr Burns,' she said, without looking at me. 'I can take care of Ogden very well by myself.'

'In the case of an – ah – ordinary boy, Mrs Sheridan, I should not hesitate to leave you in sole charge as you have very kindly offered to stay and help me in this matter. But we must recollect not only – I speak frankly – not only the peculiar – ah – dis-

158

position of this particular lad, but also the fact that those ruffians who visited the house that night may possibly seize the opportunity to make a fresh attack. I should not feel – ah – justified in thrusting so heavy a reponsibility upon you.'

There was reason in what he said. Audrey made no reply. I heard her pen tapping on the desk and deduced her feelings. I, myself, felt like a prisoner who, having filed through the bars of his cell, is removed to another on the eve of escape. I had so braced myself up to endure till the end of term and no longer that this postponement of the day of release had a crushing effect.

Mr Abney coughed and lowered his voice confidentially.

'I would stay myself, but the fact is, I am called to London on very urgent business, and shall be unable to return for a day or so. My late pupil, the – ah – the Earl of Buxton, has been – I can rely on your discretion, Mr Burns – has been in trouble with the authorities at Eton, and his guardian, an old college friend of mine – the – in fact, the Duke of Bessborough, who, rightly or wrongly, places – er – considerable reliance on my advice, is anxious to consult me on the matter. I shall return as soon as possible, but you will readily understand that, in the circumstances, my time will not be my own. I must place myself unreservedly at – ah – Bessborough's disposal.'

He pressed the bell.

'In the event of your observing any suspicious characters in the neighbourhood, you have the telephone and can instantly communicate with the police. And you will have the assistance of – '

The door opened and Smooth Sam Fisher entered.

'You rang, sir?'

'Ah! Come in, White, and close the door. I have something to say to you. I have just been informing Mr Burns that Mr Ford has written asking me to allow his son to stay on at the school for the first few days of the vacation.'

He turned to Audrey.

'You will doubtless be surprised, Mrs Sheridan, and possibly – ah – somewhat startled, to learn the peculiar nature of White's position at Sanstead House. You have no objection to my

159

informing Mrs Sheridan, White, in consideration of the fact that you will be working together in this matter? Just so. White is a detective in the employment of Pinkerton's Agency. Mr Ford' – a slight frown appeared on his lofty brow – 'Mr Ford obtained his present situation for him in order that he might protect his son in the event of – ah – in fact, any attempt to remove him.'

I saw Audrey start. A quick flush came into her face. She uttered a little exclamation of astonishment.

'Just so,' said Mr Abney, by way of comment on this. 'You are naturally surprised. The whole arrangement is excessively unusual, and, I may say – ah – disturbing. However, you have your duty to fulfil to your employer, White, and you will, of course, remain here with the boy.'

'Yes, sir.'

I found myself looking into a bright brown eye that gleamed with genial triumph. The other was closed. In the exuberance of the moment, Smooth Sam had had the bad taste to wink at me.

'You will have Mr Burns to help you, White. He has kindly consented to postpone his departure during the short period in which I shall be compelled to be absent.'

I had no recollection of having given any kind consent, but I was very willing to have it assumed, and I was glad to see that Mr Fisher, though Mr Abney did not observe it, was visibly taken aback by this piece of information. But he made one of his swift recoveries.

'It is very kind of Mr Burns,' he said in his fruitiest voice, 'but I hardly think it will be necessary to put him to the inconvenience of altering his plans. I am sure that Mr Ford would prefer the entire charge of the affair to be in my hands.'

He had not chosen a happy moment for the introduction of the millionaire's name. Mr Abney was a man of method, who hated any dislocation of the fixed routine of life; and Mr Ford's letter had upset him. The Ford family, father and son, were just then extremely unpopular with him.

He crushed Sam.

'What Mr Ford would or would not prefer is, in this particular matter, beside the point. The responsibility for the boy, while he remains on the school premises, is – ah – mine, and I shall take such precautions as seem fit and adequate to – him – myself, irrespective of those which, in your opinion, might suggest themselves to Mr Ford. As I cannot be here myself, owing to – ah – urgent business in London, I shall certainly take advantage of Mr Burns's kind offer to remain as my deputy.'

He paused and blew his nose, his invariable custom after these occasional outbursts of his. Sam had not wilted beneath the storm. He waited, unmoved, till all was over:

'I am afraid I shall have to be more explicit,' he said: 'I had hoped to avoid scandal and unpleasantness, but I see it is impossible.'

Mr Abney's astonished face emerged slowly from behind his handkerchief.

'I quite agree with you, sir, that somebody should be here to help me look after the boy, but not Mr Burns. I am sorry to have to say it, but I do not trust Mr Burns.'

Mr Abney's look of astonishment deepened. I, too, was surprised. It was so unlike Sam to fling away his chances on a blundering attack like this.

'What do you mean?' demanded Mr Abney.

'Mr Burns is after the boy himself. He came to kidnap him.'

Mr Abney, as he had every excuse for doing, grunted with amazement. I achieved the ringing laugh of amused innocence. It was beyond me to fathom Sam's mind. He could not suppose that any credence would be given to his wild assertion. It seemed to me that disappointment had caused him momentarily to lose his head.

'Are you mad, White?'

'No, sir. I can prove what I say. If I had not gone to London with him that last time, he'd have got away with the boy then, for certain.'

For an instant an uneasy thought came to me that he might have something in reserve, something unknown to me, which had encouraged him to this direct attack. I dismissed the notion. There could be nothing.

Mr Abney had turned to me with a look of hopeless bewilderment. I raised my eyebrows.

'Ridiculous,' I said.

That this was the only comment seemed to be Mr Abney's view. He turned on Sam with the pettish anger of the mild man.

'What do you *mean*, White, by coming to me with such a preposterous story?'

'I don't say Mr Burns wished to kidnap the boy in the ordinary way,' said Sam imperturbably, 'like those men who came that night. He had a special reason. Mr and Mrs Ford, as of course you know, sir, are divorced. Mr Burns was trying to get the boy away and take him back to his mother.'

I heard Audrey give a little gasp. Mr Abney's anger became modified by a touch of doubt. I could see that these words, by lifting the accusation from the wholly absurd to the somewhat plausible, had impressed him. Once again I was gripped by the uneasy feeling that Sam had an unsuspected card to play. This might be bluff, but it had a sinister ring.

'You might say,' went on Sam smoothly, 'that this was creditable to Mr Burns's heart. But, from my employer's viewpoint and yours, too, it was a chivalrous impulse that needed to be checked. Will you please read this, sir?'

He handed a letter to Mr Abney, who adjusted his glasses and began to read – at first in a detached, judicial way, then with startled eagerness.

'I felt it necessary to search among Mr Burns's papers, sir, in the hope of finding – '

And then I knew what he had found. From the first the blue-grey notepaper had had a familiar look. I recognized it now. It was Cynthia's letter, that damning document which I had been mad enough to read to him in London. His prediction that the luck would change had come amazingly true.

I caught Sam's eye. For the second time he was unfeeling enough to wink. It was a rich, comprehensive wink, as expressive and joyous as a college yell.

Mr Abney had absorbed the letter and was struggling for speech. I could appreciate his emotion. If he had not actually

162

been nurturing a viper in his bosom, he had come, from his point of view, very near it. Of all men, a schoolmaster necessarily looks with the heartiest dislike on the would-be kidnapper.

As for me, my mind was in a whirl. I was entirely without a plan, without the very beginnings of a plan, to help me cope with this appalling situation. I was crushed by a sense of the utter helplessness of my position. To denounce Sam was impossible; to explain my comparative innocence was equally out of the question. The suddenness of the onslaught had deprived me of the power of coherent thought. I was routed.

Mr Abney was speaking.

'Is your name Peter, Mr Burns?'

I nodded. Speech was beyond me.

'This letter is written by – ah – by a lady. It asks you in set terms to – ah – hasten to kidnap Ogden Ford. Do you wish me to read it to you? Or do you confess to knowing its contents?'

He waited for a reply. I had none to make.

'You do not deny that you came to Sanstead House for the deliberate purpose of kidnapping Ogden Ford?'

I had nothing to say. I caught a glimpse of Audrey's face, cold and hard, and shifted my eyes quickly. Mr Abney gulped. His face wore the reproachful expression of a cod-fish when jerked out of the water on the end of a line. He stared at me with pained repulsion. That scoundrelly old buccaneer Sam did the same. He looked like a shocked bishop.

'I – ah – trusted you implicitly,' said Mr Abney.

Sam wagged his head at me reproachfully. With a flicker of spirit I glared at him. He only wagged the more.

It was, I think, the blackest moment of my life. A wild desire for escape on any terms surged over me. That look on Audrey's face was biting into my brain like an acid.

'I will go and pack,' I said.

'This is the end of all things,' I said to myself.

I had suspended my packing in order to sit on my bed and brood. I was utterly depressed. There are crises in a man's life when Reason fails to bring the slightest consolation. In vain I tried to tell myself that what had happened was, in essence, precisely what, twenty-four hours ago, I was so eager to bring about. It amounted to this, that now, at last, Audrey had definitely gone out of my life. From now on I could have no relations with her of any sort. Was not this exactly what, twenty-four hours ago, I had wished? Twenty-four hours ago had I not said to myself that I would go away and never see her again? Undoubtedly. Nevertheless, I sat there and groaned in spirit.

It was the end of all things.

A mild voice interrupted my meditations.

'Can I help?'

Sam was standing in the doorway, beaming on me with invincible good-humour.

'You are handling them wrong. Allow me. A moment more and you would have ruined the crease.'

I became aware of a pair of trousers hanging limply in my grasp. He took them from me, and, folding them neatly, placed them in my trunk.

'Don't get all worked up about it, sonny,' he said. 'It's the fortune of war. Besides, what does it matter to you? Judging by that very snug apartment in London, you have quite enough money for a young man. Losing your job here won't break you. And, if you're worrying about Mrs Ford and her feelings, don't! I guess she's probably forgotten all about the Nugget by this time. So cheer up. *You're* all right!'

He stretched out a hand to pat me on the shoulder, then thought better of it and drew it back.

'Think of *my* happiness, if you want something to make you feel good. Believe me, young man, it's *some*. I could sing! Gee, when I think that it's all plain sailing now and no more troubles, I could dance! You don't know what it means to me, putting through this deal. I wish you knew Mary! That's her name. You must come and visit us, sonny, when we're fixed up in the home. There'll always be a knife and fork for *you*. We'll make you one of the family! Lord! I can see the place as plain as I can see you. Nice frame house with a good porch . . . Me in a rocker in my shirt-sleeves, smoking a cigar and reading the baseball news;

164

Mary in another rocker, mending my socks and nursing the cat! We'll sure have a cat. Two cats. I like cats. And a goat in the front garden. Say, it'll be *great*!'

And on the word, emotion overcoming prudence, he brought his fat hand down with a resounding smack on my bowed shoulders.

There is a limit. I bounded to my feet.

'Get out!' I yelped. 'Get out of here!'

'Sure,' he replied agreeably. He rose without haste and regarded me compassionately. 'Cheer up, son! Be a sport!'

There are moments when the best of men become melodramatic. I offer this as excuse for my next observation.

Clenching my fists and glaring at him, I cried, 'I'll foil you yet, you hound!'

Some people have no soul for the dramatic. He smiled tolerantly.

'Sure,' he said. 'Anything you like, Desperate Desmond. Enjoy yourself!'

And he left me.

Chapter 13

I evacuated Sanstead House unostentatiously, setting off on foot down the long drive. My luggage, I gathered, was to follow me to the station in a cart. I was thankful to Providence for the small mercy that the boys were in their classrooms and consequently unable to ask me questions. Augustus Beckford alone would have handled the subject of my premature exit in a manner calculated to bleach my hair.

It was a wonderful morning. The sky was an unclouded blue, and a fresh breeze was blowing in from the sea. I think that something of the exhilaration of approaching spring must have stirred me, for quite suddenly the dull depression with which I had started my walk left me, and I found myself alert and full of schemes.

Why should I feebly withdraw from the struggle? Why should I give in to Smooth Sam in this tame way? The memory of that wink came back to me with a tonic effect. I would show him that I was still a factor in the game. If the house was closed to me, was there not the 'Feathers'? I could lie in hiding there, and observe his movements unseen.

I stopped on reaching the inn, and was on the point of entering and taking up my position at once, when it occurred to me that this would be a false move. It was possible that Sam would not take my departure for granted so readily as I assumed. It was Sam's way to do a thing thoroughly, and the probability was that, if he did not actually come to see me off, he would at least make inquiries at the station to find out if I had gone. I walked on.

He was not at the station. Nor did he arrive in the cart with my trunk. But I was resolved to risk nothing. I bought a ticket for London, and boarded the London train. It had been my intention to leave it at Guildford and catch an afternoon train back to Stanstead; but it seemed to me, on reflection, that this was unnecessary. There was no likelihood of Sam making any move in the matter of the Nugget until the following day. I could take my time about returning.

I spent the night in London, and arrived at Sanstead by an early morning train with a suit-case containing, among other things, a Browning pistol. I was a little ashamed of this purchase. To the Buck MacGinnis type of man, I suppose, a pistol is as commonplace a possession as a pair of shoes, but I blushed as I entered the gun-shop. If it had been Buck with whom I was about to deal, I should have felt less self-conscious. But there was something about Sam which made pistols ridiculous.

My first act, after engaging a room at the inn and leaving my suit-case, was to walk to the school. Before doing anything else, I felt I must see Audrey and tell her the facts in the case of Smooth Sam. If she were on her guard, my assistance might not be needed. But her present state of trust in him was fatal.

A school, when the boys are away, is a lonely place. The deserted air of the grounds, as I slipped cautiously through the trees, was almost eerie. A stillness brooded over everything, as if the place had been laid under a spell. Never before had I been so impressed with the isolation of Sanstead House. Anything might happen in this lonely spot, and the world would go on its way in ignorance. It was with quite distinct relief that, as I drew nearer the house, I caught sight of the wire of the telephone among the trees above my head. It had a practical, comforting look.

A tradesman's cart rattled up the drive and disappeared round the side of the house. This reminder, also, of the outside world was pleasant. But I could not rid myself of the feeling that the atmosphere of the place was sinister. I attributed it to the fact that I was a spy in an enemy's country. I had to see without being seen. I did not imagine that Johnson, grocer, who had just passed in his cart, found anything wrong with the atmosphere. It was created for me by my own furtive attitude.

Of Audrey and Ogden there were no signs. That they were out somewhere in the grounds this mellow spring morning I

167

took for granted; but I could not make an extended search. Already I had come nearer to the house than was prudent.

My eye caught the telephone wire again and an idea came to me. I would call her up from the inn and ask her to meet me. There was the risk that the call would be answered by Smooth Sam, but it was not great. Sam, unless he had thrown off his role of butler completely – which would be unlike the artist that he was – would be in the housekeeper's room, and the ringing of the telephone, which was in the study, would not penetrate to him.

I chose a moment when dinner was likely to be over and Audrey might be expected to be in the drawing-room.

I had deduced her movements correctly. It was her voice that answered the call.

'This is Peter Burns speaking.'

There was a perceptible pause before she replied. When she did, her voice was cold.

'Yes?'

'I want to speak to you on a matter of urgent importance.'

'Well?'

'I can't do it through the telephone. Will you meet me in half an hour's time at the gate?'

'Where are you speaking from?'

'The "Feathers". I am staying there.'

'I thought you were in London.'

'I came back. Will you meet me?'

She hesitated.

'Why?'

'Because I have something important to say to you – important to you.'

There was another pause.

'Very well.'

'In half an hour, then. Is Ogden Ford in bed?'

'Yes.'

'Is his door locked?'

'No.'

'Then lock it and bring the key with you.'

'Why?'

168

'I will tell you when we meet.'

'I will bring it.'

'Thank you. Good-bye.'

I hung up the receiver and set out at once for the school.

She was waiting in the road, a small, indistinct figure in the darkness.

'Is that you – Peter?'

Her voice had hesitated at the name, as if at some obstacle. It was a trivial thing, but, in my present mood, it stung me.

'I'm afraid I'm late. I won't keep you long. Shall we walk down the road? You may not have been followed, but it is as well to be on the safe side.'

'Followed? I don't understand.'

We walked a few paces and halted.

'Who would follow me?'

'A very eminent person of the name of Smooth Sam Fisher.'

'Smooth Sam Fisher?'

'Better known to you as White.'

'I don't understand.'

'I should be surprised if you did. I asked you to meet me here so that I could make you understand. The man who poses as a Pinkerton's detective. and is staying in the house to help you take care of Ogden Ford, is Smooth Sam Fisher, a professional kidnapper.'

'But – but – '

'But what proof have I? Was that what you were going to say? None. But I had the information from the man himself. He told me in the train that night going to London.'

She spoke quickly. I knew from her tone that she thought she had detected a flaw in my story.

'Why did he tell you?'

'Because he needed me as an accomplice. He wanted my help. It was I who got Ogden away that day. Sam overheard me giving money and directions to him, telling him how to get away from the school and where to go, and he gathered – correctly – that I was in the same line of business as himself. He suggested a partnership which I was unable to accept.'

'Why?'

'Our objects were different. My motive in kidnapping Ogden was not to extract a ransom.'

She blazed out at me in an absolutely unexpected manner. Till now she had listened so calmly and asked her questions with such a notable absence of emotion that the outburst overwhelmed me.

'Oh, I know what your motive was. There is no need to explain that. Isn't there any depth to which a man who thinks himself in love won't stoop? I suppose you told yourself you were doing something noble and chivalrous? A woman of her sort can trick a man into whatever meanness she pleases, and, just because she asks him, he thinks himself a kind of knighterrant. I suppose she told you that he had ill-treated her and didn't appreciate her higher self, and all that sort of thing? She looked at you with those big brown eyes of hers – I can see her – and drooped, and cried, till you were ready to do anything she asked you.'

'Whom do you mean?'

'Mrs Ford, of course. The woman who sent you here to steal Ogden. The woman who wrote you that letter.'

'She did not write that letter. But never mind that. The reason why I wanted you to come here was to warn you against Sam Fisher. That was all. If there is any way in which I can help you, send for me. If you like, I will come and stay at the house till Mr Abney returns.'

Before the words were out of my mouth, I saw that I had made a mistake. The balance of her mind was poised between suspicion and belief, and my offer turned the scale.

'No, thank you,' she said curtly.

'You don't trust me?'

'Why should I? White may or may not be Sam Fisher. I shall be on my guard, and I thank you for telling me. But why should I trust you? It all hangs together. You told me you were engaged to be married. You come here on an errand which no man would undertake except for a woman, and a woman with whom he was very much in love. There is that letter, imploring you to steal the boy. I know what a man will do for a woman he is fond of. Why should I trust you?'

'There is this. You forget that I had the opportunity to steal Ogden if I had wanted to. I had got him away to London. But I brought him back. I did it because you had told me what it meant to you.'

She hesitated, but only for an instant. Suspicion was too strong for her.

'I don't believe you. You brought him back because this man whom you call Fisher got to know of your plans. Why should you have done it because of me? Why should you have put my interests before Mrs Ford's? I am nothing to you.'

For a moment a mad impulse seized me to cast away all restraint, to pour out the unspoken words that danced like imps in my brain, to make her understand, whatever the cost, my feelings towards her. But the thought of my letter to Cynthia checked me. That letter had been the irrevocable step. If I was to preserve a shred of self-respect I must be silent.

'Very well,' I said, 'good night.' And I turned to go.

'Peter!'

There was something in her voice which whirled me round, thrilling, despite my resolution.

'Are you going?'

Weakness would now be my undoing. I steadied myself and answered abruptly.

'I have said all I came to say. Good night.'

I turned once more and walked quickly off towards the village. I came near to running. I was in the mood when flight alone can save a man. She did not speak again, and soon I was out of danger, hurrying on through the friendly darkness, beyond the reach of her voice.

The bright light from the doorway of the 'Feathers', was the only illumination that relieved the blackness of the Market Square. As I approached, a man came out and stopped in the entrance to light a cigar. His back was turned towards me as he crouched to protect the match from the breeze, but something in his appearance seemed familiar.

I had only a glimpse of him as he straightened himself and

walked out of the pool of light into the Square, but it was enough.

It was my much-enduring acquaintance, Mr Buck Mac-Ginnis.

Chapter 14

I

At the receipt of custom behind the bar sat Miss Benjafield, stately as ever, relaxing her massive mind over a penny novelette.

'Who was the man who just left, Miss Benjafield?' I asked.

She marked the place with a shapely thumb and looked up.

'The man? Oh, *him*! He's – why, weren't you in here, Mr Burns, one evening in January when – '

'That American?'

'That's him. What he's doing here I don't know. He disappeared quite a while back, and I haven't seen him since. *Nor* want. Tonight up he turns again like a bad ha'penny. I'd like to know what he's after. No good, if you ask *me*.'

Miss Benjafield's prejudices did not easily dissolve. She prided herself, as she frequently observed, on knowing her own mind.

'Is he staying here?'

'Not at the "Feathers". We're particular who we have here.'

I thanked her for the implied compliment, ordered beer for the good of the house, and, lighting a pipe, sat down to meditate on this new development.

The vultures were gathered together with a vengeance. Sam within, Buck without, it was quite like old times, with the difference that now, I, too, was on the wrong side of the school door.

It was not hard to account for Buck's reappearance. He would, of course, have made it his business to get early information of Mr Ford's movements. It would be easy for him to discover that the millionaire had been called away to the north and that the Nugget was still an inmate of Sanstead

House. And here he was preparing for the grand attack.

I had been premature in removing Buck's name from the list of active combatants. Broken legs mend. I ought to have remembered that.

His presence on the scene made, I perceived, a vast difference to my plan of campaign. It was at this point that my purchase of the Browning pistol lost its absurdity and appeared in the light of an acute strategic move. With Sam the only menace, I had been prepared to play a purely waiting game, watching proceedings from afar, ready to give my help if necessary. To check Buck, more strenuous methods were called for.

My mind was made up. With Buck, that stout disciple of the frontal attack, in the field, there was only one place for me. I must get into Sanstead House and stay there on guard.

Did he intend to make an offensive movement tonight? That was the question which occupied my mind. From the point of view of an opponent, there was this merit about Mr MacGinnis, that he was not subtle. He could be counted on with fair certainty to do the direct thing. Sooner or later he would make another of his vigorous frontal attacks upon the stronghold. The only point to be decided was whether he would make it that night. Would professional zeal cause him to omit his beauty sleep?

I did not relish the idea of spending the night patrolling the grounds, but it was imperative that the house be protected. Then it occurred to me that the man for the vigil was Smooth Sam. If the arrival of Mr MacGinnis had complicated matters in one way, it had simplified them in another, for there was no more need for the secrecy which had been, till now, the basis of my plan of action. Buck's arrival made it possible for me to come out and fight in the open, instead of brooding over Sanstead House from afar like a Providence. Tomorrow I proposed to turn Sam out. Tonight I would use him. The thing had resolved itself into a triangular tournament, and Sam and Buck should play the first game.

Once more I called up the house on the telephone. There was

a long delay before a reply came. It was Mr Fisher's voice that spoke. Audrey, apparently, had not returned to the house immediately after leaving me.

'Hullo!' said Sam.

'Good evening, Mr Fisher.'

'Gee! Is that you, young fellow-me-lad? Are you speaking from London?'

'No. I am at the "Feathers".'

He chuckled richly.

'Can't tear yourself away? Hat still in the ring? Say, what's the use? Why not turn it up, sonny? You're only wasting your time.'

'Do you sleep lightly, Mr Fisher?'

'I don't get you.'

'You had better do so tonight. Buck MacGinnis is back again.'

There was silence at the other end of the wire. Then I heard him swear softly. The significance of the information had not been lost on Mr Fisher.

'Is that straight?'

'It is.'

'You're not stringing me?'

'Certainly not.'

'You're sure it was Buck?'

'Is Buck's the sort of face one forgets?'

He swore again.

'You seem disturbed,' I said.

'Where did you see him?' asked Sam.

'Coming out of the "Feathers", looking very fierce and determined. The Berserk blood of the MacGinnises is up. He's going to do or die. I'm afraid this means an all-night sitting for you, Mr Fisher.'

'I thought you had put him out of business!'

There was a somewhat querulous note in his voice.

'Only temporarily. I did my best, but he wasn't even limping when I saw him.'

He did not speak for a moment. I gathered that he was pondering over the new development.

'Thanks for tipping me off, sonny. It's a thing worth knowing. Why did you do it?'

'Because I love you, Samuel. Good night.'

I rose late and breakfasted at my leisure. The peace of the English country inn enveloped me as I tilted back my chair and smoked the first pipe of the morning. It was a day to hearten a man for great deeds, one of those days of premature summer which comes sometimes to help us bear the chill winds of early spring. The sun streamed in through the open window. In the yard below fowls made their soothing music. The thought of violence seemed very alien to such a morning.

I strolled out into the Square. I was in no hurry to end this interlude of peace and embark on what, for all practical purposes, would be a siege.

After lunch, I decided, would be time enough to begin active campaigning.

The clock on the church tower was striking two as I set forth, carrying my suit-case, on my way to the school. The light-heartedness of the morning still lingered with me. I was amused at the thought of the surprise I was about to give Mr Fisher. That wink still rankled.

As I made my way through the grounds I saw Audrey in the distance, walking with the Nugget. I avoided them and went on into the house.

About the house there was the same air of enchanted quiet which pervaded the grounds. Perhaps the stillness indoors was even more insistent. I had grown so accustomed to the never-ending noise and bustle of the boys' quarters that, as I crossed the silent hall, I had an almost guilty sense of intrusion. I felt like a burglar.

Sam, the object of my visit, would, I imagined, if he were in the house at all, be in the housekeeper's room, a cosy little apartment off the passage leading to the kitchen. I decided to draw that first, and was rewarded, on pushing open the half-closed door, by the sight of a pair of black-trousered legs stretched out before me from the depths of a wicker-work arm-chair. His portly middle section, rising beyond like a small hill,

176

heaved rhythmically. His face was covered with a silk handkerchief, from beneath which came, in even succession, faint and comfortable snores. It was a peaceful picture – the good man taking his rest; and for me it had an added attractiveness in that it suggested that Sam was doing by day what my information had prevented him from doing in the night. It had been some small consolation to me, as I lay trying to compose my anxious mind for sleep on the previous night, that Mr Fisher also was keeping his vigil.

Pleasing as Sam was as a study in still life, pressure of business compelled me to stir him into activity. I prodded him gently in the centre of the rising territory beyond the black trousers. He grunted discontentedly and sat up. The handkerchief fell from his face, and he blinked at me, first with the dazed glassiness of the newly awakened, then with a 'Soul's Awakening' expression, which spread over his face until it melted into a friendly smile.

'Hello, young man!'

'Good afternoon. You seem tired.'

He yawned cavernously.

'Lord! What a night!'

'Did Buck drop in?'

'No, but I thought he had every time I heard a board creak. I didn't dare close my eyes for a minute. Have you ever stayed awake all night, waiting for the goblins that get you if you don't watch out? Well, take it from me it's no picnic.'

His face split in another mammoth yawn. He threw his heart into it, as if life held no other tasks for him. Only in alligators have I ever seen its equal.

I waited till the seismic upheaval had spent itself. Then I came to business.

'I'm sorry you had a disturbed night, Mr Fisher. You must make up for it this afternoon. You will find the beds very comfortable.'

'How's that?'

'At the "Feathers". I should go there, if I were you. The charges are quite reasonable, and the food is good. You will like the "Feathers".'

'I don't get you, sonny.'

'I was trying to break it gently to you that you are about to move from this house. Now. At once. Take your last glimpse of the old home, Sam, and out into the hard world.'

He looked at me inquiringly.

'You seem to be talking, young man; words appear to be fluttering from you; but your meaning, if any, escapes me.'

'My meaning is that I am about to turn you out. I am coming back here, and there is not room for both of us. So, if you do not see your way to going quietly, I shall take you by the back of the neck and run you out. Do I make myself fairly clear now?'

He permitted himself a rich chuckle.

'You have gall, young man. Well, I hate to seem unfriendly. I like you, sonny. You amuse me – but there are moments when one wants to be alone. I have a whole heap of arrears of sleep to make up. Trot along, kiddo, and quit disturbing uncle. Tie a string to yourself and disappear. Bye-bye.'

The wicker-work creaked as he settled his stout body. He picked up the handkerchief.

'Mr Fisher,' I said, 'I have no wish to propel your grey hairs at a rapid run down the drive, so I will explain further. I am physically stronger than you. I mean to turn you out. How can you prevent it? Mr Abney is away. You can't appeal to him. The police are at the end of the telephone, but you can't appeal to them. So what *can* you do, except go? Do you get me now?'

He regarded the situation in thoughtful silence. He allowed no emotion to find expression in his face, but I knew that the significance of my remarks had sunk in. I could almost follow his mind as he tested my position point by point and found it impregnable.

When he spoke it was to accept defeat jauntily.

'You *are* my jinx, young man. I said it all along. You're really set on my going? Say no more. I'll go. After all, it's quiet at the inn, and what more does a man want at my time of life?'

I went out into the garden to interview Audrey.

She was walking up and down on the tennis-lawn. The

178

Nugget, lounging in a deck-chair, appeared to be asleep.

She caught sight of me as I came out from the belt of trees, and stopped. I had the trying experience of walking across open country under hostile observation.

The routing of Sam had left me alert and self-confident. I felt no embarrassment. I greeted her briskly.

'Good afternoon. I have been talking to Sam Fisher. If you wait, you will see him passing away down the drive. He is leaving the house. I am coming back.'

'Coming back?'

She spoke incredulously, or, rather, as if my words had conveyed no meaning. It was so that Sam had spoken. Her mind, like his, took time to adjust itself to the unexpected.

She seemed to awake to my meaning with a start.

'Coming back?' Her eyes widened. The flush deepened on her cheeks. 'But I told you – '

'I know what you told me. You said you did not trust me. It doesn't matter. I am coming back whether you trust me or not. This house is under martial law, and I am in command. The situation has changed since I spoke to you last night. Last night I was ready to let you have your way. I intended to keep an eye on things from the inn. But it's different now. It is not a case of Sam Fisher any longer. You could have managed Sam. It's Buck MacGinnis now, the man who came that night in the automobile. I saw him in the village after I left you. He's dangerous.'

She looked away, past me, in the direction of the drive. I followed her gaze. A stout figure, carrying a suit-case, was moving slowly down it.

I smiled. Her eyes met mine, and I saw the anger that had been lying at the back of them flash out. Her chin went up with the old defiant tilt. I was sorry I had smiled. It was my old fault, the complacency that would not be hidden.

'I don't believe you!' she cried. 'I don't trust you!'

It is curious how one's motive for embarking on a course of conduct changes or disappears altogether as the action develops. Once started on an enterprise it is as if one proceeded with it automatically, irrespective of one's original motives. I had

179

begun what I might call the second phase of this matter of the Little Nugget, the abandoning of Cynthia's cause in favour of Audrey's, with a clear idea of why I was doing it. I had set myself to resist the various forces which were trying to take Ogden from Audrey, for one simple reason, because I loved Audrey and wished to help her. That motive, if it still existed at all, did so only in the form of abstract chivalry. My personal feelings towards her seemed to have undergone a complete change, dating from our parting in the road the night before. I found myself now meeting hostility with hostility. I looked at her critically and told myself that her spell was broken at last, that, if she disliked me, I was at least indifferent to her.

And yet, despite my altered feelings, my determination to help her never wavered. The guarding of Ogden might be – primarily – no business of mine, but I had adopted it as my business.

'I don't ask you to trust me,' I said. 'We have settled all that. There's no need to go over old ground. Think what you please about this. I've made up my mind.'

'If you mean to stay, I suppose I can't prevent you.'

'Exactly.'

Sam appeared again in a gap in the trees, walking slowly and pensively, as one retreating from his Moscow. Her eyes followed him till he was out of sight.

'If you like,' I said bitterly, 'you may put what I am doing down to professional rivalry. If I am in love with Mrs Ford and am here to steal Ogden for her, it is natural for me to do all I can to prevent Buck MacGinnis getting him. There is no need for you to look on me as an ally because we are working together.'

'We are not working together.'

'We shall be in a very short time. Buck will not let another night go by without doing something.'

'I don't believe that you saw him.'

'Just as you please,' I said, and walked away. What did it matter to me what she believed?

The day dragged on. Towards evening the weather broke

suddenly, after the fashion of spring in England. Showers of rain drove me to the study.

It must have been nearly ten o'clock when the telephone rang.

It was Mr Fisher.

'Hello, is that you, sonny?'

'It is. Do you want anything?'

'I want a talk with you. Business. Can I come up?'

'If you wish it.'

'I'll start right away.'

It was some fifteen minutes later that I heard in the distance the engines of an automobile. The headlights gleamed through the trees, and presently the car swept round the bend of the drive and drew up at the front door. A portly figure got down and rang the bell. I observed these things from a window on the first floor, overlooking the front steps; and it was from this window that I spoke.

'Is that you, Mr Fisher?'

He backed away from the door.

'Where are you?'

'Is that your car?'

'It belongs to a friend of mine.'

'I didn't know you meant to bring a party.'

'There's only three of us. Me, the chauffeur, and my friend – MacGinnis.'

The possibility, indeed the probability, of Sam seeking out Buck and forming an alliance had occurred to me, and I was prepared for it. I shifted my grip on the automatic pistol in my hand.

'Mr Fisher.'

'Hello!'

'Ask your friend MacGinnis to be good enough to step into the light of that lamp and drop his gun.'

There was a muttered conversation. I heard Buck's voice rumbling like a train going under a bridge. The request did not appear to find favour with him. Then came an interlude of soothing speech from Mr Fisher. I could not distinguish the words, but I gathered that he was pointing out to him that, on

181

this occasion only, the visit being for the purposes of parley and not of attack, pistols might be looked on as non-essentials. Whatever his arguments, they were successful, for, finally, humped as to the back and muttering, Buck moved into the light.

'Good evening, Mr MacGinnis,' I said. 'I'm glad to see your leg is all right again. I won't detain you a moment. Just feel in your pockets and shed a few of your guns, and then you can come in out of the rain. To prevent any misunderstanding, I may say I have a gun of my own. It is trained on you now.'

'I ain't got no gun.'

'Come along. This is no time for airy persiflage. Out with them.'

A moment's hesitation, and a small black pistol fell to the ground.

'No more?'

'Think I'm a regiment?'

'I don't know what you are. Well, I'll take your word for it. You will come in one by one, with your hands up.'

I went down and opened the door, holding my pistol in readiness against the unexpected.

II

Sam came first. His raised hands gave him a vaguely pontifical air (Bishop Blessing Pilgrims), and the kindly smile he wore heightened the illusion. Mr MacGinnis, who followed, suggested no such idea. He was muttering moodily to himself, and he eyed me askance.

I showed them into the classroom and switched on the light. The air was full of many odours. Disuse seems to bring out the inky-chalky, appley-deal-boardy bouquet of a classroom as the night brings out the scent of flowers. During the term I had never known this classroom smell so exactly like a classroom. I made use of my free hand to secure and light a cigarette.

Sam rose to a point of order.

'Young man,' he said. 'I should like to remind you that we are here, as it were, under a flag of truce. To pull a gun on us
182

and keep us holding our hands up this way is raw work. I feel sure I speak for my friend Mr MacGinnis.'

He cocked an eye at his friend Mr MacGinnis, who seconded the motion by expectorating into the fireplace. I had observed at a previous interview his peculiar gift for laying bare his soul by this means of mode of expression. A man of silent habit, judged by the more conventional standard of words, he was almost an orator in expectoration.

'Mr MacGinnis agrees with me,' said Sam cheerfully. 'Do we take them down? Have we your permission to assume Position Two of these Swedish exercises? All we came for was a little friendly chat among gentlemen, and we can talk just as well – speaking for myself, better – in a less strained attitude. A little rest, Mr Burns! A little folding of the hands? Thank you.'

He did not wait for permission, nor was it necessary. Sam and the melodramatic atmosphere was as oil and water. It was impossible to blend them. I laid the pistol on the table and sat down. Buck, after one wistful glance at the weapon, did the same. Sam was already seated, and was looking so cosy and at home that I almost felt it remiss of me not to have provided sherry and cake for this pleasant gathering.

'Well,' I said, 'what can I do for you?'

'Let me explain,' said Sam. 'As you have, no doubt, gathered, Mr MacGinnis and I have gone into partnership. The Little Nugget Combine!'

'I gathered that – well?'

'Judicious partnerships are the soul of business. Mr MacGinnis and I have been rivals in the past, but we both saw that the moment had come for the genial smile, the hearty handshake, in fact, for an alliance. We form a strong team, sonny. My partner's speciality is action. I supply the strategy. Say, can't you see you're up against it? Why be foolish?'

'You think you're certain to win?'

'It's a cinch.'

'Then why trouble to come here and see me?'

I appeared to have put into words the smouldering thought which was vexing Mr MacGinnis. He burst into speech.

'Ahr chee! Sure! What's de use? Didn't I tell youse? What's

de use of wastin' time? What are we spielin' away here for?
Let's get busy.'

Sam waved a hand towards him with the air of a lecturer
making a point.

'You see! The man of action! He likes trouble. He asks for it.
He eats it alive. Now I prefer peace. Why have a fuss when you
can get what you want quietly? That's my motto. That's why
we've come. It's the old proposition. We're here to buy you out.
Yes, I know you have turned the offer down before, but things
have changed. Your stock has fallen. In fact, instead of letting
you in on sharing terms, we only feel justified now in offering a
commission. For the moment you may seem to hold a strong
position. You are in the house, and you've got the boy. But
there's nothing to it really. We could get him in five minutes if
we cared to risk having a fuss. But it seems to me there's no
need of any fuss. We should win dead easy all right, if it came
to trouble; but, on the other hand, you've a gun, and there's a
chance some of us might get hurt, so what's the good when we
can settle it quietly? How about it, sonny?'

Mr MacGinnis began to rumble, preparatory to making
further remarks on the situation, but Sam waved him down and
turned his brown eyes inquiringly on me.

'Fifteen per cent is our offer,' he said.

'And to think it was once fifty-fifty!'

'Strict business!'

'Business? It's sweating!'

'It's our limit. And it wasn't easy to make Buck here agree to
that. He kicked like a mule.'

Buck shuffled his feet and eyed me disagreeably. I suppose it
is hard to think kindly of a man who has broken your leg. It was
plain that, with Mr MacGinnis, bygones were by no means
bygones.

I rose.

'Well, I'm sorry you should have had the trouble of coming
here for nothing. Let me see you out. Single file, please.'

Sam looked aggrieved.

'You turn it down?'

'I do.'

'One moment. Let's have this thing clear. Do you realize what you're up against? Don't think it's only Buck and me you've got to tackle. All the boys are here, waiting round the corner, the same gang that came the other night. Be sensible, sonny. You don't stand a dog's chance. I shouldn't like to see you get hurt. And you never know what may not happen. The boys are pretty sore at you because of what you did that night. I shouldn't act like a bonehead, sonny – honest.'

There was a kindly ring in his voice which rather touched me. Between him and me there had sprung up an odd sort of friendship. He meant business; but he would, I knew, be genuinely sorry if I came to harm. And I could see that he was quite sincere in his belief that I was in a tight corner and that my chances against the Combine were infinitesimal. I imagine that, with victory so apparently certain, he had had difficulty in persuading his allies to allow him to make his offer.

But he had overlooked one thing – the telephone. That he should have made this mistake surprised me. If it had been Buck, I could have understood it. Buck's was a mind which lent itself to such blunders. From Sam I had expected better things, especially as the telephone had been so much in evidence of late. He had used it himself only half an hour ago.

I clung to the thought of the telephone. It gave me the quiet satisfaction of the gambler who holds the unforeseen ace. The situation was in my hands. The police, I knew, had been profoundly stirred by Mr MacGinnis's previous raid. When I called them up, as I proposed to do directly the door had closed on the ambassadors, there would be no lack of response. It would not again be a case of Inspector Bones and Constable Johnson to the rescue. A great cloud of willing helpers would swoop to our help.

With these thoughts in my mind, I answered Sam pleasantly but firmly.

'I'm sorry I'm unpopular, but all the same – '

I indicated the door.

Emotion that could only be expressed in words and not through his usual medium welled up in Mr MacGinnis. He sprang forward with a snarl, falling back as my faithful automatic caught his eye.

'Say, you! Listen here! You'll – '

Sam, the peaceable, plucked at his elbow.

'Nothing doing, Buck. Step lively.'

Buck wavered, then allowed himself to be drawn away. We passed out of the classroom in our order of entry.

An exclamation from the stairs made me look up. Audrey was leaning over the banisters. Her face was in the shadow, but I gathered from her voice that the sight of our little procession had startled her. I was not surprised. Buck was a distinctly startling spectacle, and his habit of growling to himself, as he walked, highly disturbing to strangers.

'Good evening, Mrs Sheridan,' said Sam suavely.

Audrey did not speak. She seemed fascinated by Buck.

I opened the front door and they passed out. The automobile was still purring on the drive. Buck's pistol had disappeared. I supposed the chauffeur had picked it up, a surmise which was proved correct a few moments later, when, just as the car was moving off, there was a sharp crack and a bullet struck the wall to the right of the door. It was a random shot, and I did not return it. Its effect on me was to send me into the hall with a leap that was almost a back-somersault. Somehow, though I was keyed up for violence and the shooting of pistols, I had not expected it at just that moment, and I was disagreeably surprised at the shock it had given me. I slammed the door and bolted it. I was intensely irritated to find that my fingers were trembling.

Audrey had left the stairs and was standing beside me.

'They shot at me,' I said.

By the light of the hall lamp I could see that she was very pale.

'It missed by a mile.' My nerves had not recovered and I spoke abruptly. 'Don't be frightened.'

'I – I was not frightened,' she said, without conviction.

'I was,' I said, with conviction. 'It was too sudden for me. It's the sort of thing one wants to get used to gradually. I shall be ready for it another time.'

I made for the stairs.

'Where are you going?'

'I'm going to call up the police-station.'

'Peter.'

'Yes?'

'Was – was that man the one you spoke of?'

'Yes, that was Buck MacGinnis. He and Sam have gone into partnership.'

She hesitated.

'I'm sorry,' she said.

I was half-way up the stairs by this time. I stopped and looked over the banisters.

'Sorry?'

'I didn't believe you this afternoon.'

'Oh, that's all right,' I said. I tried to make my voice indifferent, for I was on guard against insidious friendliness. I had bludgeoned my mind into an attitude of safe hostility towards her, and I saw the old chaos ahead if I allowed myself to abandon it.

I went to the telephone and unhooked the receiver.

There is apt to be a certain leisureliness about the methods of country telephone-operators, and the fact that a voice did not immediately ask me what number I wanted did not at first disturb me. Suspicion of the truth came to me, I think, after my third shout into the receiver had remained unanswered. I had suffered from delay before, but never such delay as this.

I must have remained there fully two minutes, shouting at intervals, before I realized the truth. Then I dropped the receiver and leaned limply against the wall. For the moment I was as stunned as if I had received a blow. I could not even think. It was only by degrees that I recovered sufficiently to understand that Audrey was speaking to me.

'What is it? Don't they answer?'

It is curious how the mind responds to the need for making an effort for the sake of somebody else. If I had had only myself to think of, it would, I believe, have been a considerable time before I could have adjusted my thoughts to grapple with this disaster. But the necessity of conveying the truth quietly to

187

Audrey and of helping her to bear up under it steadied me at once. I found myself thinking quite coolly how best I might break to her what had happened.

'I'm afraid,' I said, 'I have something to tell you which may –'

She interrupted me quickly.

'What is it? Can't you make them answer?'

I shook my head. We looked at each other in silence.

Her mind leaped to the truth more quickly than mine had done.

'They have cut the wire!'

I took up the receiver again and gave another call. There was no reply.

'I'm afraid so,' I said.

Chapter 15

'What shall we do?' said Audrey.

She looked at me hopefully, as if I were a mine of ideas. Her voice was level, without a suggestion of fear in it. Women have the gift of being courageous at times when they might legitimately give way. It is part of their unexpectedness.

This was certainly such an occasion. Daylight would bring us relief, for I did not suppose that even Buck MacGinnis would care to conduct a siege which might be interrupted by the arrival of tradesmen's carts; but while the darkness lasted we were completely cut off from the world. With the destruction of the telephone wire our only link with civilization had been snapped. Even had the night been less stormy than it was, there was no chance of the noise of our warfare reaching the ears of anyone who might come to the rescue. It was as Sam had said, Buck's energy united to his strategy formed a strong combination.

Broadly speaking, there are only two courses open to a beleaguered garrison. It can stay where it is, or it can make a sortie. I considered the second of these courses.

It was possible that Sam and his allies had departed in the automobile to get reinforcements, leaving the coast temporarily clear; in which case, by escaping from the house at once, we might be able to slip unobserved through the grounds and reach the village in safety. To support this theory there was the fact that the car, on its late visit, had contained only the chauffeur and the two ambassadors, while Sam had spoken of the remainder of Buck's gang as being in readiness to attack in the event of my not coming to terms. That might mean that they were waiting at Buck's headquarters, wherever those might be – at one of the cottages down the road, I imagined; and, in the interval before the attack began, it might be possible for us to make our sortie with success.

'Is Ogden in bed?' I asked.

'Yes.'

'Will you go and get him up as quickly as you can?'

I strained my eyes at the window, but it was impossible to see anything. The rain was still falling heavily. If the drive had been full of men they would have been invisible to me.

Presently Audrey returned, followed by Ogden. The Little Nugget was yawning the aggrieved yawns of one roused from his beauty sleep.

'What's all this?' he demanded.

'Listen,' I said. 'Buck MacGinnis and Smooth Sam Fisher have come after you. They are outside now. Don't be frightened.'

He snorted derisively.

'Who's frightened? I guess they won't hurt *me*. How do you know it's them?'

'They have just been here. The man who called himself White, the butler, was really Sam Fisher. He has been waiting an opportunity to get you all the term.'

'White! Was he Sam Fisher?' He chuckled admiringly. 'Say, he's a wonder!'

'They have gone to fetch the rest of the gang.'

'Why don't you call the cops?'

'They have cut the wire.'

His only emotions at the news seemed to be amusement and a renewed admiration for Smooth Sam. He smiled broadly, the little brute.

'He's a wonder!' he repeated. 'I guess he's smooth, all right. He's the limit! He'll get me all right this trip. I bet you a nickel he wins out.'

I found his attitude trying. That he, the cause of all the trouble, should be so obviously regarding it as a sporting contest got up for his entertainment, was hard to bear. And the fact that, whatever might happen to myself, he was in no danger, comforted me not at all. If I could have felt that we were in any way companions in peril, I might have looked on the bulbous

190

boy with quite a friendly eye. As it was, I nearly kicked him.

'We had better waste no time,' suggested Audrey, 'if we are going.'

'I think we ought to try it,' I said.

'What's that?' asked the Nugget. 'Go where?'

'We are going to steal out through the back way and try to slip through to the village.'

The Nugget's comment on the scheme was brief and to the point. He did not embarrass me with fulsome praise of my strategic genius.

'Of all the fool games!' he said simply. 'In this rain? No, sir!'

This new complication was too much for me. In planning out my manoeuvres I had taken his cooperation for granted. I had looked on him as so much baggage – the impedimenta of the retreating army. And, behold, a mutineer!

I took him by the scruff of the neck and shook him. It was a relief to my feelings and a sound move. The argument was one which he understood.

'Oh, all right,' he said. 'Anything you like. Come on. But it sounds to me like darned foolishness!'

If nothing else had happened to spoil the success of that sortie, the Nugget's depressing attitude would have done so. Of all things, it seems to me, a forlorn hope should be undertaken with a certain enthusiasm and optimism if it is to have a chance of being successful. Ogden threw a gloom over the proceedings from the start. He was cross and sleepy, and he condemned the expedition unequivocally. As we moved towards the back door he kept up a running stream of abusive comment. I silenced him before cautiously unbolting the door, but he had said enough to damp my spirits. I do not know what effect it would have had on Napoleon's tactics if his army – say, before Austerlitz – had spoken of his manoeuvres as a 'fool game' and of himself as a 'big chump', but I doubt if it would have stimulated him.

The back door of Sanstead House opened on to a narrow yard, paved with flagstones and shut in on all sides but one by walls. To the left was the outhouse where the coal was stored, a squat barnlike building: to the right a wall that appeared to have been erected by the architect in an outburst of pure whimsicality. It just stood there. It served no purpose that I had ever been able to discover, except to act as a cats' club-house.

Tonight, however, I was thankful for this wall. It formed an important piece of cover. By keeping in its shelter it was possible to work round the angle of the coal-shed, enter the stable-yard, and, by making a detour across the football field, avoid the drive altogether. And it was the drive, in my opinion, that might be looked on as the danger zone.

The Nugget's complaints, which I had momentarily succeeded in checking, burst out afresh as the rain swept in at the open door and lashed our faces. Certainly it was not an ideal night for a ramble. The wind was blowing through the opening at the end of the yard with a compressed violence due to the confined space. There was a suggestion in our position of the Cave of the Winds under Niagara Falls, the verisimilitude of which was increased by the stream of water that poured down from the gutter above our heads. The Nugget found it unpleasant, and said so shrilly.

I pushed him out into the storm, still protesting, and we began to creep across the yard. Half-way to the first point of importance of our journey, the corner of the coal-shed, I halted the expedition. There was a sudden lull in the wind, and I took advantage of it to listen.

From somewhere beyond the wall, apparently near the house, sounded the muffled note of the automobile. The siege-party had returned.

There was no time to be lost. Apparently the possibility of a sortie had not yet occurred to Sam, or he would hardly have left the back door unguarded; but a general of his astuteness was certain to remedy the mistake soon, and our freedom of action might be a thing of moments. It behoved us to reach the stable-yard as quickly as possible. Once there, we should be practically through the enemy's lines.

Administering a kick to the Nugget, who showed a disposition to linger and talk about the weather, I moved on, and we reached the corner of the coal-shed in safety.

We had now arrived at the really perilous stage in our journey. Having built his wall to a point level with the end of the coal-shed, the architect had apparently wearied of the thing and given it up; for it ceased abruptly, leaving us with a matter of half a dozen yards of open ground to cross, with nothing to screen us from the watchers on the drive. The flagstones, moreover, stopped at this point. On the open space was loose gravel. Even if the darkness allowed us to make the crossing unseen, there was the risk that we might be heard.

It was a moment for a flash of inspiration, and I was waiting for one, when that happened which took the problem out of my hands. From the interior of the shed on our left there came a sudden scrabbling of feet over loose coal, and through the square opening in the wall, designed for the peaceful purpose of taking in sacks, climbed two men. A pistol cracked. From the drive came an answering shout. We had been ambushed.

I had misjudged Sam. He had not overlooked the possibility of a sortie.

It is the accidents of life that turn the scale in a crisis. The opening through which the men had leaped was scarcely a couple of yards behind the spot where we were standing. If they had leaped fairly and kept their feet, they would have been on us before we could have moved. But Fortune ordered it that, zeal outrunning discretion, the first of the two should catch his foot in the woodwork and fall on all fours, while the second, unable to check his spring, alighted on top of him, and, judging from the stifled yell which followed, must have kicked him in the face.

In the moment of their downfall I was able to form a plan and execute it.

'The stables!'

I shouted the words to Audrey in the act of snatching up the Nugget and starting to run. She understood. She did not hesitate in the direction of the house for even the instant which might have undone us, but was with me at once; and we were across the open space and in the stable-yard before the first of the men in the drive loomed up through the darkness. Half of the wooden double-gate of the yard was open, and the other half

193

served us as a shield. They fired as they ran – at random, I think, for it was too dark for them to have seen us clearly – and two bullets slapped against the gate. A third struck the wall above our heads and ricocheted off into the night. But before they could fire again we were in the stables, the door slammed behind us, and I had dumped the Nugget on the floor, and was shooting the heavy bolts into their places. Footsteps clattered over the flagstones and stopped outside. Some weighty body plunged against the door. Then there was silence. The first round was over.

The stables, as is the case in most English country-houses, had been, in its palmy days, the glory of Sanstead House. In whatever other respect the British architect of that period may have fallen short, he never scamped his work on the stables. He built them strong and solid, with walls fitted to repel the assaults of the weather, and possibly those of men as well, for the Boones in their day had been mighty owners of race-horses at a time when men with money at stake did not stick at trifles, and it was prudent to see to it that the spot where the favourite was housed had something of the nature of a fortress. The walls were thick, the door solid, the windows barred with iron. We could scarcely have found a better haven of refuge.

Under Mr Abney's rule, the stables had lost their original character. They had been divided into three compartments, each separated by a stout wall. One compartment became a gymnasium, another the carpenter's shop, the third, in which we were, remained a stable, though in these degenerate days no horse ever set foot inside it, its only use being to provide a place for the odd-job man to clean shoes. The mangers which had once held fodder were given over now to brushes and pots of polish. In term-time, bicycles were stored in the loose-box which had once echoed to the tramping of Derby favourites.

I groped about among the pots and brushes, and found a candle-end, which I lit. I was running a risk, but it was necessary to inspect our ground. I had never troubled really to examine this stable before, and I wished to put myself in touch with its geography.

I blew out the candle, well content with what I had seen. The only two windows were small, high up, and excellently barred. Even if the enemy fired through them there were half a dozen spots where we should be perfectly safe. Best of all, in the event of the door being carried by assault, we had a second line of defence in a loft. A ladder against the back wall led to it, by way of a trap-door. Circumstances had certainly been kind to us in driving us to this apparently impregnable shelter.

On concluding my inspection, I became aware that the Nugget was still occupied with his grievances. I think the shots must have stimulated his nerve centres, for he had abandoned the languid drawl with which, in happier moments, he was wont to comment on life's happenings, and was dealing with the situation with a staccato briskness.

'Of all the darned fool lay-outs I ever struck, this is the limit. What do those idiots think they're doing, shooting us up that way? It went within an inch of my head. It might have killed me. Gee, and I'm all wet. I'm catching cold. It's all through your blamed foolishness, bringing us out here. Why couldn't we stay in the house?'

'We could not have kept them out of the house for five minutes,' I explained. 'We can hold this place.'

'Who wants to hold it? I don't. What does it matter if they do get me? *I* don't care. I've a good mind to walk straight out through that door and let them rope me in. It would serve Dad right. It would teach him not to send me away from home to any darned school again. What did he want to do it for? I was all right where I was. I – '

A loud hammering on the door cut off his eloquence. The intermission was over, and the second round had begun.

It was pitch dark in the stable now that I had blown out the candle, and there is something about a combination of noise and darkness which tries the nerves. If mine had remained steady, I should have ignored the hammering. From the sound, it appeared to be made by some wooden instrument – a mallet from the carpenter's shop I discovered later – and the door could be relied on to hold its own without my intervention. For a novice to violence, however, to maintain a state of calm inaction is the most difficult feat of all. I was irritated and worried by the noise, and exaggerated its importance. It seemed to me that it must be stopped at once.

A moment before, I had bruised my shins against an empty packing-case, which had found its way with other lumber into the stable. I groped for this, swung it noiselessly into position beneath the window, and, standing on it, looked out. I found the catch of the window, and opened it. There was nothing to be seen, but the sound of the hammering became more distinct; and pushing an arm through the bars, I emptied my pistol at a venture.

As a practical move, the action had flaws. The shots cannot have gone anywhere near their vague target. But as a demonstration, it was a wonderful success. The yard became suddenly full of dancing bullets. They struck the flagstones, bounded off, chipped the bricks of the far wall, ricocheted from those, buzzed in all directions, and generally behaved in a manner calculated to unman the stoutest hearted.

The siege-party did not stop to argue. They stampeded as one man. I could hear them clattering across the flagstones to every point of the compass. In a few seconds silence prevailed, broken only by the swish of the rain. Round two had been brief, hardly worthy to be called a round at all, and, like round one, it had ended wholly in our favour.

I jumped down from my packing-case, swelling with pride. I had had no previous experience of this sort of thing, yet here I was handling the affair like a veteran. I considered that I had a right to feel triumphant. I lit the candle again, and beamed protectively upon the garrison.

The Nugget was sitting on the floor, gaping feebly, and awed for the moment into silence. Audrey, in the far corner, looked pale but composed. Her behaviour was perfect. There was nothing for her to do, and she was doing it with a quiet self-control which won my admiration. Her manner seemed to me exactly suited to the exigencies of the situation. With a super-competent dare-devil like myself in charge of affairs, all she had to do was to wait and not get in the way.

'I didn't hit anybody,' I announced, 'but they ran like rabbits. They are all over Hampshire.'

I laughed indulgently. I could afford an attitude of tolerant amusement towards the enemy.

'Will they come back?'

'Possibly. And in that case' – I felt in my left-hand coat-pocket – 'I had better be getting ready.' I felt in my right-hand coat-pocket. 'Ready,' I repeated blankly. A clammy coldness took possession of me. My voice trailed off into nothingness. For in neither pocket was there a single one of the shells with which I had fancied that I was abundantly provided. In moments of excitement man is apt to make mistakes. I had made mine when, starting out on the sortie, I had left all my ammunition in the house.

II

I should like to think that it was an unselfish desire to spare my companions anxiety that made me keep my discovery to myself. But I am afraid that my reticence was due far more to the fact that I shrank from letting the Nugget discover my imbecile carelessness. Even in times of peril one retains one's human weaknesses; and I felt that I could not face his comments. If he had permitted a certain note of querulousness to creep into his conversation already, the imagination recoiled from the thought of the caustic depths he would reach now should I reveal the truth.

I tried to make things better with cheery optimism.

'*They* won't come back!' I said stoutly, and tried to believe it.

The Nugget as usual struck the jarring note.

'Well, then, let's beat it,' he said. 'I don't want to spend the night in this darned icehouse. I tell you I'm catching cold. My chest's weak. If you're so dead certain you've scared them away, let's quit.'

I was not prepared to go as far as this.

'They may be somewhere near, hiding.'

'Well, what if they are? I don't mind being kidnapped. Let's go.'

'I think we ought to wait,' said Audrey.

'Of course,' I said. 'It would be madness to go out now.'

'Oh, pshaw!' said the Little Nugget; and from this point onwards punctuated the proceedings with a hacking cough.

I had never really believed that my demonstration had brought the siege to a definite end. I anticipated that there would be some delay before the renewal of hostilities, but I was too well acquainted with Buck MacGinnis's tenacity to imagine that he would abandon his task because a few random shots had spread momentary panic in his ranks. He had all the night before him, and sooner or later he would return.

I had judged him correctly. Many minutes dragged wearily by without a sign from the enemy, then, listening at the window, I heard footsteps crossing the yard and voices talking in cautious undertones. The fight was on once more.

A bright light streamed through the window, flooding the opening and spreading in a wide circle on the ceiling. It was not difficult to understand what had happened. They had gone to the automobile and come back with one of the head-lamps, an astute move in which I seemed to see the finger of Sam. The danger-spot thus rendered harmless, they renewed their attack on the door with a reckless vigour. The mallet had been superseded by some heavier instrument – of iron this time. I think it must have been the jack from the automobile. It was a more formidable weapon altogether than the mallet, and even our good oak door quivered under it.

A splintering of wood decided me that the time had come to retreat to our second line of entrenchments. How long the door would hold it was impossible to say, but I doubted if it was more than a matter of minutes.

Relighting my candle, which I had extinguished from motives of economy, I caught Audrey's eye and jerked my head towards the ladder.

'You go first,' I whispered.

The Nugget watched her disappear through the trap-door, then turned to me with an air of resolution.

'If you think you're going to get *me* up there, you've another guess coming. I'm going to wait here till they get in, and let them take me. I'm about tired of this foolishness.'

198

It was no time for verbal argument. I collected him, a kicking handful, bore him to the ladder, and pushed him through the opening. He uttered one of his devastating squeals. The sound seemed to encourage the workers outside like a trumpet-blast. The blows on the door redoubled.

I climbed the ladder and shut the trap-door behind me.

The air of the loft was close and musty and smelt of mildewed hay. It was not the sort of spot which one would have selected of one's own free will to sit in for any length of time. There was a rustling noise, and a rat scurried across the rickety floor, drawing a startled gasp from Audrey and a disgusted 'Oh, piffle!' from the Nugget. Whatever merits this final refuge might have as a stronghold, it was beyond question a noisome place.

The beating on the stable-door was working up to a crescendo. Presently there came a crash that shook the floor on which we sat and sent our neighbours, the rats, scuttling to and fro in a perfect frenzy of perturbation. The light of the automobile lamp poured in through the numerous holes and chinks which the passage of time had made in the old boards. There was one large hole near the centre which produced a sort of searchlight effect, and allowed us for the first time to see what manner of place it was in which we had entrenched ourselves. The loft was high and spacious. The roof must have been some seven feet above our heads. I could stand upright without difficulty.

In the proceedings beneath us there had come a lull. The mystery of our disappearance had not baffled the enemy for long, for almost immediately the rays of the lamp had shifted and begun to play on the trap-door. I heard somebody climb the ladder, and the trap-door creaked gently as a hand tested it. I had taken up a position beside it, ready, if the bolt gave way, to do what I could with the butt of my pistol, my only weapon. But the bolt, though rusty, was strong, and the man dropped to the ground again. Since then, except for occasional snatches of whispered conversation, I had heard nothing.

Suddenly Sam's voice spoke.

'Mr Burns!'

I saw no advantage in remaining silent.

'Well?'

'Haven't you had enough of this? You've given us a mighty good run for our money, but you can see for yourself that you're through now. I'd hate like anything for you to get hurt. Pass the kid down, and we'll call it off.'

He paused.

'Well?' he said. 'Why don't you answer?'

'I did.'

'Did you? I didn't hear you.'

'I smiled.'

'You mean to stick it out? Don't be foolish, sonny. The boys here are mad enough at you already. What's the use of getting yourself in bad for nothing? We've got you in a pocket. I know all about that gun of yours, young fellow. I had a suspicion what had happened, and I've been into the house and found the shells you forgot to take with you. So, if you were thinking of making a bluff in that direction forget it!'

The exposure had the effect I had anticipated.

'Of all the chumps!' exclaimed the Nugget caustically. 'You ought to be in a home. Well, I guess you'll agree to end this foolishness now? Let's go down and get it over and have some peace. I'm getting pneumonia.'

'You're quite right, Mr Fisher,' I said. 'But don't forget I still have the pistol, even if I haven't the shells. The first man who tries to come up here will have a headache tomorrow.'

'I shouldn't bank on it, sonny. Come along, kiddo! You're done. Be good, and own it. We can't wait much longer.'

'You'll have to try.'

Buck's voice broke in on the discussion, quite unintelligible except that it was obviously wrathful.

'Oh well!' I heard Sam say resignedly, and then there was silence again below.

I resumed my watch over the trap-door, encouraged. This parleying, I thought, was an admission of failure on the part of the besiegers. I did not credit Sam with a real concern for my welfare – thereby doing him an injustice. I can see now that he spoke perfectly sincerely. The position, though I was unaware of it, really was hopeless, for the reason that, like most positions, it had a flank as well as a front. In estimating the possibilities of attack, I had figured assaults as coming only from below. I had omitted from my calculations the fact that the loft had a roof.

It was a scraping on the tiles above my head that first brought the new danger-point to my notice. There followed the sound of heavy hammering, and with it came a sickening realization of the truth of what Sam had said. We were beaten.

I was too paralysed by the unexpectedness of the attack to form any plan; and, indeed, I do not think that there was anything that I could have done. I was unarmed and helpless. I stood there, waiting for the inevitable.

Affairs moved swiftly. Plaster rained down on to the wooden floor. I was vaguely aware that the Nugget was speaking, but I did not listen to him.

A gap appeared in the roof and widened. I could hear the heavy breathing of the man as he wrenched at the tiles.

And then the climax arrived, with anticlimax following so swiftly upon it that the two were almost simultaneous. I saw the worker on the roof cautiously poise himself in the opening, hunched up like some strange ape. The next moment he had sprung.

As his feet touched the floor there came a rending, splintering crash; the air was filled with a choking dust, and he was gone. The old worn out boards had shaken under my tread. They had given way in complete ruin beneath this sharp onslaught. The rays of the lamp, which had filtered in like pencils of light through crevices, now shone in a great lake in the centre of the floor.

In the stable below all was confusion. Everybody was speaking at once. The hero of the late disaster was groaning horribly, for which he certainly had good reason: I did not know the extent of his injuries, but a man does not do that sort of thing with impunity. The next of the strange happenings of the night now occurred.

I had not been giving the Nugget a great deal of my attention for some time, other and more urgent matters occupying me.

His action at this juncture, consequently, came as a complete and crushing surprise.

I was edging my way cautiously towards the jagged hole in the centre of the floor, in the hope of seeing something of what was going on below, when from close beside me his voice screamed. 'It's me, Ogden Ford. I'm coming!' and, without further warning, he ran to the hole, swung himself over, and dropped.

Manna falling from the skies in the wilderness never received a more whole-hearted welcome. Howls and cheers and ear-splitting whoops filled the air. The babel of talk broke out again. Some exuberant person found expression of his joy in emptying his pistol at the ceiling, to my acute discomfort, the spot he had selected as a target chancing to be within a foot of where I stood. Then they moved off in a body, still cheering. The fight was over.

I do not know how long it was before I spoke. It may have been some minutes. I was dazed with the swiftness with which the final stages of the drama had been played out. If I had given him more of my attention, I might have divined that Ogden had been waiting his opportunity to make some such move; but, as it was, the possibility had not even occurred to me, and I was stunned.

In the distance I heard the automobile moving off down the drive. The sound roused me.

'Well, we may as well go,' I said dully. I lit the candle and held it up. Audrey was standing against the wall, her face white and set.

I raised the trap-door and followed her down the ladder.

The rain had ceased, and the stars were shining. After the closeness of the loft, the clean wet air was delicious. For a moment we stopped, held by the peace and stillness of the night.

Then, quite suddenly, she broke down.

It was the unexpectedness of it that first threw me off my balance. In all the time I had known her, I had never before seen Audrey in tears. Always, in the past, she had borne the blows of fate with a stoical indifference which had alternately attracted and repelled me, according as my mood led me to think it courage or insensibility. In the old days, it had done much, this trait of hers, to rear a barrier between us. It had made her seem aloof and unapproachable. Subconsciously, I suppose, it had offended my egoism that she should be able to support herself in times of trouble, and not feel it necessary to lean on me.

And now the barrier had fallen. The old independence, the almost aggressive self-reliance, had vanished. A new Audrey had revealed herself.

She was sobbing helplessly, standing quite still, her arms hanging and her eyes staring blankly before her. There was something in her attitude so hopeless, so beaten, that the pathos of it seemed to cut me like a knife.

'Audrey!'

The stars glittered in the little pools among the worn flagstones. The night was very still. Only the steady drip of water from the trees broke the silence.

A great wave of tenderness seemed to sweep from my mind everything in the world but her. Everything broke abruptly that had been checking me, stifling me, holding me gagged and bound since the night when our lives had come together again after those five long years. I forgot Cynthia, my promise, everything.

'Audrey!'

She was in my arms, clinging to me, murmuring my name. The darkness was about us like a cloud.

And then she had slipped from me, and was gone.

Chapter 16

In my recollections of that strange night there are wide gaps. Trivial incidents come back to me with extraordinary vividness; while there are hours of which I can remember nothing. What I did or where I went I cannot recall. It seems to me, looking back, that I walked without a pause till morning; yet, when day came, I was still in the school grounds. Perhaps I walked, as a wounded animal runs, in circles. I lost, I know, all count of time. I became aware of the dawn as something that had happened suddenly, as if light had succeeded darkness in a flash. It had been night; I looked about me, and it was day – a steely, cheerless day, like a December evening. And I found that I was very cold, very tired, and very miserable.

My mind was like the morning, grey and overcast. Conscience may be expelled, but, like Nature, it will return. Mine, which I had cast from me, had crept back with the daylight. I had had my hour of freedom, and it was now for me to pay for it.

I paid in full. My thoughts tore me. I could see no way out. Through the night the fever and exhilaration of that mad moment had sustained me, but now the morning had come, when dreams must yield to facts, and I had to face the future.

I sat on the stump of a tree, and buried my face in my hands. I must have fallen asleep, for, when I raised my eyes again, the day was brighter. Its cheerlessness had gone. The sky was blue, and birds were singing.

It must have been about half an hour later that the first beginnings of a plan of action came to me. I could not trust myself to reason out my position clearly and honestly in this place where Audrey's spell was over everything. The part of me that was struggling to be loyal to Cynthia was overwhelmed here. London called to me. I could think there, face my position quietly, and make up my mind.

I turned to walk to the station. I could not guess even remotely what time it was. The sun was shining through the trees, but in the road outside the grounds there were no signs of workers beginning the day.

It was half past five when I reached the station. A sleepy porter informed me that there would be a train to London, a slow train, at six.

I remained in London two days, and on the third went down to Sanstead to see Audrey for the last time. I had made my decision.

I found her on the drive, close by the gate. She turned at my footstep on the gravel; and, as I saw her, I knew that the fight which I had thought over was only beginning.

I was shocked at her appearance. Her face was very pale, and there were tired lines about her eyes.

I could not speak. Something choked me. Once again, as on that night in the stable-yard, the world and all that was in it seemed infinitely remote.

It was she who broke the silence.

'Well, Peter,' she said listlessly.

We walked up the drive together.

'Have you been to London?'

'Yes. I came down this morning.' I paused. 'I went there to think,' I said.

She nodded.

'I have been thinking, too.'

I stopped, and began to hollow out a groove in the wet gravel with my heel. Words were not coming readily.

Suddenly she found speech. She spoke quickly, but her voice was dull and lifeless.

'Let us forget what has happened, Peter. We were neither of us ourselves. I was tired and frightened and disappointed. You were sorry for me just at the moment, and your nerves were strained, like mine. It was all nothing. Let us forget it.'

I shook my head.

'No,' I said. 'It was not that. I can't let you even pretend you think that was all. I love you. I always have loved you, though I did not know how much till you had gone away. After a time, I thought I had got over it. But when I met you again down here, I knew that I had not, and never should. I came back to say good-bye, but I shall always love you. It is my punishment for being the sort of man I was five years ago.'

'And mine for being the sort of woman I was five years ago.' She laughed bitterly. 'Woman! I was just a little fool, a sulky child. My punishment is going to be worse than yours, Peter. You will not be always thinking that you had the happiness of two lives in your hands, and threw it away because you had not the sense to hold it.'

'It is just that that I shall always be thinking. What happened five years ago was my fault, Audrey, and nobody's but mine. I don't think that, even when the loss of you hurt most, I ever blamed you for going away. You had made me see myself as I was, and I knew that you had done the right thing. I was selfish, patronizing – I was insufferable. It was I who threw away our happiness. You put it in a sentence that first day here, when you said that I had been kind – sometimes – when I happened to think of it. That summed me up. You have nothing to reproach yourself for. I think we have not had the best of luck; but all the blame is mine.'

A flush came into her pale face.

'I remember saying that. I said it because I was afraid of myself. I was shaken by meeting you again. I thought you must be hating me – you had every reason to hate me, and you spoke as if you did – and I did not want to show you what you were to me. It wasn't true, Peter. Five years ago I may have thought it, but not now. I have grown to understand the realities by this time. I have been through too much to have any false ideas left. I have had some chance to compare men, and I realize that they are not all kind, Peter, even sometimes, when they happen to think of it.'

'Audrey,' I said – I had never found myself able to ask the question before – 'was – was – he – was Sheridan kind to you?'

She did not speak for a moment, and I thought she was resenting the question.

'No!' she said abruptly.

She shot out the monosyllable with a force that startled and silenced me. There was a whole history of unhappiness in the word.

'No,' she said again, after a pause, more gently this time. I understood. She was speaking of a dead man.

'I can't talk about him,' she went on hurriedly. 'I expect most of it was my fault. I was unhappy because he was not you, and he saw that I was unhappy and hated me for it. We had nothing in common. It was just a piece of sheer madness, our marriage. He swept me off my feet. I never had a great deal of sense, and I lost it all then. I was far happier when he had left me.'

'Left you?'

'He deserted me almost directly we reached America.' She laughed. 'I told you I had grown to understand the realities. I began then.'

I was horrified. For the first time I realized vividly all that she had gone through. When she had spoken to me before of her struggles that evening over the study fire, I had supposed that they had begun only after her husband's death, and that her life with him had in some measure trained her for the fight. That she should have been pitched into the arena, a mere child, with no experience of life, appalled me. And, as she spoke, there came to me the knowledge that now I could never do what I had come to do. I could not give her up. She needed me. I tried not to think of Cynthia.

I took her hand.

'Audrey,' I said, 'I came here to say good-bye. I can't. I want you. Nothing matters except you. I won't give you up.'

'It's too late,' she said, with a little catch in her voice. 'You are engaged to Mrs Ford.'

'I am engaged, but not to Mrs Ford. I am engaged to someone you have never met – Cynthia Drassilis.'

She pulled her hand away quickly, wide-eyed, and for some moments was silent.

'Do you love her?' she asked at last.

'No.'

'Does she love you?'

Cynthia's letter rose before my eyes, that letter that could have had no meaning, but one.

'I am afraid she does,' I said.

She looked at me steadily. Her face was very pale.

'You must marry her, Peter.'

I shook my head.

'You must. She believes in you.'

'I can't. I want you. And you need me. Can you deny that you need me?'

'No.'

She said it quite simply, without emotion. I moved towards her, thrilling, but she stepped back.

'She needs you too,' she said.

A dull despair was creeping over me. I was weighed down by a premonition of failure. I had fought my conscience, my sense of duty and honour, and crushed them. She was raising them up against me once more. My self-control broke down.

'Audrey,' I cried, 'for God's sake can't you see what you're doing? We have been given a second chance. Our happiness is in your hands again, and you are throwing it away. Why should we make ourselves wretched for the whole of our lives? What does anything else matter except that we love each other? Why should we let anything stand in our way? I won't give you up.'

She did not answer. Her eyes were fixed on the ground. Hope began to revive in me, telling me that I had persuaded her. But when she looked up it was with the same steady gaze, and my heart sank again.

'Peter,' she said, 'I want to tell you something. It will make you understand, I think. I haven't been honest, Peter. I have not fought fairly. All these weeks, ever since we met, I have been trying to steal you. It's the only word. I have tried every little miserable trick I could think of to steal you from the girl you had promised to marry. And she wasn't here to fight for herself. I didn't think of her. I was wrapped up in my own selfishness. And then, after that night, when you had gone away, I thought

208

it all out. I had a sort of awakening. I saw the part I had been playing. Even then I tried to persuade myself that I had done something rather fine. I thought, you see, at that time that you were infatuated with Mrs Ford – and I know Mrs Ford. If she is capable of loving any man, she loves Mr Ford, though they are divorced. I knew she would only make you unhappy. I told myself I was saving you. Then you told me it was not Mrs Ford, but this girl. That altered everything. Don't you see that I can't let you give her up now? You would despise me. I shouldn't feel clean. I should feel as if I had stabbed her in the back.'

I forced a laugh. It rang hollow against the barrier that separated us. In my heart I knew that this barrier was not to be laughed away.

'Can't you see, Peter? You must see.'

'I certainly don't. I think you're overstrained, and that you have let your imagination run away with you. I – '

She interrupted me.

'Do you remember that evening in the study?' she asked abruptly. 'We had been talking. I had been telling you how I had lived during those five years.'

'I remember.'

'Every word I spoke was spoken with an object – calculated ... Yes, even the pauses. I tried to make *them* tell, too. I knew you, you see, Peter. I knew you through and through, because I loved you, and I knew the effect those tales would have on you. Oh, they were all true. I was honest as far as that goes. But they had the mean motive at the back of them. I was playing on your feelings. I knew how kind you were, how you would pity me. I set myself to create an image which would stay in your mind and kill the memory of the other girl; the image of a poor, ill-treated little creature who should work through to your heart by way of your compassion. I knew you, Peter, I knew you. And then I did a meaner thing still. I pretended to stumble in the dark. I meant you to catch me and hold me, and you did. And ...'

Her voice broke off.

'I'm glad I have told you,' she said. 'It makes it a little better. You understand now how I feel, don't you?'

She held out her hand.

'Good-bye.'

'I am not going to give you up,' I said doggedly.

'Good-bye,' she said again. Her voice was a whisper.

I took her hand and began to draw her towards me.

'It is not good-bye. There is no one else in the world but you, and I am not going to give you up.'

'Peter!' she struggled feebly. 'Oh, let me go.'

I drew her nearer.

'I won't let you go,' I said.

But, as I spoke, there came the sound of automobile wheels on the gravel. A large red car was coming up the drive. I dropped Audrey's hand, and she stepped back and was lost in the shrubbery. The car slowed down and stopped beside me. There were two women in the tonneau. One, who was dark and handsome, I did not know. The other was Mrs Drassilis.

Chapter 17

I was given no leisure for wondering how Cynthia's mother came to be in the grounds of Sanstead House, for her companion, almost before the car had stopped, jumped out and clutched me by the arm, at the same time uttering this cryptic speech: 'Whatever he offers I'll double!'

She fixed me, as she spoke, with a commanding eye. She was a woman, I gathered in that instant, born to command. There seemed, at any rate, no doubt in her mind that she could command *me*. If I had been a black beetle she could not have looked at me with a more scornful superiority. Her eyes were very large and of a rich, fiery brown colour, and it was these that gave me my first suspicion of her identity. As to the meaning of her words, however, I had no clue.

'Bear that in mind,' she went on. 'I'll double it if it's a million dollars.'

'I'm afraid I don't understand,' I said, finding speech.

She clicked her tongue impatiently.

'There's no need to be so cautious and mysterious. This lady is a friend of mine. She knows all about it. I asked her to come. I'm Mrs Elmer Ford. I came here directly I got your letter. I think you're the lowest sort of scoundrel that ever managed to keep out of gaol, but that needn't make any difference just now. We're here to talk business, Mr Fisher, so we may as well begin.'

I was getting tired of being taken for Smooth Sam.

'I am not Smooth Sam Fisher.'

I turned to the automobile. 'Will you identify me, Mrs Drassilis?'

She was regarding me with wide-open eyes.

211

'What on earth are you doing down here? I have been trying everywhere to find you, but nobody – '

Mrs Ford interrupted her. She gave me the impression of being a woman who wanted a good deal of the conversation, and who did not care how she got it. In a conversational sense she thugged Mrs Drassilis at this point, or rather she swept over her like some tidal wave, blotting her out.

'Oh,' she said fixing her brown eyes, less scornful now but still imperious, on mine. 'I must apologize. I have made a mistake. I took you for a low villain of the name of Sam Fisher. I hope you will forgive me. I was to have met him at this exact spot just about this time, by appointment, so, seeing you here, I mistook you for him.'

'If I might have a word with you alone?' I said.

Mrs Ford had a short way with people. In matters concerning her own wishes, she took their acquiescence for granted.

'Drive on up to the house, Jarvis,' she said, and Mrs Drassilis was whirled away round the curve of the drive before she knew what had happened to her.

'Well?'

'My name is Burns,' I said.

'Now I understand,' she said. 'I know who you are now.' She paused, and I was expecting her to fawn upon me for my gallant service in her cause, when she resumed in quite a different strain.

'I can't think what you can have been about, Mr Burns, not to have been able to do what Cynthia asked you. Surely in all these weeks and months ... And then, after all, to have let this Fisher scoundrel steal him away from under your nose ...!'

She gave me a fleeting glance of unfathomable scorn. And when I thought of all the sufferings I had gone through that term owing to her repulsive son and, indirectly, for her sake, I felt that the time had come to speak out.

'May I describe the way in which I allowed your son to be stolen away from under my nose?' I said. And in well-chosen words, I sketched the outline of what had happened. I did not omit to lay stress on the fact that the Nugget's departure with the enemy was entirely voluntary.

She heard me out in silence.

'That was too bad of Oggie,' she said tolerantly, when I had ceased dramatically on the climax of my tale.

As a comment it seemed to me inadequate.

'Oggie was always high-spirited,' she went on. 'No doubt you have noticed that?'

'A little.'

'He could be led, but never driven. With the best intentions, no doubt, you refused to allow him to leave the stables that night and return to the house, and he resented the check and took the matter into his own hands.' She broke off and looked at her watch. 'Have you a watch? What time is it? Only that? I thought it must be later. I arrived too soon. I got a letter from this man Fisher, naming this spot and this hour for a meeting, when we could discuss terms. He said that he had written to Mr Ford, appointing the same time.' She frowned. 'I have no doubt he will come,' she said coldly.

'Perhaps this is his car,' I said.

A second automobile was whirring up the drive. There was a shout as it came within sight of us, and the chauffeur put on the brake. A man sprang from the tonneau. He jerked a word to the chauffeur, and the car went on up the drive.

He was a massively built man of middle age, with powerful shoulders, and a face – when he had removed his motor-goggles – very like any one of half a dozen of those Roman emperors whose features have come down to us on coins and statues, square-jawed, clean-shaven, and aggressive. Like his late wife (who was now standing, drawn up to her full height, staring haughtily at him) he had the air of one born to command. I should imagine that the married life of these two must have been something more of a battle even than most married lives. The clashing of those wills must have smacked of a collision between the immovable mass and the irresistible force.

He met Mrs Ford's stare with one equally militant, then turned to me.

'I'll give you double what she has offered you,' he said. He paused, and eyed me with loathing. 'You damned scoundrel,' he added.

Custom ought to have rendered me immune to irritation, but it had not. I spoke my mind.

'One of these days, Mr Ford,' I said, 'I am going to publish a directory of the names and addresses of the people who have mistaken me for Smooth Sam Fisher. I am *not* Sam Fisher. Can you grasp that? My name is Peter Burns, and for the past term I have been a master at this school. And I may say that, judging from what I know of the little brute, any one who kidnapped your son as long as two days ago will be so anxious by now to get rid of him that he will probably want to pay you for taking him back.'

My words almost had the effect of bringing this divorced couple together again. They made common cause against me. It was probably the first time in years that they had formed even a temporary alliance.

'How dare you talk like that!' said Mrs Ford. 'Oggie is a sweet boy in every respect.'

'You're perfectly right, Nesta,' said Mr Ford. 'He may want intelligent handling, but he's a mighty fine boy. I shall make inquiries, and if this man has been ill-treating Ogden, I shall complain to Mr Abney. Where the devil is this man Fisher?' he broke off abruptly.

'On the spot,' said an affable voice. The bushes behind me parted, and Smooth Sam stepped out on to the gravel.

I had recognized him by his voice. I certainly should not have done so by his appearance. He had taken the precaution of 'making up' for this important meeting. A white wig of indescribable respectability peeped out beneath his black hat. His eyes twinkled from under two penthouses of white eyebrows. A white moustache covered his mouth. He was venerable to a degree.

He nodded to me, and bared his white head gallantly to Mrs Ford.

'No worse for our little outing, Mr Burns, I am glad to see. Mrs Ford, I must apologize for my apparent unpunctuality, but

I was not really behind time. I have been waiting in the bushes. I thought it just possible that you might have brought unwelcome members of the police force with you, and I have been scouting, as it were, before making my advance. I see, however, that all is well, and we can come at once to business. May I say, before we begin, that I overheard your recent conversation, and that I entirely disagree with Mr Burns. Master Ford is a charming boy. Already I feel like an elder brother to him. I am loath to part with him.'

'How much?' snapped Mr Ford. 'You've got me. How much do you want?'

'I'll give you double what he offers,' cried Mrs Ford.

Sam held up his hand, his old pontifical manner intensified by the white wig.

'May I speak? Thank you. This is a little embarrassing. When I asked you both to meet me here, it was not for the purpose of holding an auction. I had a straight-forward business proposition to make to you. It will necessitate a certain amount of plain and somewhat personal speaking. May I proceed? Thank you. I will be as brief as possible.'

His eloquence appeared to have had a soothing effect on the two Fords. They remained silent.

'You must understand,' said Sam, 'that I am speaking as an expert. I have been in the kidnapping business many years, and I know what I am talking about. And I tell you that the moment you two got your divorce, you said good-bye to all peace and quiet. Bless you' – Sam's manner became fatherly – 'I've seen it a hundred times. Couple get divorced, and, if there's a child, what happens? They start in playing battledore-and-shuttlecock with him. Wife sneaks him from husband. Husband sneaks him back from wife. After a while along comes a gentleman in my line of business, a professional at the game, and he puts one across on both the amateurs. He takes advantage of the confusion, slips in, and gets away with the kid. That's what has happened here, and I'm going to show you the way to stop it another time. Now I'll make you a proposition. What you want to do' – I have never heard anything so soothing, so suggestive of the old family friend healing an unfortunate breach, as

Sam's voice at this juncture – 'what you want to do is to get together again right quick. Never mind the past. Let bygones be bygones. Kiss and be friends.'

A snort from Mr Ford checked him for a moment, but he resumed.

'I guess there were faults on both sides. Get together and talk it over. And when you've agreed to call the fight off and start fair again, that's where I come in. Mr Burns here will tell you, if you ask him, that I'm anxious to quit this business and marry and settle down. Well, see here. What you want to do is to give me a salary – we can talk figures later on – to stay by you and watch over the kid. Don't snort – I'm talking plain sense. You'd a sight better have me with you than against you. Set a thief to catch a thief. What I don't know about the fine points of the game isn't worth knowing. I'll guarantee, if you put me in charge, to see that nobody comes within a hundred miles of the kid unless he has an order-to-view. You'll find I earn every penny of that salary ... Mr Burns and I will now take a turn up the drive while you think it over.'

He linked his arm in mine and drew me away. As we turned the corner of the drive I caught a glimpse over my shoulder of the Little Nugget's parents. They were standing where we had left them, as if Sam's eloquence had rooted them to the spot.

'Well, well, well, young man,' said Sam, eyeing me affectionately, 'it's pleasant to meet you again, under happier conditions than last time. You certainly have all¹ the luck, sonny, or you would have been badly hurt that night. I was getting scared how the thing would end. Buck's a plain rough-neck, and his gang are as bad as he is, and they had got mighty sore at you, mighty sore. If they had grabbed you, there's no knowing what might not have happened. However, all's well that ends well, and this little game has surely had the happy ending. I shall get that job, sonny. Old man Ford isn't a fool, and it won't take him long, when he gets to thinking it over, to see that I'm right. He'll hire me.'

'Aren't you rather reckoning without your partner?' I said. 'Where does Buck MacGinnis come in on the deal?'

Sam patted my shoulder paternally.

'He doesn't, sonny, he doesn't. It was a shame to do it – it was like taking candy from a kid – but business is business, and I was reluctantly compelled to double-cross poor old Buck. I sneaked the Nugget away from him next day. It's not worth talking about; it was too easy. Buck's all right in a rough-and-tumble, but when it comes to brains he gets left, and so he'll go on through life, poor fellow. I hate to think of it.'

He sighed. Buck's misfortunes seemed to move him deeply.

'I shouldn't be surprised if he gave up the profession after this. He has had enough to discourage him. I told you about what happened to him that night, didn't I? No? I thought I did. Why, Buck was the guy who did the Steve Brodie through the roof; and, when we picked him up, we found he'd broken his leg again! Isn't that enough to jar a man? I guess he'll retire from the business after that. He isn't intended for it.'

We were approaching the two automobiles now, and, looking back, I saw Mr and Mrs Ford walking up the drive. Sam followed my gaze, and I heard him chuckle.

'It's all right,' he said. 'They've fixed it up. Something in the way they're walking tells me they've fixed it up.'

Mrs Drassilis was still sitting in the red automobile, looking piqued but resigned. Mrs Ford addressed her.

'I shall have to leave you, Mrs Drassilis,' she said. 'Tell Jarvis to drive you wherever you want to go. I am going with my husband to see my boy Oggie.'

She stretched out a hand towards the millionaire. He caught it in his, and they stood there, smiling foolishly at each other, while Sam, almost purring, brooded over them like a stout fairy queen. The two chauffeurs looked on woodenly.

Mr Ford released his wife's hand and turned to Sam.

'Fisher.'

'Sir?'

'I've been considering your proposition. There's a string tied to it.'

'Oh no, sir, I assure you!'

'There is. What guarantee have I that you won't double-cross me?'

Sam smiled, relieved.

'You forget that I told you I was about to be married, sir. My wife won't let me!'

Mr Ford waved his hand towards the automobile.

'Jump in,' he said briefly, 'and tell him where to drive to. You're engaged!'

Chapter 18

'No manners!' said Mrs Drassilis. 'None whatever. I always said so.'

She spoke bitterly. She was following the automobile with an offended eye as it moved down the drive.

The car rounded the corner. Sam turned and waved a farewell. Mr and Mrs Ford, seated close together in the tonneau, did not even look round.

Mrs Drassilis sniffed disgustedly.

'She's a friend of Cynthia's. Cynthia asked me to come down here with her to see you. I came, to oblige her. And now, without a word of apology, she leaves me stranded. She has no manners whatever.'

I offered no defence of the absent one. The verdict more or less squared with my own opinion.

'Is Cynthia back in England?' I asked, to change the subject.

'The yacht got back yesterday. Peter, I have something of the utmost importance to speak to you about.' She glanced at Jarvis the chauffeur, leaning back in his seat with the air, peculiar to chauffeurs in repose, of being stuffed. 'Walk down the drive with me.'

I helped her out of the car, and we set off in silence. There was a suppressed excitement in my companion's manner which interested me, and something furtive which brought back all my old dislike of her. I could not imagine what she could have to say to me that had brought her all these miles.

'How *do* you come to be down here?' she said. 'When Cynthia told me you were here, I could hardly believe her. Why are you a master at this school? I cannot understand it!'

'What did you want to see me about?' I asked.

She hesitated. It was always an effort for her to be direct. Now, apparently, the effort was too great. The next moment she had rambled off on some tortuous bypath of her own, which, though it presumably led in the end to her destination, was evidently a long way round.

'I have known you for so many years now, Peter, and I don't know of anybody whose character I admire more. You are so generous – quixotic in fact. You are one of the few really unselfish men I have ever met. You are always thinking of other people. Whatever it cost you, I know you would not hesitate to give up anything if you felt that it was for someone else's happiness. I do admire you so for it. One meets so few young men nowadays who consider anybody except themselves.'

She paused, either for breath or for fresh ideas, and I took advantage of the lull in the rain of bouquets to repeat my question.

'What *did* you want to see me about?' I asked patiently.

'About Cynthia. She asked me to see you.'

'Oh!'

'You got a letter from her.'

'Yes.'

'Last night, when she came home, she told me about it, and showed me your answer. It was a beautiful letter, Peter. I'm sure I cried when I read it. And Cynthia did, I feel certain. Of course, to a girl of her character that letter was final. She is so loyal, dear child.'

'I don't understand.'

As Sam would have said, she seemed to be speaking; words appeared to be fluttering from her; but her meaning was beyond me.

'Once she has given her promise, I am sure nothing would induce her to break it, whatever her private feelings. She is so loyal. She has such character.'

'Would you mind being a little clearer?' I said sharply. 'I really don't understand what it is you are trying to tell me. What do you mean about loyalty and character? I don't understand.'

She was not to be hustled from her bypath. She had chosen

her route, and she meant to travel by it, ignoring short-cuts.

'To Cynthia, as I say, it was final. She simply could not see that the matter was not irrevocably settled. I thought it so fine of her. But I am her mother, and it was my duty not to give in and accept the situation as inevitable while there was anything I could do for her happiness. I knew your chivalrous, unselfish nature, Peter. I could speak to you as Cynthia could not. I could appeal to your generosity in a way impossible, of course, for her. I could put the whole facts of the case clearly before you.'

I snatched at the words.

'I wish you would. What are they?'

She rambled off again.

'She has such a rigid sense of duty. There is no arguing with her. I told her that, if you knew, you would not dream of standing in her way. You are so generous, such a true friend, that your only thought would be for her. If her happiness depended on your releasing her from her promise, you would not think of yourself. So in the end I took matters into my own hands and came to see you. I am truly sorry for you, dear Peter, but to me Cynthia's happiness, of course, must come before everything. You *do* understand, don't you?'

Gradually, as she was speaking, I had begun to grasp hesitatingly at her meaning, hesitatingly, because the first hint of it had stirred me to such a whirl of hope that I feared to risk the shock of finding that, after all, I had been mistaken. If I were right – and surely she could mean nothing else – I was free, free with honour. But I could not live on hints. I must hear this thing in words.

'Has – has Cynthia – ' I stopped, to steady my voice. 'Has Cynthia found – ' I stopped again. I was finding it absurdly difficult to frame my sentence. 'Is there someone else?' I concluded with a rush.

Mrs Drassilis patted my arm sympathetically.

'Be brave, Peter!'

'There is?'

'Yes.'

The trees, the drive, the turf, the sky, the birds, the house, the automobile, and Jarvis, the stuffed chauffeur, leaped together for an instant in one whirling, dancing mass of which I was the centre. And then, out of the chaos, as it separated itself once more into its component parts, I heard my voice saying, 'Tell me.'

The world was itself again, and I was listening quietly and with a mild interest which, try as I would, I could not make any stronger. I had exhausted my emotion on the essential fact: the details were an anticlimax.

'I liked him directly I saw him,' said Mrs Drassilis. 'And, of course, as he was such a friend of yours, we naturally – '

'A friend of mine?'

'I am speaking of Lord Mountry.'

'Mountry? What about him?' Light flooded in on my numbed brain. 'You don't mean – Is it Lord Mountry?'

My manner must have misled her. She stammered in her eagerness to dispel what she took to be my misapprehension.

'Don't think that he acted in anything but the most honourable manner. Nothing could be farther from the truth. He knew nothing of Cynthia's engagement to you. She told him when he asked her to marry him, and he – as a matter of fact, it was he who insisted on dear Cynthia writing that letter to you.'

She stopped, apparently staggered by this excursion into honesty.

'Well?'

'In fact, he dictated it.'

'Oh!'

'Unfortunately, it was quite the wrong sort of letter. It was the very opposite of clear. It can have given you no inkling of the real state of affairs.'

'It certainly did not.'

'He would not allow her to alter it in any way. He is very obstinate at times, like so many shy men. And when your answer came, you see, things were worse than before.'

'I suppose so.'

'I could see last night how unhappy they both were. And when Cynthia suggested it, I agreed at once to come to you and tell you everything.'

She looked at me anxiously. From her point of view, this was the climax, the supreme moment. She hesitated. I seemed to see her marshalling her forces, the telling sentences, the persuasive adjectives; rallying them together for the grand assault.

But through the trees I caught a glimpse of Audrey, walking on the lawn; and the assault was never made.

'I will write to Cynthia tonight,' I said, 'wishing her happiness.'

'Oh, Peter!' said Mrs Drassilis.

'Don't mention it,' said I.

Doubts appeared to mar her perfect contentment.

'You are sure you can convince her?'

'Convince her?'

'And – er – Lord Mountry. He is so determined not to do anything – er – what he would call unsportsmanlike.'

'Perhaps I had better tell her I am going to marry some one else,' I suggested.

'I think that would be an excellent idea,' she said, brightening visibly. 'How clever of you to have thought of it.'

She permitted herself a truism.

'After all, dear Peter, there are plenty of nice girls in the world. You have only to look for them.'

'You're perfectly right,' I said. 'I'll start at once.'

A gleam of white caught my eye through the trees by the lawn. I moved towards it.